Twilight

Look for these titles by *Ally Blue*

Now Available:
Willow Bend
Love's Evolution
Eros Rising (A *Hearts from the Ashes* story)
Catching a Buzz (A *Midsummer Night's Steam* story)
Fireflies
Untamed Heart

Bay City Paranormal Investigations:
Oleander House (Book 1)
What Hides Inside (Book 2)
Twilight (Book 3)

Coming Soon:
The Happy Onion
Where the Heart Is

Bay City Paranormal Investigations:
Closer (Book 4)
An Inner Darkness (Book 5)

Twilight

Ally Blue

A Samhain Publishing, Ltd. publication.

Samhain Publishing, Ltd.
577 Mulberry Street, Suite 1520
Macon, GA 31201
www.samhainpublishing.com

Twilight
Copyright © 2008 by Ally Blue
Print ISBN: 978-1-59998-838-2
Digital ISBN: 1-59998-620-5

Editing by Sasha Knight
Cover by Scott Carpenter

First Samhain Publishing, Ltd. electronic publication: October 2007
First Samhain Publishing, Ltd. print publication: August 2008

Dedication

To my critique group, as always, for helping me make this a story worth reading, and for listening to me whine whenever I was having a hard time with it.

Chapter One

Sam Raintree shifted in his chair, his video camera trained on the faint outline of the door to the large room. He glanced at the fluorescent hands of his watch. Eleven-thirty p.m.

Come on, he thought, his foot tapping an impatient rhythm on the carpet. *We can only stay in here until midnight, then we have to meet the rest of the group. Please show up.*

As if in response to his thought, a glowing mist began to gather against the closed door. In a few seconds, it resolved itself into a wispy female figure with short, sleek black hair and delicate features. She wore a deep red dress which brushed the floor and left her white shoulders bare.

"Holy shit," whispered the young man sitting at the other side of the little round table. "It's her. It's the Lady in Red."

Sam nodded, his gaze flicking between the camera's display screen and the apparition drifting toward the bed. "Sure enough." He flashed a grin at his companion. "Exciting, isn't it?"

The young man—Toby something, Sam could never remember his last name—didn't say anything, but the look on his face was answer enough. His awestruck expression was obvious even in the faint light cast by the camera. Sam swallowed a laugh. He understood how the boy felt. Hell, this was only the second true apparition Sam had ever seen. He was nearly as excited as Toby.

The Lady in Red had been haunting Asheville, North Carolina's Kimberley Inn for eighty years, ever since she was murdered in her bed back in the nineteen-twenties. She'd been seen by countless guests and most of the staff. According to the Inn's owners, she had interacted with some of the witnesses but had never harmed anyone.

The same could be said of the other spirits rumored to inhabit the one hundred and twenty-five year old building. Which was why Bay City Paranormal Investigations had decided to make the Kimberley Inn one of their biannual investigation trips for amateur ghost hunters. They could teach a group of interested—and paying—guests the basics of paranormal investigation, with almost guaranteed ghost sightings and no chance of anyone being harmed. At least not by ghosts.

Toby squeaked when the Lady turned her blurry white face toward him, stopped and hovered in the air at the end of the bed. "What's she doing?" he hissed, cutting a panicked glance at Sam. "Don't let her hurt me!"

"She won't hurt you," Sam murmured, keeping the camera rolling. "Just stay calm, Toby. She's been known to interact with people before, you know that. She's never hurt anyone, she's just being friendly."

The Lady floated closer. She smiled, her lips stretching a bit too wide and revealing yellow, uneven teeth. The effect was rather ghastly. Sam shuddered, even though he didn't believe for a second she would hurt either of them. The psychic energy he sensed from her was perfectly benign.

She stretched out a translucent hand to Toby, who cringed away. "Sam..."

"Relax." Sam zoomed in for a close-up on her face. "Come on, this is why you're here, right?"

"I didn't think any of the ghosts would touch me."

"She won't hurt you." Panning out again, Sam shot Toby an irritated look. "Just hold still and don't engage her. Maybe she'll leave you alone and go to the bed like she usually does."

Toby looked doubtful, but he froze in place, lips pressed together. The Lady, it seemed, wasn't giving up so easily. Her hand shot out, and slim white fingers grasped at Toby's arm. They passed right through, insubstantial as they were, but Toby shrieked as if he'd been skewered.

"Fuck!" He leapt from the chair, sending the EMF detector which had been on his lap crashing to the floor, and ran across the room. Flinging the door open, he dashed down the hallway as if a pack of rabid dogs was after him.

Sam sighed and rubbed his eyes. "Amateurs." It was an unkind thing to say, but he didn't care. Toby had been nervous and jumpy every step of the way so far. They'd only been here two days, but Toby's attitude was already getting on his nerves.

Worst of all, Toby's hysterics had apparently disturbed the Lady in Red. Instead of lying down on the bed and slowly disappearing as witnesses said she usually did, she abruptly vanished from the spot where she'd been hovering in front of Toby's chair.

"Well, that's just great." Switching the camera off, Sam set it on the table, leaned back in the chair and shut his eyes. He'd taken Toby along to investigate the Lady in Red's room because he thought she'd scare Toby less than any of the other spirits they'd potentially encounter. *Boy, was I ever wrong about that.*

He wondered if he had any ibuprofen left. The headache coming on promised to be a monster.

The door swung shut with a faint squeak. The lock snicked, and light footfalls sounded across the room. Sam smiled. "Hi, Bo."

"How'd you know it was me?" A warm body straddled Sam's

lap, knees pressing on either side of his hips. "Could've been anyone."

Opening his eyes, Sam smiled at the silhouette of Dr. Bo Broussard's head. "I recognized your walk."

"My walk?"

"Yeah." Sam slipped his arms around Bo's waist and aimed a kiss at where his mouth should be, landing half on and half off his bottom lip. "You walk like a cat. All quiet and slinky."

Bo laughed. "What did you do to Toby? He ran out of here like a horde of demons was chasing him."

"I didn't do a damn thing. He scared himself, like always."

"Does that mean the Lady in Red showed up?"

"She sure did." Sliding his hands lower, Sam grabbed Bo's ass and squeezed, drawing a surprised sound from his boss and lover. "She liked Toby, but he didn't like her much."

Bo wriggled his ass in Sam's grip, settling more firmly astride him. "You know, if I'd had any idea that boy was going to be so easily spooked I would've given his spot to someone else."

"I hear you. It's kind of hard to screen people just from emails and online forms, though. He said in his application that seeing a real ghost was his lifelong dream."

"Maybe we should revamp our screening process for these trips." Bo began rocking his hips back and forth between Sam's grasping hands and his belly. "I don't want to end up with someone really unstable one of these days."

Sam licked his lips, trying to concentrate on the conversation. It wasn't easy, with Bo's butt muscles flexing in his palms and Bo's crotch rubbing against his abdomen. God, the man knew just how to drive him crazy. "Um...they have to sign a waiver."

"Yes, but Toby's behavior has me rethinking the whole process." Bo dipped his head, brushing his lips against Sam's neck. "Maybe we should only bring people local to Mobile, so we can meet them beforehand."

"Or just conduct all these amateur investigations locally." Sam groaned when Bo's teeth sank into his flesh at the juncture of neck and shoulder. "Bo, unless you're prepared to throw me on that bed and fuck me right now and explain to the group later what we were doing all this time, you'd better stop it."

Bo laughed, but Sam felt the sudden tension in his body. No one except their coworkers and friends at Bay City Paranormal Investigations knew they were a couple. It wasn't ideal, as far as Sam was concerned. He'd much rather be completely open in their relationship. But Bo had what he felt were valid reasons to keep their secret from all but their closest friends, and Sam respected that. After nearly losing Bo during the South Bay High investigation two months earlier, Sam had decided he could deal with a little secrecy as long as they were both alive, and together.

"Sorry," Bo said, moving off Sam's lap. He stood, outlined in the faint light bleeding around the door. "I can't get you off my mind today."

"Just today?" Sam rose to his feet, crossed the room and flipped on the lights. "Seems to me like you've been all over me ever since we got here."

"I think it's being here at the Inn. Being alone in a room with you every single night." Bo tugged on the waist-length black braid hanging over one shoulder. "You'd think all that sex would calm my libido down, but it seems to be having the opposite effect. I can't get enough of you."

The reminder that soon they'd be back in their room, alone

and horny, made Sam's groin twitch. He loved the frequent sex, but what he loved more was simply having Bo with him. Being able to hold him close while they slept, to wake up with Bo in his arms and make love in the early morning light. It was a rare thing for them, and Sam cherished every second. Thank God for the Kimberley's exorbitant prices, which made sharing rooms necessary for all the BCPI staff.

Closing the distance between them, Sam pulled Bo into his arms and kissed him. "Good, because I can never get enough of your cock in my ass."

Bo's cheeks flushed, his dark eyes glazing. "Christ, I can't believe the things you say sometimes."

Sam leaned over until his lips brushed Bo's cheek. "You mean things like how much I'd like to spread your legs and eat your asshole right now? Or how much I love it when you shove your cock down my throat and fuck my mouth? Things like that?" He flicked his tongue into Bo's ear, chuckling at the sharp gasp that caused. "You know you love it."

Bo didn't answer, but the way he shook in Sam's embrace said it all. Sam grinned against Bo's neck. Discovering how turned on Bo got when Sam talked dirty to him had been a delightful surprise. It had only taken Sam a couple of weeks to convince Bo that it was nothing to be embarrassed about. Now, describing in minute and graphic detail what he'd like to do to Bo at any given time had become his favorite method of turning the man into a shivering puddle of lust.

The best thing about it was, he could do it at any time. Just last night, he'd kept whispering to Bo during dinner at the Kimberley Inn's posh restaurant, telling him all the depraved things he could do to Sam's body later. They'd barely made it through dessert before Bo dragged him back to their room, yanked his pants down just enough to expose the necessary area and fucked him so hard his teeth rattled.

Who knew that underneath that cool, professional exterior lurked a sex-crazed hedonist?

My sex-crazed hedonist. Sam hummed and buried his face in Bo's neck.

"Sam," Bo breathed, stroking Sam's back. "We...we still have to do tonight's wrap-up. We're going to be late if we don't go."

"You started it." Yanking Bo's head back by his braid, Sam took his mouth in a deep, probing kiss.

Bo melted against Sam with a soft sigh, just like Sam had known he would. In public, no one would ever guess they were a couple. They treated one another with the utmost professional respect, always, and never touched each other in a way which could be construed as indicating anything beyond friendship.

When they were alone, however, Bo morphed into a completely different person. Lusty, sensual and surprisingly aggressive once he'd gotten over his initial uncertainty about his own sexual skills. It amazed Sam sometimes, that the man he'd once thought would be repressed and full of hang-ups in bed had turned out to be such an uninhibited and creative lover.

Sam was starting to wonder whether they could get away with a quickie against the wall when a light rap sounded on the door. Breaking the kiss with some difficulty, Sam cleared his throat. "Yes?"

"Sam? Is Bo in there with you? We're ready to start the wrap-up early, and we need y'all."

Bo shot a half-annoyed, half-ashamed look at Sam. "I told you we'd be late," he murmured, giving Sam's butt a hard smack before pulling out of the embrace. "I'm here, David," he called. "We'll be right out."

On the other side of the door, BCPI's lead tech specialist, David Broom, snickered like the twelve-year-old Sam often suspected him of being underneath his thirty-something disguise. "Oooh, is there some man-on-man action going on in there?"

Sam laughed, and Bo glared at him. "Oh, come on, Bo," Sam said. "It's just David. You know he wouldn't say that if anyone else could hear."

Bo's sharp gaze softened, and he sighed. Striding to the door, Bo unlocked it and threw it open. "No, David, there is no action of any sort going on in here."

"Sorry to disappoint you," Sam added, doing his best to look sincere. "I know you keep hoping to catch us at it."

"Sam, I love y'all both, but I do not ever—*ever*—want to see you two fucking. I'd have to scrub my eyeballs with steel wool and then Cecile would yell at me." David sauntered into the room and looked them both up and down with a smirk. "I just barely stopped y'all from doing the horizontal Hustle right here on the carpet, didn't I?"

Groaning, Bo covered his face with both hands. "Go away, David."

"And that's the thanks I get." With an exaggerated sigh, David walked out into the hallway. "See you in a few minutes. Oh, and Sam? What the hell did you do to Toby?"

Sam rubbed his temples. His headache, which had subsided when he was busy kissing Bo, was coming back with a vengeance. "I'll tell you what happened later. Go on, we'll be right there."

"Okay. Don't be too long. Everybody's tired and they want to get to bed. Which I expect the two of you understand just fine." Quirking an eyebrow at them, David strolled off down the hall and turned the corner toward the elevators.

Bo shook his head as he watched David go. "Sometimes I wonder if I'm running a business or an elementary school."

"Amen to that. At least Cecile and Andre act like adults most of the time."

"Good thing, since Dean's just as bad as David is." Crossing the room, Bo picked up the EMF detector Toby had dropped. "Although, even the two of them are always careful with the equipment. Did Toby leave this on the floor?"

"He dropped it when he went tearing out of the room." Sam walked over to retrieve his camera and the canvas duffle bag containing the rest of the equipment. "Please tell me it's not broken."

Bo inspected it with a critical eye as he and Sam left the room. "It seems to be all right, luckily for Toby."

"Good." Sam turned off the lights and shut the door behind them. "I doubt he has the cash left to buy us a new one, after paying for this trip."

"True." Glancing around the empty hallway, Bo leaned over and planted a swift kiss on the corner of Sam's mouth. "Come on. Let's get downstairs."

Sam followed Bo to the elevator, a big smile spread across his face.

CR

When Sam woke the next morning, Bo was already in the shower. Sam lay there for a few minutes, staring at the closed bathroom door and smiling. His hips ached and the sheets tangled around his naked body smelled like sex. God, he loved it when Bo fucked him to within an inch of his life. It was well worth every one of the little aches and pains the next morning.

A vision flashed into Sam's mind—Bo flat on his back, legs up and spread, Sam's cock buried to the root in his ass. Sam shoved it impatiently away. Bo wasn't ready to bottom yet, and Sam wasn't about to push him.

Yawning, Sam slid out of bed, shuffled to the bathroom door and opened it as quietly as he could. Citrus-scented steam billowed out. He could hear Bo singing softly, a lilting minor-key ballad in French.

Sam grinned. Bo's penchant for singing in the shower had been another interesting quirk he'd discovered since becoming Bo's lover. The man was chock-full of surprises. Not all of those surprises were pleasant ones, but Sam didn't care. He'd fallen in love with all of Bo, not just the easy parts.

Moving silently, Sam pulled the shower curtain aside and stepped into the shower. Bo stood with his head tilted under the spray, rinsing shampoo out of his long black hair. His eyes were closed, his lips shaping the quiet syllables of the song. Sam shook his head. He supposed Bo's nearly tone-deaf singing voice was the price he had to pay for being so physically stunning.

"Couldn't wait your turn, huh, Sam?"

"What, when I know you're in here naked and wet? Hell no." Stepping closer, Sam wound an arm around Bo's waist and kissed his chin. "You are so fucking gorgeous."

Bo laughed. Straightening up, he opened his eyes and molded his body to Sam's. "So are you. Kiss me."

Sam happily obeyed. He pressed his mouth to Bo's and opened for Bo's tongue, loving the soft, slick feel of it tangling with his own. Bo moaned, his cock firming against Sam's hip. The sound made Sam burn inside.

Following a sudden, familiar urge, Sam broke the kiss, dropped to his knees and took Bo's cock into his mouth. Bo let out a sharp cry. His hands slid into Sam's hair and his hips began to move. Sam groaned with his mouth full. He loved sucking Bo off. Loved the way Bo's cock slid between his lips and deep into his throat, the tang of precome on the back of his tongue, the way Bo's moans rose in pitch as orgasm began to overtake him. He loved taking Bo to a different plane, driving him out of his mind with pleasure.

"Oh, oh fuck, Sam," Bo breathed, and came in a rush of salty-bitter warmth down Sam's throat.

Sam swallowed every drop, then climbed to his feet and swept Bo into a hard kiss. Bo's hand found Sam's shaft, his fingers stroking in a practiced rhythm. It didn't take long before Sam felt the orgasm building inside him. It was always like that. Bo's touch undid him, every time. Sam came with a shudder and a moan, one hand clamped onto Bo's ass and the other buried in his hair.

"You're a bad influence," Bo murmured, smiling against Sam's mouth.

"Oh, really?"

"Really."

Sam chuckled. "You love it."

"I do." Framing Sam's face in his hands, Bo stared straight into his eyes. "I love you."

Sam's chest constricted. Almost two months to the day since Bo had first said those words to him, hearing it still had the power to reduce him to tears. Unwinding his hand from Bo's hair, he caressed Bo's wet, flushed cheek. "And I love you. So much."

The tender shine in Bo's eyes made Sam's spirit soar. Bo brushed his fingertips across Sam's lips. "Sam…"

When Bo's lips met his again, Sam closed his eyes and let

the kiss carry him away. If they were a few minutes late to the morning's planning meeting, so what? They had to be so careful back home, mostly to keep Bo's estranged wife, Janine, from finding out about their relationship. A leisurely shower together wasn't something they got to do together often, and Sam intended to enjoy every second.

℆

"They noticed."

"No, they didn't."

"Some of them did."

"Like who?"

"Tessa."

Sam sighed. If any of their group was going to notice Sam and Bo had been not only late to the meeting, but rather flushed and disheveled as well, it would've been Tessa. She was a journalist, keen-eyed and observant, and shrewd enough to be a little scary. But Sam didn't think even she had thought anything of their slightly late, slightly rushed arrival to the meeting.

"She didn't notice, Bo." They emerged from the quiet hallway where the meeting room was located into the rustic yet elegant lobby, and Sam dropped his voice low. "Even if she did, I don't think she'd mention it to anyone else."

Bo shot him a worried look. "What if she does?"

"Well, then, I guess everyone will think Tessa has an overactive imagination."

"But what if they don't think that? What if they believe her?"

"If they do, so what?" Exasperated, Sam stopped in an alcove between two stone pillars and planted his hands on his hips. "None of these people live anywhere near Mobile, Bo. What does it matter if some of them are suspicious that we might be closer than we let on? Even if any of them knew Janine or any of the folks we do business with—which I seriously doubt they do—I don't think they're going to run to those people and say, 'Hey, Bo and Sam are fucking, you better stay away or you might catch gayness!'"

"Keep your voice down," Bo hissed, shooting a furtive look around the lobby.

"I am!" Sam exclaimed. Bo raised an eyebrow at him, and he sighed. "I am," he repeated more quietly. He started to lay a hand on Bo's shoulder, then thought better of it. "Look, Bo, I know you don't want anyone else to find out, and I understand why, believe me. But I think you're worrying for no reason in this case. Two of this group have family members who are gay, and it doesn't bother them any. Nobody else seemed bothered by it either."

"Looks can be deceiving, Sam. Just because someone doesn't speak up and say they have a problem doesn't mean they don't." A couple walked past them, headed down the hallway they'd just exited. Bo fell silent, watching them go. "I don't want to find out the hard way that one of these people is dangerously homophobic," he continued after the couple was out of earshot. "They could destroy BCPI with a few well-placed words to the right people. And if Janine found out…"

"Yeah, I know." Sam made a face. Janine had threatened more than once to dig up any dirt she could on Bo in an effort to keep their two sons, Sean and Adrian, away from him. Sam didn't believe she could legally use Bo's sexual orientation against him, but Bo wasn't about to take any chances. Even though Sam understood it, he sometimes thought Bo was being

21

overly paranoid for no good reason.

Like now.

Shaking his head, Sam leaned against the thick stone pillar behind him. "Look, it doesn't matter anyway. If Tessa or anyone else suspect anything, there's not much we can do other than watch ourselves in public, which we're already doing. And don't even suggest that one of us switch rooms," he added, recognizing the particular way Bo's mouth twisted when he thought he needed to do something unpleasant for the greater good. "Everyone's sharing rooms. It'll look even more suspicious if we change roommates now."

Bo gave him a sharp look, then unexpectedly burst out laughing. "Sam, it's scary how well you've got me figured out."

Sam grinned. "Don't worry, nobody but me could possibly figure you out."

Whatever Bo was going to say to that was cut off by a male voice ringing loud and clear across the lobby. "There they are! Hey, guys, wait up!"

They exchanged an amused look as their coworker and friend, Dean Delapore, weaved his way through the crowd. David and the rest of the BCPI crew followed in his wake.

"Hey, y'all," Dean greeted them as the group approached. Flashing a wide smile, Dean thumped Sam on the back hard enough to make him cough. "That was some awesome footage you got of the Lady in Red, Sam."

"Oh, you watched it already? When?"

"This morning," David mumbled, yawning. "Bastard came banging on our door at the ass-crack of damn dawn, wanting to go over the footage from last night."

"David!" Cecile Langlois, who'd been dating David for five months now, nudged him with her hip. "Don't be crude."

He gave her a fond look. "Yes, dear."

"I told him to go wake you," said Andre Meloy, co-owner and manager of Bay City Paranormal. "This may be a tour to make money for the business, but that doesn't mean we're going to slack off on our investigative techniques." He pointed a thick finger at David. "You slept in half the morning yesterday, while Dean was up early and working. Can't let you get away with that two days in a row."

Andre's tone was stern, but his dark eyes twinkled and his expression said he was trying hard not to laugh. Sam studied his face, relieved to see only the faintest trace of the sadness Andre had radiated for the last five months. Ever since Oleander House and the dimensional gateway, and the thing Sam had accidentally let loose via his psychokinetic abilities. The thing which had killed Andre's lover and Bo's business partner and friend, Amy Landry. The same sort of thing which had almost killed Bo at South Bay High.

Sam shuddered. He still had nightmares about that day during the investigation of the high school, and the days following. The other-dimensional creature biting Bo's thigh, Bo's face flushed with fever and rapidly advancing infection, the doctor's grave voice as he told Sam and the others Bo might not live. Sam thought he'd never stop hearing those words, never stop seeing Bo lying still and silent in that damn ICU bed.

Stop it. That's all behind you. Bo's fine now. Andre's fine, or as fine as can be expected. Don't dwell on it.

Fighting the urge to wrap Bo in a protective embrace, Sam shook himself and focused on the conversation going on around him.

"Andre and I have felt out all the spots where paranormal activity has been reported here," Cecile was saying. Andre's psychic abilities were stronger than Cecile's or Sam's, but Cecile was by far the most experienced in the practical application of those abilities, so she was default leader when it came to the psychic portion of the investigations. "I'm not finding any malevolent energy anywhere in this building. In fact, I believe most of the hauntings here are probably residuals. The Lady in Red is probably the one true apparition here."

Sam grimaced. "Wish I'd sent Toby along with you last night, Dean. If the butler's ghost in the pantry is a residual haunting, he wouldn't have interacted with Toby the way the Lady did, and the little wuss wouldn't have run off."

"I don't know." Dean ran a hand through his blond-streaked hair, gray-green eyes thoughtful. "The butler's definitely a residual. But it's pretty hair-raising to see him chop his own hand off with a meat cleaver and go running around the kitchen."

David rolled his eyes. "Jesus, Toby would've had a whole herd of cows."

"Yeah, I guess you're right." Sam glanced at Bo, who was unusually quiet. He was staring intently at the front desk, which was about ten feet from where they stood. "Bo? What are you looking at?"

"That woman at the desk just mentioned my name." Eyes narrowing, Bo stepped closer to the desk. "Yes, she just said it again. I wonder what she wants?"

The group looked at each other and fell silent by unspoken consensus. Sam stepped up next to Bo, listening as hard as he could.

"I really need to speak with him," the woman at the desk said. "It's very important. I promise not to disturb their work, but I have to see him."

Sam studied the stranger. She was short, with a rounded figure hidden by loose jeans and a thick jacket. She wore sturdy, mud-caked hiking boots. Two shoulder-length brown braids hung from beneath a dark red knit cap. In profile, her face looked young and harmless, with a snub nose and round, rosy cheeks.

Bo and Sam glanced at each other. Sam shrugged at the question in Bo's eyes. He'd never seen the woman before in his life, and evidently Bo hadn't either.

The worker at the desk looked distinctly skeptical. He leaned toward the woman. Sam heard him say something, but couldn't make out what it was. Whatever he said, however, it did not make the woman happy. She slammed one petite fist on the gleaming wooden counter.

"Fine," she said, her voice rising. "I'll just sit right out here and wait. You can't stop me from doing that."

The desk worker's face darkened. "Ma'am, I'm afraid I'll have to ask you to leave."

The woman blinked, a stricken expression crossing her face. She seemed at a loss for words. Shoulders slumping, she turned around and started toward the lobby doors. If she saw Bo and the others, she gave no sign of recognizing them.

Bo watched her, biting his lip and pulling on his braid. Just as the woman reached the doors, decision hardened in his eyes. "Come with me, Sam. We're going to talk to her."

With a quick glance at his coworkers, Sam trotted after Bo, who was striding across the lobby as fast as his long legs would take him. The rest of the group stayed put. They didn't seem surprised, any more than Sam was. It would be completely unlike Bo not to find out what was behind the stranger's demands to see him.

They caught up to her as she was descending the wide stone steps from the verandah in front of the Inn. "Excuse me, miss?" Bo jogged the last few feet and touched the woman's shoulder.

She turned around, wide blue eyes questioning. "Yes?"

"I'm Dr. Bo Broussard," Bo said. "I'm sorry, but I overheard you asking the man at the desk if you could speak with me."

The woman's face lit up with a wide smile. This close, the fine laugh lines around her eyes and mouth and the streaks of gray in her braids told Sam she was likely older than Bo or himself. "Dr. Broussard, I'm so happy to meet you." Grasping Bo's hand, she pumped it hard. "I'm Alexa Bledsoe, call me Lex. Hi."

"And you can call me Bo." Returning Lex's infectious smile, Bo let go of her hand and glanced at Sam. "This is Sam Raintree, one of the investigators at Bay City Paranormal."

"Nice to meet you, Lex." Sam took her hand, and bit back a yelp when her fingers closed around his. Damn, but the woman had a grip like a wrestler.

"Why don't we go back into the lobby?" Bo suggested. "It's cold out here."

Lex shot a nervous glance at the door. "Do you think it's okay? I don't want to get in trouble."

"I'm sure it'll be fine." Taking her elbow, Bo steered her through the massive wooden door and into the warmth of the lobby. "What did you want to see me about, Lex?"

"I need you to investigate my place," she answered. "Sunset Lodge. My guests are being frightened away and I don't know what to do."

Bo's gaze cut to Sam before settling on Lex again. "Please don't take this the wrong way, Lex, but why us? I know of at least two investigative agencies in this general area. They both have good reputations in the business. Plus we're in the midst of an investigation here at the Kimberley Inn. Is there some reason you needed us in particular, rather than one of the other agencies?"

She glanced around, then leaned close to Bo and Sam. "I've heard about Oleander House, and South Bay High," she whispered. "I think that's what's happening at Sunset Lodge. I think there's an interdimensional gateway."

Chapter Two

Ten minutes later, Lex was nestled in a large chair in the corner of the tremendous lobby, with a mug of Irish coffee in her hand and the BCPI team gathered around her.

"So, Lex," Andre said, leaning forward with his elbows resting on his knees. "Tell us about your place. Sunset Lodge, right?"

"That's right." Lex sipped from her steaming mug. "My husband and I bought Sunset Lodge ten years ago, when the previous owners became unable to keep up with it."

"I imagine running a business like that would be a lot of work," Cecile observed.

"Especially this one." Lex grinned. "It's located at the top of one of the highest peaks in the western North Carolina mountains, almost at the Tennessee border. There's no electricity, and it's only accessible by foot or horseback."

David let out a low whistle. "Dang. No offense or anything, Lex, but I don't blame the former owners for letting it go. Sounds pretty rough."

"It is, in a way. But the beds are big and warm, the food's out of this world, and the view is not to be believed, especially watching the sun go down from Sunset Rock. People come from all over the country for the experience. We stay fully booked up to a year ahead."

"It sounds fantastic." Setting his coffee mug on the table between the sofa and Lex's chair, Sam leaned on the arm of the couch and gave Lex a keen look. "Why don't you tell us why you believe you have an interdimensional gateway?"

She stared into her coffee for a moment. *Please don't be another one,* Sam thought. If it really was a gateway, he knew he wouldn't be able to walk away from it. He'd promised himself he'd do his best to permanently close any gateway he found, and he intended to honor that promise. But the thought of facing another gateway, of having those alien beings inside his mind, made him feel sick.

He refused to think of what might happen to his friends, or to Bo, if Lex's suspicion was correct. The temptation to run the other way would be too strong to fight if he let himself dwell on it.

"In the past two weeks, several guests at the Lodge have seen strange things in the woods around Sunset Rock," Lex finally spoke up, her voice so soft Sam could barely hear her over the buzz of conversation around them. "It's about a twenty minute hike between the Lodge and the Rock. People have caught glimpses of what they say is a strange animal in the woods on the way back to the Lodge after the sunset. It's always at the same spot, in the trees to the left of the path about halfway between the Rock and the Lodge. A couple of people thought it must've been a bear, only it didn't make any noise." She glanced up, blue gaze locking onto Bo's face. "Only one person got a really good look at it, just the day before yesterday. She said it looked...wrong. Twisted, somehow. She took her family and left at first light the next morning. None of them slept. Her youngest son saw it too. She said he had nightmares from it."

The BCPI group all looked at one another with identical horrified expressions. An icy lump lodged itself in Sam's gut. *It's*

29

a gateway. Another one. Fuck.

"I came into town yesterday afternoon," Lex continued. She scraped at a chip in the handle of her mug with one short, ragged thumbnail. "I'd read about your previous gateway cases online, and what's happening at Sunset Lodge sounds awfully similar. I was going to call you and ask you to come investigate. It was just dumb luck you happened to be here in town already."

"How'd you hear about our cases?" Dean wondered, fixing Lex with a bright, curious gaze. "I know you don't get internet on top of the mountain."

Lex smiled. "No, we don't. But Carl—that's my husband— and I don't spend all our time up there. We generally go for a few days each month, and leave it to the regular staff the rest of the time. We live in Maggie Valley, a little ways west of here."

Scooting to the edge of the sofa, Bo leaned forward, braid swinging over his shoulder. "Lex, has anyone been injured since these sightings began?"

She shook her head. "No, thank God. I'd like to keep it that way."

"Have there been any other unusual events preceding the start of the sightings?" Bo asked.

Lex gave him an odd look. "Funny you should ask that. One of our employees went missing just before these sightings started."

Andre's eyebrows went up. "What were the circumstances surrounding the disappearance?"

"He went down the mountain to get a prescription filled, and he never came back. The police searched for him, of course, but they didn't find him. I have no reason to think his disappearance was connected to whatever people have been seeing, but you asked." Biting her lip, Lex looked around at the group. "So, what do you say? Can you help us?"

Sam turned to look at Bo. His brow was furrowed, his fingers restlessly twirling the end of his braid. Everyone else stared at him, clearly waiting for his verdict.

"I'd like to take the case," Bo said, speaking slowly. "But it'll have to wait a few days. We're in the middle of an investigation here. We have a group of amateur investigators with us who've paid for a ghost hunting trip. We have an obligation to give them what they paid for."

Lex hunched her shoulders. "I expected you'd say that. The thing is, there's a winter storm predicted to hit in the next couple of days. We're considering canceling the reservations that haven't already been canceled because of it, but even if we do, Carl and I and our staff will be trapped up there. If there's really a gateway, and those things are coming through..."

She didn't need to finish. Chills raced up Sam's spine. He knew what the creatures were capable of. They all knew. He glanced at Andre. His friend's deep brown skin had an ashen hue, and his eyes were haunted. *He's thinking of Amy.* Sam's heart went out to him.

"Is there a number where I could reach you in the morning?" Bo asked. "I think we need to discuss this as a group and come to a consensus."

"Yes, of course." Reaching into the pocket of her jeans, Lex pulled out a rather battered business card. "Do you have a pen?"

Cecile flipped open her purse, dug around for a moment and came out with a green ballpoint. "Here you go."

"Thanks." Taking the pen, Lex scribbled a string of numbers on the card and handed it to Bo. "Here's my cell number. Call me as soon as you can tomorrow. I'm at the Days Inn a few miles down the road. I'll be checking out around ten and heading back up the mountain. The only way to reach me at the Lodge is by radio."

"Okay." Bo took the card, stood and tucked it into his jeans pocket. "I'll call you first thing in the morning with our decision."

Rising to her feet, Lex held out her hand. "Thanks for your time, Bo. It's good to meet you. All of you."

"Same here," Bo said. "Talk to you tomorrow."

Everyone stood to shake hands with Lex, then she left with a smile and a wave. Sam watched her go. The tension in her shoulders said quite clearly she didn't expect them to take the case soon enough to do any good.

"She doesn't think we'll get to her in time," Dean observed, unknowingly echoing Sam's thoughts. "She thinks by the time we get up there, it'll be too late. That something bad'll happen first."

No one answered, but Sam could tell by the looks on his friends' faces that they were thinking the same thing he was— Dean was right. If they waited, they'd be too late.

Without thinking, Sam reached out and took Bo's hand. To his surprise, Bo didn't let go, but curled his fingers around Sam's and squeezed.

"Let's all go back to mine and Sam's room," he said. "We need to talk."

Bo pulled his hand from Sam's grip as they left their relatively secluded corner, and Sam mourned the loss of that comforting touch. A hard knot of dread formed in his belly as he followed Bo to the elevators.

I can't let him go up there. I couldn't handle it if anything happened to him.

A hand landed on his shoulder, making him jump. He

turned to meet Dean's concerned gaze.

"You okay, Sam?" Dean murmured. "You look kind of pale."

"I'm fine," Sam lied.

Behind him, David snorted. "Yeah, right. Like the whole world can't tell you're worried about Bo getting hurt again."

Heat suffused Sam's face. "Yeah, well—"

"It's okay," Cecile reassured him. "We're all worried. But you know what he's going to want to do."

"And we won't be able to talk him out of it," Andre added. "Not that any of us would've tried, I think. We all know what this might mean."

"I can hear y'all, you know," Bo said without turning around. "Keep it to yourselves until we get upstairs."

The group fell silent. Sam watched Bo's ramrod-straight back, long ebony braid swinging like a pendulum, and wished more than ever that they could be open as a couple. The need to hold Bo right then was a burning ache deep in his core. He desperately wanted to reassure himself that Bo was safe and whole, and would stay that way forever.

No such thing as forever, Sam. Especially now that people are coming to us with these interdimensional gateway cases. You can't keep him safe, and he'd hate you for trying, so just stop.

As much as he hated it, Sam knew it was true. Bo would never turn away a possible gateway case out of fear, and Sam risked losing his respect if he asked him to do such a thing. Yet Sam knew he couldn't just agree to take the case without at least trying to get Bo to stay behind. It was a conundrum Sam had no idea how to solve.

No one said a word until they reached the airy, high-ceilinged room Sam and Bo shared. The second the door clicked shut behind Andre, everyone except Bo and Sam started talking at once. Sitting cross-legged on the tremendous four-poster bed, Sam listened to the cacophony with only half an ear. Most of his attention remained focused on Bo, who was pacing the floor and pulling on his braid.

"All right, everybody settle down," Bo ordered, giving the entire group a sharp look. Quiet descended instantly. Bo chuckled and shook his head. "Okay, let's get this out of the way first thing. I'm fine. The bite healed ages ago, the infection's long gone, and I'm completely back to normal." Crossing his arms, he arched a brow at Sam. "And I'm not about to let what happened at South Bay keep me away from a case. Is that clear?"

Everyone nodded. Sam thought they looked like a bunch of chastised schoolchildren. Knowing it was a bad idea before he even opened his mouth, Sam spoke up anyway. "It's not clear to me."

A flush crept up Bo's neck. His eyes glittered with a look Sam knew well and had learned to dread. The look that meant he was in for a fight if he kept pushing. Sam held his gaze without flinching. He wasn't ready to back down. Not without so much as a discussion.

"I think we should take this case," Bo said, his tone clipped and careful. "We all know what might happen if this is a real gateway. We can't take that chance."

"I agree with you." Sam kept his voice calm in spite of the frustration and fear boiling inside him. "We should definitely take the case."

Five pairs of eyes widened in tandem, and Sam had to laugh. Was he really so predictable that they were all this surprised by what he'd said?

"Well, good." Clearly flustered, Bo yanked the rubber band from the end of his braid and started unraveling it. He eyed

Sam warily. "I have to say, Sam, I thought you'd argue about this."

Sam gave him a wry smile. "I'm not done yet."

Sighing, Bo plopped onto the bed beside him and fixed him with an expectant look. "Okay. You think we should take the case. So what's the argument?"

Taking Bo's hand, Sam wound their fingers together. "I don't think you should go," he said quietly. "I think you should stay here."

A crackling silence fell. Sam waited, staring at his lap, resigned to his fate. When Bo remained unmoving and unspeaking after several endless seconds, Sam risked a glance at his face. To his surprise, Bo was gazing at him with solemn sympathy in his eyes.

"If we take this case—and I think we all know we're going to—we *will* need to split up," Andre mused, rubbing the back of his neck. "We can't risk waiting for someone to get hurt up at the Lodge."

Nodding, Cecile wound an arm around David's waist and leaned against him. "I'd suggest that half of us stay here with the tour group and finish the Kimberley Inn investigation, and half of us go to Sunset Lodge."

"I'll volunteer for the Sunset Lodge detail," Dean offered. "I have some training in wilderness medicine. Might come in handy."

"Excellent idea." Bo smiled, but the expression in his eyes remained troubled. "Okay, here's what I'd like to do. Andre, I'd like you, Cecile and David to stay here, since you three are the most capable of handling this bunch. Dean, Sam and I will head up to Sunset Lodge tomorrow."

Sam held his tongue with an effort. Letting go of his hand, Bo stood and herded the rest of the group out the door. He didn't look at Sam. Dean shot a worried glance at Sam as he left, then the door closed and Sam and Bo were alone.

For a moment, neither of them spoke. Bo walked over to the window and stood staring out at the city below them. Sam picked at a loose thread in the thick royal blue comforter and watched Bo from under lowered lashes.

"Go on and say it, Sam," Bo said finally. "I know you want to."

"I don't want you to go," Sam told him. "I know it's stupid. I know it doesn't make any sense, and I know you hate it when I get all protective. But I can't help it. I can't stand the thought of anything happening to you."

Turning from the window, Bo perched on the end of the bed and met Sam's gaze. "I understand that. I don't want anything to happen to you either. But, Sam, you know people's lives could be at stake here. Not just yours or mine, but lives of people who have no idea what they might be facing. At least you and I, and Dean, know what we're getting into, and we have some idea of how to defeat it." One corner of his mouth lifted in a bitter half smile. "I'd leave you here in a hot minute, if that were an option. But it isn't. You're the only one who can close the damn things. So I can't make you stay here, no matter how much I'd like to."

"I know, but..." Sam's throat constricted, and he had to force the next words out. "You almost died, Bo. I have never felt more scared or more helpless in my life than when I saw you unconscious in that hospital bed, and I didn't know if you'd ever wake up. I can't face that again. I just can't."

Bo didn't answer. For a long moment, they sat there, neither moving, neither talking. Then Bo crawled up to Sam, and without a word put his arms around him and pulled him close. Slipping his arms around Bo, Sam buried his face in his lover's neck, closed his eyes and breathed in Bo's scent.

Chapter Three

Bo called Lex the next morning as soon as he and Sam woke up. At breakfast, the group discussed the plans for the upcoming days. Andre would be in charge of the overall investigation at the Kimberley Inn, while David and Cecile would each lead a team of three in each day's activities. Bo, Sam and Dean would ride to one of the Lodge's trailheads with Lex, and Andre would pick them up in the BCPI van in four days. They couldn't stay any longer than that, since they only had rooms at the Kimberley for five more days.

Sam hoped they would be able to resolve the case at Sunset Lodge one way or another by then. With any luck, what the people had seen would turn out to be a bear after all. Twilight shadows often played tricks on the eye, making ordinary things seem weird and frightening, and Sam fervently hoped that would turn out to be the explanation in this case. It wouldn't be the first time they'd set out to investigate a possible gateway, only to find something much more benign at the heart of it.

He wished he could ignore the inner voice whispering that none of those other cases had sounded so uncomfortably close to their experiences at Oleander House and South Bay High.

At ten o'clock, the group stood on the rambling verandah in front of the Kimberley Inn, waiting for Lex. David and Dean had their heads together, talking in low tones while they reviewed the contents of the big equipment bag Dean carried. Bo stood talking to Andre. Going over last minute details, from what Sam could hear. Sam stared up at the heavy gray sky, feeling unaccountably left out.

Slipping a hand into the crook of Sam's elbow, Cecile leaned close. "Y'all are going to contact us, aren't you?"

Sam nodded. "Yeah. There's a radio in the manager's office here. Bo talked to her and arranged for us to call and talk to Andre in a couple of days."

"Good. That makes me feel better."

"Me too."

Cecile glanced at Bo. "I know you're not happy about this, Sam. Are you and Bo okay?"

He knew what she meant, and he appreciated it. Smiling, he patted her hand. "We're fine. At least, we're not fighting, which is something. I think we're both getting better at the fine art of compromise."

Cecile laughed. "Yes, I've noticed."

At that moment, a dark blue, mud-splattered SUV pulled up in front of the Inn. The driver's side door opened, and Lex hurried around the front. "Hi, guys," she called. "Come on, we need to get started. I need to get back to the Lodge in time to help with dinner. We're one short without Harry."

"Is that the guy who disappeared?" Dean asked, trotting down the steps to the SUV.

"Yes, it is. Harry Norton." Lex shook her head. "Terrible thing. He's worked at the Lodge for eighteen years. Such a sweet, wonderful man. It's been awful, not knowing what happened to him, and Carl and I have hesitated to hire anyone to fill his position, since we're still hoping he'll turn up."

"Good God, your employees don't live up there all the time,

do they?" David's expression reflected horrified disbelief.

Opening the back of the SUV for the team's equipment, Lex shot David an amused look. "No, they don't. They're usually on the mountain for two weeks and off for one. It's an unusual type of schedule, which makes it difficult to hire people. Most of our employees are young people with no spouse or children. Harry was—is—our oldest worker, in both senses of the word. He just turned fifty last month."

Sam and Bo glanced at each other as they descended the steps side by side. Lex's words and the grief on her face made it clear that she wanted to believe Harry was still alive, but felt in her heart he wasn't.

"I guess that's all of our stuff," Bo said, slinging his backpack into the back of the SUV beside Sam's. He turned to Andre, David and Cecile, who stood shoulder to shoulder at the bottom of the verandah steps. "Good luck with the rest of the investigation here. Y'all know what to do. And be sure to call us on the manager's radio if there's an emergency."

David nodded. "Will do, boss-man."

Hurrying forward, Cecile hugged first Dean, then Bo and finally Sam. "Be careful, okay?"

"We will, don't worry." Sam patted her back, kissed the top of her head and let her go. "See y'all in four days."

"You have the directions to the trailhead, don't you, Andre?" Bo asked as he opened the front passenger side door of the SUV and climbed in.

Andre patted his back pocket. "Right here. I'll be there at four o'clock on Thursday."

"Okay." Bo smiled at the three remaining at the Inn. "Bye. Y'all be good."

Dean pulled open the back door of the SUV and climbed in.

Sam slid in beside him, closed the door and rolled down the window. "Bye, guys," he called as Lex hopped behind the wheel and began steering the vehicle down the narrow cobblestone drive. "See you soon!"

All three called goodbye, and Cecile blew them a kiss. Dean leaned over Sam to wave out the window at them. When they rounded a corner of the drive and lost sight of their friends, Dean settled back into his seat and buckled his seat belt. Sam rolled up the window, cutting off the flow of chilly air from outside.

"Looks like that winter weather you predicted is on the way, Lex." Dean tilted his head to frown at the sky. "You think we'll make it up the mountain before it hits?"

"Hopefully, but there's no guarantee." Lex steered the SUV onto the winding, tree-lined road running past the Kimberley Inn. "The trails can be difficult to negotiate when it's snowy or icy, but we're not supposed to get any of that until tomorrow sometime. The storm might even miss us altogether. It's coming up from the south, heading northeast, so we might or might not see any accumulation to amount to anything."

"I brought my waterproof hiking boots," Dean cheerfully informed them.

"We all did. Our whole team actually drove up here a day early so we could do some hiking, so we all had boots with us." Twisting in his seat, Bo gave Sam a questioning look. "You remembered to wear yours, right?"

Amused, Sam held up a boot-clad foot. Bo had the good grace to blush. He'd been plastered against Sam's back, mouth latched onto his neck, while Sam was attempting to lace the boots in question that morning. Sam had a tender red bruise there to prove it.

As Bo turned around again and started asking Lex

questions about Sunset Lodge, Dean nudged Sam's arm. Sam looked over at him, eyebrows raised. Darting his gaze from Sam to Bo and back again, Dean grinned and waggled his eyebrows. Sam bit the insides of his cheeks. Dean always managed to make him laugh, no matter how scared, worried or angry he was. He needed to laugh right now, and he suspected Dean knew that quite well.

Thanks, Sam mouthed.

Dean nodded and patted his thigh. Relaxing into the leather seat, Sam turned his attention to Lex.

☙

It took just over an hour to reach the small parking lot at the Birch Gap trailhead. By that time, Lex had filled them in on the history of Sunset Lodge and they'd begun to discuss sleeping arrangements.

"We've had several cancellations, but they're not all for the same days," Lex explained as they piled out of the SUV and hoisted their packs. "We'll have at least one cabin empty each night, maybe more but that's not for sure."

"How many people do the cabins sleep?" Bo asked, adjusting the straps of his backpack.

"Four, technically speaking." Lex locked the SUV and shoved the keys in her jacket pocket. "The cabins are set up with bunk beds, each level sleeping two people. So two of you would have to share a bed."

Bo shot Sam a swift, smoldering look. Heat pulsed through Sam's groin. He risked a lascivious grin at Bo, who mouthed *stop it* at him and turned to follow Lex up the trail. Sam stared at his denim-clad ass, enjoying the extra sway he knew Bo was putting in his walk for Sam's benefit.

Trotting to catch up, Sam leaned close and whispered, "Tease," in Bo's ear before dropping back to walk beside Dean. Bo gave him a *who, me?* look over his shoulder.

"We do have a staff bed available," Lex added, apparently unaware of the flirting going on behind her back. "One of you can use that if you don't want to all share one cabin."

"I'll take the staff bed," Dean spoke up. "Sam, you and Bo can have the cabin."

Turning his head, Bo gave Dean a grateful smile. "That'll be fine, Dean, thanks."

"Yeah, thanks," Sam added, squeezing Dean's arm.

"My pleasure." Dean bumped Sam's hip with his. "Hey, Lex, what time's sunset tonight?"

"Around six-fifteen, if I remember right." She glanced at her watch. "That should give you plenty of time to get settled in and take a look around the Lodge property, and still be able to watch the sunset. Dinner's normally at six, but we do work around the sunset times. That view's one of our biggest draws, after all."

"Would you be able to show us the spot where the sightings have occurred this afternoon, before sunset?" Bo wondered. "We're planning to investigate the area during the usual time of the sightings, of course, and see if we can capture it on film. But we need to look it over beforehand if possible, to get a feel for the area."

"Certainly." Lex clumped up the wooden steps of a narrow footbridge across a shallow stream. "I may not be able to take you myself, but I'll have someone show you the area and answer any questions you have. The staff knows just as much about the place as I do, they should be able to tell you anything you need to know."

Sam stopped a few seconds to watch the swift little stream chattering beneath the bridge. Fitful sunlight pierced through the clouds overhead, sparkling diamond-like on the surface of the clear flowing water and bringing out a rainbow of colors in the rocks below. The bare branches of oaks and birch hissed and rattled in a sudden burst of chill wind. The air smelled of water, earth and leaf mold.

"Hey, Sam."

Looking toward Dean's voice, Sam found himself staring into a camera lens. "Dean…"

"Say 'cheese'." Dean snapped a picture before Sam could object, then lowered the camera, eyes sparkling and a smug smile on his face. "Gotcha."

Sam shook his head. "Don't waste pictures on me, Dean. Save it for the job."

"Hey, this is my personal camera, not one of the BCPI ones. I'm gonna fill up all my memory cards with pics of the three of us and the gorgeous view, just like a tourist."

"Oh, well, that's all right then." Pushing away from the bridge's wooden rail, Sam crossed to the far bank with Dean beside him. Lex and Bo were already several yards ahead, deep in conversation. "Hey. Take a picture of Bo."

Dean looked at Bo, then back at Sam. "You mean a pic of Bo's ass."

Sam shrugged. "Maybe."

"Maybe, my perfectly toned rear end. You want pics of your man's admittedly fine ass. Don't even try to bullshit me."

Laughing, Sam nudged Dean with his elbow. "Okay, yeah. Can you blame me?"

"Not hardly. That's one smokin' hot scientist you're fucking."

"Actually, he's the one doing the fucking." The second he said it, Sam winced. No way was Dean going to let *that* go without comment.

Sure enough, Dean's jaw dropped open and he stared at Sam as if he'd sprouted a few extra limbs. "What? You mean to tell me Bo hasn't bottomed for you yet?"

Sam hunched his shoulders. His cheeks burned. "Well, no. But not everyone bottoms. You know that."

"Yeah, I know, but..." Dean pursed his lips and plucked at the zipper of his bright yellow jacket. "I know for a fact that you like to top, at least sometimes. It's been, what, a couple of months now. I just think he should've let you fuck him by now."

"He'll let me know when he's ready," Sam snapped, sounding harsher than he'd intended. "I'm not going to push him."

"I'm not saying you should." Dean glanced at him from under the blond-streaked fringe veiling his eyes. "Sorry, Sam. I didn't mean to upset you. You know me, always shoving my foot in my mouth."

Feeling contrite now, Sam laid a hand on Dean's shoulder. "And you know me, always getting defensive for no reason. Sorry."

They smiled at each other, and Sam felt better. At one time, not so long ago, he'd wished he could love Dean, because it would be so much easier than loving Bo. Now, with the perspective of time, Sam was glad he and Dean had been able to remain friends in spite of everything that had happened between them. He treasured Dean's friendship every bit as much as he treasured Bo's love.

From the curve of the trail ahead, Bo turned and called to them. "Y'all okay back there?"

"Translation: hurry the fuck up," Dean muttered.

"We're fine," Sam answered, biting back laughter. "Just stopped to take a picture."

"Well, come on. We have a long way to go." Bo's words were short, but his tone was mild, and Sam saw the indulgent shine in his eyes.

Sam smiled, warmth washing through him as it always did when he looked at his lover. "We're coming."

Settling his heavy pack more firmly on his shoulders, Sam picked up his pace. Soon enough, he and Dean caught up with Bo and Lex, and the four of them struck out for the top of the mountain.

CR

The hike to Sunset Lodge took just over four hours. The trail grew narrower and steeper the closer they got to the top. It wound back and forth like a rocky ribbon across the face of the mountain. Dean stopped every time the trees opened up to take pictures of the breathtaking view. Below them, patches of fog shrouded the leafless forest. Ahead, a ridge of rock and broken firs grew closer with every step.

Dean let out a whoop when they rounded a huge shoulder of stone and the rugged path leveled out into a wide lane strewn with wood chips. "Oh my God, I thought that hike was gonna kill me. Lex, please tell me we're there."

Laughing, she dropped back to walk beside him. "Yes, Dean, we're here. The Lodge office is just up the path."

"Excellent." Thumbing on the camera hanging around his neck, Dean began flipping through the pictures he'd taken. "I got some great shots on the way up, though. That's a hell of a view from the trail."

"Wait till you see the view from Sunset Rock." Lex patted Dean's shoulder, then strode forward. "Come on, not far now."

As they walked, Bo drifted back to Sam's side. "That was quite a hike," he said, smiling at Sam. "Probably nothing to you, though, as much running as you do."

"Yeah, but I try to avoid running five miles up steep, rocky mountains. I have a feeling I'm going to be sore later."

"I can promise you will be," Bo said, with an evil grin.

Sam let out a yip of surprise when Bo grabbed his ass and squeezed. He turned to Bo, intent on teasing, and frowned when he noticed Bo favoring his right leg. That leg still bore scars from poisoned needle teeth and emergency surgery.

"Bo, is your leg bothering you?" Sam murmured.

Bo grimaced. "It hurts, yes. But it's not that bad. I'm sure it'll settle down after I get a chance to rest it."

"I'm sorry. I should've known this climb would be too much for your leg."

"I told you, it's fine. I just need to rest it a bit."

"You should stay at the Lodge and let Dean and me check out the property."

"I don't think that'll be necessary." With a frustrated sigh, Bo leaned against Sam's shoulder. "I have to admit, I never considered how the hike might affect my leg. It never bothers me at home, and it really didn't bother me when we went for that hike in Pisgah Forest when we first arrived in Asheville."

"Don't worry. You know Dean and I can do anything you can't. We'll make sure the investigation doesn't suffer."

"I know. I can always count on y'all to take care of things." Bo glanced ahead. Lex and Dean were out of sight around a bend in the path. With no one to see, he hooked a hand around the back of Sam's neck, pulled his face down and planted a hard, swift kiss on his mouth. "I'm a lucky man, Sam."

Sam licked his lips, wishing he could sweep Bo into his arms and devour his mouth. "So am I."

They walked along in silence for a moment. When they rounded the next turn, Dean and Lex were there waiting for them. Dean lifted the camera and snapped a picture of them. "That's a good one, y'all. Remind me to show you later."

Shaking his head, Sam slipped an arm between the frame of Bo's pack and the small of his back. "Lean on me."

Bo nestled into the curve of Sam's arm, and in that moment, life for Sam was perfect.

A couple minute's walk brought them to a slight rise in the path. On the other side of the rise, the trail wound downhill and took a sharp turn to the right. Sam let out a soft "oh" as they rounded the curve and walked out of the trees into the open. "Wow. Look at this."

"Yeah." Pulling away from Sam, Bo limped over to a steep drop-off ahead and to the left. "Beautiful."

Sam went to stand beside Bo, gazing out at the slopes rising into the hazy distance. The mountainside fell away practically at their feet and tumbled into a wide valley far below. To their right, a large, rambling structure of wood perched at the edge of the drop. Its narrow porch overlooked the valley. The clouds had scattered and the sunshine felt wonderful, though Sam figured it still wasn't above thirty-five degrees here.

"Hey, come on, y'all!" Dean called, bounding up to them. "We have to check in and get our key, and Lex says there's coffee and hot chocolate in the dining hall. That's the building right there on the edge of the damn cliff."

Chuckling, Bo turned around to face Dean. "We're coming. I just had to get a good look at this view."

"Yeah, well, you can see it even better from the deck outside the office." Cocking his head, Dean frowned. "Bo, you're limping."

Bo made a face. "Yes, my leg's hurting some. It'll be okay."

"Aw, damn. Here, let me get your pack. I left mine up at the office."

Before Bo could object, Dean had sidled around behind him and was working the heavy pack off Bo's shoulders. Sam laughed at the mix of amusement and irritation on Bo's face. "Give it up. You know you can't talk Dean out of something he's set his mind to."

"What Sam said." Dean wrestled the pack onto his own back. "Oof. Damn, no wonder your leg hurts. This is *really* heavy."

"Yes, well, since we had to carry everything in and you insisted on having the equipment bag, I put some of the equipment in my pack."

Dean's eyebrows went up. "Huh. I thought that bag felt lighter than usual. I figured I was just turning into a big, strong he-man. How disappointing."

"No danger of you ever turning into one of those testosterone-poisoned hunks," Sam teased.

Rubbing his chin, Dean started toward the office, which lay just on the other side of the path. "Is that good or bad?"

"Good. Believe me." Turning to Bo, Sam rested his hand on his lover's back. "You need help?"

Bo shook his head. "No, I'm fine. Thanks."

The way Bo winced when he put his weight on his right leg said otherwise, but Sam knew better than to argue. During Bo's convalescence two months before, Sam had learned right off the bat how useless it was to try to overcome Bo's independent streak. Fighting the man's stubborn insistence on doing everything himself was like running a toy car into a concrete wall. All you got was a wrecked toy; the wall never changed.

"Stop looking at me like that," Bo muttered as they followed Dean up a gentle, grassy slope to the shallow slate steps set in the ground.

Sam almost protested that he wasn't looking at Bo any particular way, but then decided there was no point. Bo knew him too well. "Let me help you up to the office, and I'll stop looking worried."

Bo shot him a sly smile. "That's blackmail, you know."

"I know. I'm not above stooping to underhanded tactics to force you to look after yourself for a change."

Bo stopped and gazed up at the rustic office building. He groaned. The building was a two-story wood frame structure built on a steep section of the slope, with a wide deck wrapped around two sides of the upper story. A narrow door was set in the wall of the lower level, underneath the deck. The slate steps in the ground led to the bottom of a set of wooden stairs climbing two flights up to the deck.

"Okay, you win." Drawing a deep breath, Bo slung an arm across Sam's shoulders. "Help me up. But then you have to promise not to be a mother hen after this, okay?"

"Deal." Sam put his arm around Bo's waist and gripped the wrist hanging over his shoulder. "Here we go. Let me know if you need to stop and rest."

Bo gave him a thunderous look, but kept quiet. Sam bit back a laugh. Bo hated being babied, and Sam knew it.

They made it up the short flight of stone steps without incident. Dean met them at the bottom of the stairs to the office deck, having already taken Bo's pack up to the office. "Y'all okay?"

"Fine." Sam glanced up at the deck, where Lex stood talking to a tall, balding man. "Who's that?"

"Carl, Lex's husband. I think they're discussing who to send to babysit us this afternoon."

"Okay. Good." Bo put his free hand against the wall of the building and looked at Dean. "Go on up and tell them we'll be right there. They're looking kind of worried."

"'Kay." Dean scampered up the steps and trotted over to Lex and Carl.

Leaning heavily on Sam, Bo stepped gingerly on his injured leg, and he and Sam began making their way up the steps. It didn't take long, once they got their rhythm. At the top, Lex hurried over to them.

"I'm so sorry, Bo." Taking his arm, she led him away from Sam's side and over to the rocking chairs sitting in a row in front of the deck railing. "Dean said your leg was bothering you from an old injury. I would have rented you a horse to ride if I'd known. We would've had to take a longer trail, one more suitable for horses, but that would've been just fine. Why didn't you tell me?"

"I honestly didn't think of it myself. My leg never bothers me at home." Bo sank into a rocking chair, leaned his head against the graying wooden backrest and tilted his face up to the sun. "It should be just fine with a little rest. There's nothing really wrong with it, the muscles just aren't as strong as they used to be before the surgery."

Lex still looked worried, but she nodded. "Bo, Sam, I'd like you both to meet my husband, Carl. Sweetheart, this is Sam Raintree and Dr. Bo Broussard. They're Dean's coworkers from Bay City Paranormal Investigations."

Carl grabbed Sam's hand and pumped it hard. "Sam, nice to meet you. Welcome to Sunset Lodge. And you too, Bo," he added, leaning down to shake Bo's hand. "We're glad to have you folks here."

Bo smiled. "We're glad to be here, Carl. This place is absolutely beautiful."

"Thank you very much. We love it here." Carl squinted, fine lines crinkling around his hazel eyes. He swept a wiry arm toward the wooden cabins dotting the clearing to their right. "Sunset Rock is just over that way, beyond that stand of firs. See that mound of rock sticking up?"

Shading his eyes, Sam gazed in the direction Carl indicated. "Yes, I see it."

"You can't tell from here, but there's a really wide, flat place on the western side of the rock, and that's where everyone goes to watch the sunset." Carl planted his hands on his hips and beamed. "Be sure to bring your cameras. Trust me, you'll want to get pictures."

"I'm on it." Dean plopped into the chair beside Bo's and put his feet up on the deck rail. "Bo, you and Sam just sit on the rock looking photogenic, I'll take the pictures."

Sam laughed. "Suits me."

"Me too." Shooting Dean a quick grin, Bo twisted in his seat to talk to Lex, who still stood behind him on the deck. "Lex, I know you and Carl have things you need to do. You'd said something about having one of your employees show us around?"

"Yes. I think Anne's free this afternoon, isn't she, Carl?"

Carl nodded. "She's inside reading. I'll go get her."

"Thanks, honey." Rising on tiptoe, Lex gave her husband a kiss. "I'm heading to the kitchen. Jerome and Sandra need my help with dinner. The kitchen's just inside the dining hall, please come get me there if you need me."

"Sure thing. Thanks, Lex." Sam waved at Lex as she hurried down the steps, then moved to stand behind Bo's chair. Leaning down, he brushed a light kiss across the top of Bo's head. "I wish we could be here without a case to work on. This is a hell of a vacation spot."

"It sure is." Bo tilted his head back to smile at Sam. "Maybe we'll come back one day, huh?"

"I'd like that," Sam answered, stroking Bo's braid.

"Oh my God, you two are the best couple ever," Dean sighed, a faraway look in his eyes. "I am *so* taking pictures of y'all watching the sunset together tonight."

Bo chuckled. "You're such a romantic, Dean."

Behind them, the wooden door creaked open. Sam straightened up before Bo could shrug him off. Turning around, he saw a tall, shapely young woman with a cap of rich brown curls and a wide smile walking out of the office.

"Hi, I'm Anne Tallant," she said, holding out a slender, calloused hand. "Carl asked me to show y'all around the Lodge."

Sam took her hand and shook. "Nice to meet you, Anne. I'm Sam Raintree."

Dean jumped up from his chair and took Anne's hand the second Sam released it. "Dean Delapore." Dean flashed his most flirtatious smile. "Charmed."

She laughed, warm brown eyes shining. "Hi, Dean."

Pushing himself out of the rocking chair, Bo hobbled around to take his turn at shaking Anne's hand. "I'm Bo Broussard. Thanks for taking the time to show us the property, Anne. We really appreciate it."

"No problem. The Lodge is great, I love showing it off." She nodded toward their backpacks, which lay against the wall of the office. "I can take you to your cabins on the way, if you want."

Bo smiled at her. "That'd be great, thanks."

"Okay, cool." She stuck her hands in the back pockets of her jeans and pulled out a key attached to an orange plastic star. "Do y'all need help with your stuff?"

"No thank you," Bo answered. "We can get it."

She bit her lip. "You sure? Carl said you'd hurt your leg or something, Bo. I can carry stuff for you if you want, it's no trouble."

A muscle in Bo's jaw twitched. He opened his mouth to say something—probably, Sam figured, to tell Anne he'd hiked all the way up the mountain with his pack on his back and could damn well carry the thing to the cabin—when Dean cut him off.

"Bo won't say so, but his leg's hurting from the climb. He had major surgery on it just two months ago." Sidling closer to Anne, Dean laid a slightly-more-than-friendly hand on her shoulder. "If you could just carry his pack, that would be awesome."

A pretty pink flush crept into Anne's cheeks. She returned Dean's smile. "Sure thing, Dean."

Sam glanced at Bo. The man's expression was blank, but his dark eyes snapped with frustration. To Sam's relief, Bo kept whatever he was thinking to himself. Sam really didn't want to have to point out that a re-injury now could be disastrous to the investigation.

Slinging Bo's pack onto her back as if it weighed nothing, Anne started across the deck. "Y'all follow me. The cabin's not far. You can ditch your junk, then I'll show you around the property."

"Actually, Lex said I could stay in the extra staff bed," Dean said, grabbing his pack and the equipment bag and trotting after Anne. "Where's that?"

"In the downstairs part of this building." Anne stopped walking, turned and gave Dean a coquettish look over her shoulder. "You'll have to share a room with me, I hope that's okay."

Dean's teasing smile widened. "Oh yeah. That'll be just fine."

"Cool." Holding Dean's gaze just a little longer than was necessary, Anne turned around again and headed down the stairs.

Dean caught Sam's eye, jerked a thumb toward Anne and mouthed *hot!* before hurrying after her. Sam chuckled.

"I hope he realizes we're here to do a job, not literally charm the pants off as many staff members as possible," Bo grumbled.

"Don't worry. Sure, he's a flirt, but you know he never neglects the job." Sam hoisted his pack onto his shoulders, then wound an arm around Bo's waist. "You going to be able to tour the property?"

"I think so." Biting his lip, Bo levered himself carefully onto the first step, his hand gripping the frame of Sam's backpack. "As long as there are no more steep slopes, I think I'll be fine. Level ground is no problem. It's the up and down that hurts right now."

"Just promise me you'll tell me if you need to rest, okay?"

"Sure." Bo slid his hand down to squeeze Sam's butt. He grinned. "I know I never tell you this, Sam, but I love how you fuss over me."

Sam shot him a surprised look as they reached the landing halfway down the steps. "Really? I could've sworn you hated it."

Bo's expression turned sheepish. "I know. I'm sorry I'm so

hard to deal with sometimes. It bothers me to feel helpless, and that makes me short-tempered and I snap at people. You don't deserve that." He stopped, staring into Sam's eyes. "You've been my rock these last few months, Sam, and I've never once told you how grateful I am for that. So I'm telling you now. Thank you."

To Sam's utter shock, Bo tilted his face up and captured Sam's mouth in a soft kiss. It was swift and chaste, just a gentle brush of lips, but it was the first time Bo had ever kissed him where strangers might see. True, Anne and Dean had already disappeared into the staff quarters, but there were other guests at the Lodge and any of them might be watching. It was a huge step for Bo, and Sam knew it. Fighting the urge to crush Bo's body to his and open those silky lips with his tongue, Sam shut his eyes and savored the warm, sweet touch of Bo's mouth on his.

Bo nudged Sam's nose with his as he pulled away, making Sam smile. Neither said anything, but when their gazes locked, Sam knew they understood each other. Pressing his lips briefly to Bo's brow, he tucked his arm more firmly around his lover and they descended the steps together.

Anne and Dean emerged from a narrow door in the wall beneath the deck as Sam helped Bo from the last step onto the pathway. Dean had left his pack, but still carried the equipment bag. "Bo and Sam, you have cabin number four," Anne told them. "It's the second one on the right."

She strode down the path with Dean beside her. Trailing behind her with his arm still around Bo, Sam surveyed the area. Tiny wooden cabins dotted the gently tilted clearing, forming two staggered rows on either side of the narrow path through the grass. An old-fashioned hand pump was set in the ground beside the path. The dirt below the spout was damp.

"That's where you get your water," Anne said, waving a hand toward the pump. "There's a water bucket in your cabin. Bathrooms are down that path there." She pointed to a small building set apart from the cabins, down the slope a dozen yards or so past the dining hall. "No showers, but there's flush toilets and running water in the sinks."

"Thank God for that," Sam muttered. Bo laughed.

When she reached the second cabin on the right, Anne bounded up the three shallow steps, unlocked the door and flung it open. Sam and Bo followed her inside. Dean stood on the steps, leaning against the doorframe with his arms crossed.

"Wow, this is cute," Dean said, giving the place an appraising once-over. "Looks cozy."

Sam had to agree. The room was small, with most of the floor space taken up by a wide bunk bed in a rough-hewn wood frame. Thick red and white blankets covered the mattresses. Four plump pillows lay at the head of each bunk. A single wooden chair sat beneath the window on the left side of the room. Coarse blue curtains were tied to either side of that window, as well as a second window in the opposite wall behind the beds. To Sam's right, a narrow plank table hugged the wall. An oil lamp, a pack of matches, two metal cups, a large metal bucket and a wide white bowl covered the top of the table.

"Cabins are all propane heated." Crossing the room, Anne switched on the heater mounted on the wall. "You've got an oil lamp and matches there on the table. The bucket's for fresh water. The bowl's for washing in. Y'all brought towels and wash clothes, right?"

Bo shook his head. "No. We were at the Kimberley Inn when Lex asked us to investigate here, so we didn't have anything like that with us. Lex said she'd loan us some."

"Okay, cool. I'll bring some by later." Anne glanced from

face to face. "Do y'all need me to show you how to use the water pump?"

"Naw, I know how," Dean answered, grinning. "I'll show the city boys how to do it."

Sam slid his pack off his shoulders and hefted it onto the top bunk. "Dean, I know for a fact that you grew up in Mobile. You're more of a city boy than Bo or me."

"Yeah, but I spent part of every summer on my grandparents' farm. It was a really old property, and they still used the hand pump for water out at the barn." Dean stuck his thumbs in his front pockets, looking smug. "I'm the best of both worlds. City sophisticate *and* manly farmhand."

Giggling, Anne smacked Dean's arm. "Fine, you show them how to use the pump."

"Done." Giving Anne a slow, simmering look which made her blush to the roots of her hair, Dean sauntered into the room and set the equipment bag carefully on the floor beside the bed. "Bo, do you want to rest your leg before we see the property?"

Bo lifted his foot, flexing and straightening his right leg. "No, I think it'll be okay. Are there any steep slopes, Anne?"

"No. The path gains some elevation on the way to Sunset Rock, but it's a really shallow grade and the path's pretty smooth. You want to be careful out on the Rock, though. It isn't steep, but it's a giant rock, so the surface is uneven. All of you should watch your footing, actually."

"Sure thing," Sam said, silently vowing to keep a close eye on Bo. The man was a scientist, meticulous and careful during investigations, but he tended to be absentminded when it came to looking after himself.

Putting a hand on the bunk bed frame to steady himself, Bo rose to his feet. "Okay. Anne, if you're ready, we'd love to go ahead and see the area where your guests have spotted the animal, or whatever is it they're seeing. Sam, Dean, y'all bring still and video cameras. I'll take notes, Sam, if you'll hand me the notebook and pen."

Sam squatted on the floor and rifled through the bag until he found the sturdy, plastic-covered notebook and a blue pen. He handed them to Bo, then got out two small digital cameras—one for stills and one for video. They'd decided not to bring the cameras requiring film, and use only the digital equipment since it took up less room. Passing the still camera to Dean, he zipped the bag and stood up.

Dean snickered as he hung the official BCPI camera around his neck along with his own camera. "Two cameras. I feel like such a tourist."

Smiling, Bo flipped the notebook open and scribbled the date at the top of a fresh page. "Just remember, I wouldn't let you carry both if I thought for a second that being a tourist would distract you from the job."

"I know, Oh Exalted Bossy One, and I thank you."

Dean bowed low, and Anne laughed. "Are you guys always this much fun when you're working?"

"Oh, hell no," Dean answered, straight-faced. "Bo's a slave driver."

Bo didn't say anything, but quirked an eyebrow at Dean as he made his way outside. Sam laughed. "Don't listen to Dean. You might've noticed he's a tease and a bald-faced liar. We're serious about what we do, but yeah, we have fun with it too."

Anne shook her head. "This should be an interesting few days. Okay, let's head out."

Everyone piled back out into the thin winter sunshine. Anne locked the cabin door and handed the key to Sam. He stuck it in the front pocket of his jeans. Hanging the strap of the video camera around his neck, he followed the rest of the group up the path leading into the woods.

Chapter Four

The firs grew tall and thick around the path, plunging the group into a cold green gloom broken by the occasional splash of golden sunlight. Brown pine needles carpeted the ground, muffling their footsteps. The sharp scent of evergreens permeated the air. Hands in the pockets of his jacket, Sam drew a deep breath.

"This is gorgeous," he said, smiling up at the branches swaying in the breeze far above his head. "I love how it smells out here."

"Great, isn't it?" Anne swept an arm out in front of her. "You get kind of addicted to the fresh air up here. It's hard going back down the mountain."

"Yeah, I guess if y'all had hot showers here you'd never want to leave." Dean lifted his personal camera and pointed it at Anne. "Smile."

Anne struck a pose, one hand on her hip and the other behind her head. The camera clicked, the flash bright in the dimness. "Oh, man, that's fantastic!" Dean held up the camera for Anne to see. "You're beautiful, girl."

She waved a dismissive hand, but the flush in her cheeks and the sparkle in her eyes told Sam how flattered she was. Biting back a laugh, Sam caught Bo's eye. Bo just shook his head, an indulgent grin tugging at the corners of his mouth.

"The place where the sightings have happened is just up ahead," Anne told them. "So far, no one's seen anything at any time other than after the sunset. But then again, people usually don't even come up this path except at sunset."

Bo gave his braid a thoughtful tug. "Why is that? This is a beautiful hike, I'd think guests would want to come up here more than once."

"Well, most folks don't arrive here until mid-to-late afternoon. They generally want to rest after they get up here, and most people only stay one night so they pretty much leave after breakfast the next morning. This time of year, that doesn't really leave time for more than one trip to the Rock. Some people go up there more than once in the summer, though, 'cause the sun sets way later."

Dean turned around, walking backward in order to talk to Bo and Sam. "Are y'all thinking what I'm thinking?"

"You mean, that whatever it is might not just be around at twilight?" Sam glanced at Bo, and saw the same thought in his eyes. "Yeah."

"Sam, when we get to the spot, go ahead and take video." Clicking the pen on, Bo scribbled a note on the pad. "Dean, you take stills."

Anne's gaze darted back and forth between the three of them, curiosity bright in her eyes. "How come?"

"Sometimes things show up on film that the naked eye can't pick up," Bo explained. "We've learned a great deal in the past by taking video and still pictures of the area in question, even if we can't see or sense anything ourselves."

Frowning, Anne tilted her head to the side. "What do you mean, sense? You mean, like, psychic stuff?"

Bo and Dean both looked at Sam. He bit back a groan. "Yes, like psychic stuff. I'm psychic. I can sometimes sense things other people can't sense, even see and hear things other people can't. Things that show up on film or audio tape later," he added, noting Anne's skeptical expression. "We have two other psychics on our team, but they're back in Asheville finishing up the investigation at the Kimberley Inn."

The shuttered look vanished from Anne's face, bubbly eagerness taking its place. "Oh my God, I stayed there one time! It's awesome! Did you guys see the Lady in Red?"

Sam nodded. "Yeah, we did. I got some video of her."

"Wow, that's so cool." Anne turned and started up the path again. "I guess we better get going. I want to make sure you guys get to do everything you need to before I have to head back."

Dean fell into step beside Anne, the two of them talking with their heads together. Sam and Bo followed more slowly. Bo's gait was more hesitant than usual, and his shoulders were tight. Worried, Sam drew closer and laid a hand on Bo's back.

"Is your leg still bothering you?" he murmured. "You promised to tell me."

Bo grimaced. "Yes, actually. But it's different from before."

"Different how?"

"After the climb up the mountain, it ached, like an overworked muscle normally would. Just felt tight and sore, and it hurt to put weight on it. Now..." He shook his head, brows drawn together in thought. "I don't know. It doesn't hurt, exactly. It burns. It feels sort of like there's little bubbles bursting under my skin and inside the muscle."

Sam shot him a concerned look. "That can't be normal."

"I know." Winding the tail of his braid around his finger, Bo met Sam's gaze. "When we get back to the cabin, I'd like to take a good look at it. What I'm feeling is unusual enough that I'd like for us both to examine the old wound as closely as possible."

Letting his hand slide down Bo's arm, Sam briefly squeezed his fingers. "Maybe you should let Dean look at it too. He's the only one here with medical training."

"Yes, I think you're right. I'll have Dean take a look and give his opinion."

"Good."

At that moment, Anne stopped about fifty feet up the trail and nodded toward the trees to Sam's right. "Okay, this is it. Right here is where the sightings have been."

Bo hurried forward, with Sam at his heels. Sam noticed the faint stiffness of Bo's gait and the way his hand rubbed his right thigh, but kept quiet about it. Bo wouldn't appreciate him interrupting the investigation with concerns over Bo's discomfort, especially since they'd just finished discussing what to do about it.

"All of the sightings have been at this exact spot?" Bo twisted his braid and stared into the thicket of pines. "You're certain?"

"Uh-huh." Moving to stand beside Bo, Anne pointed into the trees. "See that rock there?"

Sam looked in the direction Anne pointed. About twenty feet from the path, a large, smooth boulder rose from a mass of brambles. It shone white in the shadows.

"Yes, I see it," Bo said. "Have the witnesses all mentioned seeing the creature near that boulder?"

"Yep. Every last one."

"Hm." Bo wrote on his notepad, then glanced at Sam. "Why don't you go ahead and start the video, Sam?"

"Sure thing." Thumbing the video camera on, Sam centered

the picture and started filming. "Dean? Stills?"

"Got it," Dean called, already snapping photos. "Hey, Anne, what exactly did the witnesses see? Where did they say the...critter, thing, whatever, where did it come from? And where did it go?"

"Everybody said it came from behind the rock someplace, ran through the woods to the left of the rock for a little ways, then took off through the trees away from the path and disappeared. We figure it only seemed like it disappeared because of the low light." Her face took on a thoughtful expression. "You know what, now that I think of it, it's kind of weird that everybody saw it go the exact same way."

"Just what I was thinking myself," Bo said. "Anne, have you seen it?"

Her eyes took on a strangely furtive look. "No. A couple of the other workers have, though."

A glance at Bo told Sam he'd gotten the same sense Sam had—that Anne was lying. *But why? It doesn't make any sense.* Resolving to talk to the other staff members when he got a chance, Sam filed the information away for later use.

Bo laid a hand on Sam's arm. "Sam, can you feel anything here?"

"Not right now. Here, take the camera and I'll see what I can pick up."

Handing the video camera to Bo, Sam shut his eyes and stretched out his senses. Something wispy and vague tugged at the edge of his mind. Whatever it was, it was nothing like the overwhelming menace and sense of purpose he'd felt in Oleander House or South Bay High.

"There's something," he murmured, his eyes still closed. "But it's very faint. And it doesn't feel threatening at all. Not like before."

He opened his eyes and met Bo's relieved gaze. Bo gave him a wide smile. "That's good. Why don't the three of us walk out to the rock? We can take some close-up pictures and video, and inspect the area." He turned to Anne. "That's okay, isn't it?"

"Sure," she said. "Just watch your step. The ground drops off pretty suddenly a few dozen yards past the boulder."

"We'll be careful." Bo glanced at Dean. "All right, let's all be on the lookout for anything unusual while we're walking out there. We'll check all around the rock, then take video and stills. Got it?"

"Got it, boss." Bumping Anne's shoulder with his, Dean moved to Bo's side. "I'm ready."

The three of them moved together, walking slow and steady. Sam took the video camera back, ready to film. He swept a keen gaze over the ground as he walked, looking for anything out of place. At the same time, he kept his psychic senses open for any further evidence of whatever he'd felt before.

When they reached the boulder, which rose above Sam's head, Bo grunted and leaned a hand against the stone. "Damn."

"Bo? What is it?" Moving closer to Bo, Sam laid a hand on his shoulder. "Your leg again?"

"Yeah. The burning's getting worse. It feels so strange. I can't even describe it." Bo rubbed a palm over his thigh. "It feels almost electrified."

Sam glanced at Dean, who looked just as worried as Sam felt. "We should go back. Let Dean look at it."

"He's right," Dean chimed in. "This doesn't sound like normal muscle strain."

The muscles in Bo's jaw tightened. "I know. But I feel like we need to finish here first. It may be our last chance to investigate this spot in the daytime, without any snow or anything to hinder us. The weather's clear right now, but that winter storm could still hit."

Sam sighed. "I'd argue, but I know what kind of chance I've got at changing your mind. Besides which, you have a point."

"At least let me and Sam walk around the back," Dean suggested. "You can check here in the front, that way you won't have to put any more strain on your leg."

Bo didn't look happy, but he nodded. "Okay. We'll do that."

Sam and Dean wasted no time trampling through the weeds and briars to the back of the boulder. Dean began perusing the ground around the base of the boulder, taking pictures every few seconds. Sam panned the camera in a slow arc from the boulder through the trees and back.

The video done, Sam switched the camera off and let it dangle from the strap around his neck. "Dean, I'm going to see what I can feel on this side of the rock, okay?"

"Gotcha. I'll keep my eyes peeled for anything, you just yell if you feel something weird."

Pressing both hands to the rock's surface, Sam closed his eyes and let his senses expand. The stone felt cold and rough under his palms, and the air smelled damp. A gust of wind moaned through the branches overhead. Sam grimaced at the sharp sting of the frigid breeze on his face and ears. He wished he'd worn a cap.

Something flickered ghost-like on the edge of Sam's inner vision. Concentrating as hard as he could, he nudged his awareness closer to it, trying to understand what it was. What he sensed confused him. It felt static. Dead and fading, like the smell of a match after it's snuffed out.

Bracken crackled to Sam's left, then he caught the spicy scent of Dean's cologne. "What're you feeling?" Dean asked, keeping his voice low as everyone in the group had learned to do when one of their psychics was working.

Sam shook his head. "I'm not sure. Like I said before, it's not threatening at all. It's barely even there."

"And it's not like at South Bay? Or Oleander House?"

It wasn't, not really. But there was a flavor of the familiar about what Sam sensed that made him reluctant to dismiss the potential link so easily. Especially in light of what the Sunset Lodge guests had seen here.

"I'm not sure, actually." Opening his eyes, Sam pushed away from the rock and stuck his chilled hands in his pockets. "It feels similar, in a way, but not the same. Like it's a faded version of what was there at Oleander House and the high school."

Leaning his back against the boulder, Dean stared thoughtfully at Sam's face. "Kind of like the difference between red and pink, huh?"

Sam laughed. "That's actually a really good analogy. If what I felt at the high school was red, this is definitely a pastel pink."

"Hmm." Dean scratched his chin. "Wonder what that means?"

"I have no idea. Did you see anything behind the rock, back in the woods?"

"Not a thing." Dean gave him an apprehensive look. "You think we should walk back there a little?"

"Bo would want us to."

"I was afraid you'd say that."

At that moment, Bo hobbled around the edge of the rock. "Okay, I didn't find anything worth seeing on that side. What about y'all?"

"Just boring old weeds and trees," Dean answered

cheerfully. "But Sam's mojo caught something."

"Pretty much what I felt before," Sam elaborated. "Vague, non-threatening, almost not there. It feels like a faded-out version of what I sensed at Oleander House."

Bo's jaw tightened. "Okay. Sam, give me the video camera. You keep the notebook and pen. I'll take video. I want you to concentrate on your psychic senses. See if what you feel grows stronger or weaker, or changes in any other way, as we go into the woods. Dean, continue to take stills."

"How many?" Dean brandished the camera. "I brought all but a couple of our memory cards, and extra batteries for the cameras and the laptop, but we can only download so many times before all our batteries die. I figure they have a generator here, but it'll be for emergencies only. We need to be careful how many pics we take."

"Damn, you're right." Bo tugged hard on his braid, teeth worrying his bottom lip. "Okay, well, for now just take stills if we see something worth taking pictures of. I'll do the same with video."

Dean nodded. Sliding an arm around Bo's waist, Sam kissed his brow. "That works. I'm ready, are y'all?"

"Ready," Dean called.

Without further comment, Bo started wading through the weeds and pine needles, deeper into the forest. He limped with every step, obviously in pain. Sam glanced at Dean, who rolled his eyes and shrugged as if to say, *What can you do?*

Shaking his head, Sam stretched out his psychic mind and followed Bo into the shadows. Dean trailed just behind him, guarding his footsteps in case his partial trance caused him to stumble.

Sam wasn't sure exactly how long they tramped through the woods. He figured they covered at least fifty square feet of ground. Bo and Dean kept glancing back, making sure they kept Anne and the trail in sight. The trace of abnormal energy lingered. Sam could pick it up easily now that he knew how it felt. It didn't seem to change at all. It remained steady the whole time, its strength the same fifty feet from the boulder and right beside it.

Finally, Bo motioned Sam and Dean to follow him back to the trail. "I guess we've done all we can for now. Let's head on back."

Sam and Dean fell into step beside Bo. "You want to bring the EMF detectors out tonight when we come for sunset?" Dean asked. "We can get some readings, then come back tomorrow and do it again and compare the readings. If the weather holds, that is."

Bo smiled. "That's a good idea. We'll do it."

They made their way back to the trail, where Anne stood talking to a dark-skinned young man in a blue knit cap and matching down jacket.

"Hey, guys," Anne called. "Did you find anything?"

"We didn't see anything," Sam answered. "But we'll have to review the pics and videos to know for sure if we got anything."

"We'd like to stop and take another look tonight after sunset." Walking up to Anne and her friend, Bo held out his hand to the young man. "Hi, I'm Bo Broussard, and this is Sam Raintree and Dean Delapore. We're from Bay City Paranormal Investigations in Mobile."

"I know. Lex mentioned you might be coming up when she radioed last night." The stranger smiled, took Bo's hand and shook. "Darren Soames. I'm a big fan of your work, especially with the portals. I'm studying theoretical physics in school, so what you folks have done is fascinating to me."

Bo's eyebrows shot up. "I'd love to talk with you at some

point, if that's okay. My doctorate is in psychology. I'm afraid I'm not really up on theoretical physics."

Darren beamed. "I'd love that."

"Great." Bo glanced at Anne. "We were just heading back to the cabins, Anne, we can find our own way if you have things you need to do."

"The stuff I have to do is back at the Lodge." She grinned. "Darren's just coming back up the mountain from a trip to town, so he's headed back that way too. We can all walk together."

Dean turned a curious look to Darren as the group started back down the path to the Lodge. "That's a big hike all the way down the mountain. Must be one hell of a party town down there."

Laughing, Darren shook his head. "Not really, no. I went to pick up some books I'd ordered." He held up a large plastic bag. "Texts on quantum physics and string theory. I'm taking a semester off school to work, but I don't want to fall behind."

Moving closer to Darren, Dean nudged the young man with his elbow. "Darren, you are *scary* smart."

Dean's eyes gleamed with the same interest he'd shown Anne, and Sam bit back a laugh. Maybe Dean really would charm the pants off the entire staff.

"I didn't think this path connected with one we took to get up here," Bo said. "Is this the horse path Lex was telling us about?"

"No, it's up closer to the Lodge. The path Darren took joins this one further on, almost at Sunset Rock." Turning around, Anne gestured toward the trail curving into the trees behind them. "Guests don't use that trail, just employees."

"I see." Bo stumbled into Sam's side, his face contorting.

"Oh. Damn."

Without thinking of what he was doing, Sam wound an arm around Bo's waist and drew him close. "You're hurting again."

Sam wasn't surprised when Bo pushed away from him, but it still hurt a little. Bo gave him a strained smile. "No, it's actually better now. I just tripped over a tree root. I'm fine."

The lie was obvious, to Sam at least, but he didn't say anything. Bo was nothing if not stoic, especially in front of people he didn't know well. At least Bo had agreed to let Dean take a look at his leg, which was more than Sam had expected.

We're only a few minutes from the cabin, he reminded himself. *And Bo's a grown man. Just leave it.*

Tamping down his irritation, Sam glanced around at the rest of their group. Just ahead, Darren, Dean and Anne were deep in conversation about what sounded like current theories on the nature of higher dimensions. Darren darted a keen look over his shoulder, dark gaze flicking between Sam and Bo. Sam recognized the furtive expression in his eyes. He'd seen it before, mostly on the faces of people who'd never been around a gay couple before. Curiosity, veiled with a vague distaste.

It was a relief, in a way. Darren would be uncomfortable if confronted with physical evidence of Sam and Bo's relationship, but he wouldn't give them any trouble over it.

Dean, however, would not be getting into the man's pants.

When they reached Sam and Bo's cabin, Bo thanked Anne for her time, everyone shook hands and Anne and Darren headed toward the kitchen. Sam watched them go. They had their heads together, holding a whispered discussion. Anne shot a glance backward as Bo unlocked the cabin, and Sam saw unveiled disgust in her eyes. His gut clenched.

Inside, Dean drew the curtains, then dug his flashlight out of the equipment bag. "Okay, Bo, let's have a look at that leg."

Without a word, Bo shucked his jacket, sat in the chair and started unlacing his hiking boots. He kept his gaze fixed on his feet. His lips were pressed together in a thin line. Sam suppressed a sigh. Bo was angry with him, probably over the incident on the trail, and Sam would be hearing all about it as soon as Dean left.

He hated that. Hated the continuing arguments over other people finding out about them. Hated being lulled into a comfortable openness around their friends, then being slapped in the face with the knowledge that what he and Bo had was still little more than a dirty secret.

Sam took off his jacket, threw it onto the bed and perched on the edge of the bottom bunk, hunched over to keep from hitting his head on the sturdy wood frame of the top bunk. He watched Bo stand and slip his jeans off. He wore dark red boxer briefs. The color brought out the rich caramel of his skintone.

As usual, the sight of Bo's smooth skin dissolved Sam's melancholy in a wash of desire. He bit his lip and forced himself to focus on the old wound in Bo's thigh.

The surgical scar ran from just above the kneecap nearly all the way to the bend of Bo's hip. Emergency surgery, the doctor had explained at the time, necessitated a larger incision, the need to remove the rapidly spreading infection taking precedence over cosmetic concerns. They'd had to remove some of the damaged subcutaneous tissue, leaving a faint depression in Bo's leg a few inches above the knee. Luckily, none of the actual thigh muscle had needed to be excised. Bo's strength and range of motion in that leg was almost as good as in the other one.

Dean knelt on the floor and handed Sam the flashlight. "Here, Sam, shine this on the scar."

Sam switched the flashlight on and trained the beam on

Bo's thigh. The puckered scars around the still-visible furrows from the creature's teeth shone in the light.

"I'm going to palpate all along your incision, Bo," Dean said. "Tell me if anything I do hurts or feels strange in any way."

Bo nodded. "Okay."

Dean worked his way down the thin pink surgical scar, pressing his fingertips gently into the muscle on either side. When he reached the old bite mark, Bo hissed, his thigh twitching away from Dean's touch. Dean stopped and raised his eyebrows at Bo.

"It didn't hurt exactly," Bo said. "It felt almost like a mild electrical shock. As if you'd touched a live wire to my leg."

Dean frowned. "Okay, that's just weird. Even if your pain was from some sort of nerve compression, what I just did shouldn't have set it off." Taking the flashlight from Sam, Dean held the beam directly over the healed wound and peered at it from inches away. "I don't see any signs of infection or impaired blood flow. I guess the scar tissue could've maybe entrapped a nerve, but it seemed like that would've manifested before now."

"So what do you think?" Sam leaned back on his hands, watching Dean's face instead of Bo's. "Is it anything to worry about?"

"I'm sure it isn't," Bo said, his voice slow and clipped like it always was when he was angry and trying not to show it. "It's probably just strained from the hike. That's the most strenuous exercise that muscle's had in a long time."

Sitting back on his heels, Dean turned the flashlight off and set it on the floor. "It isn't acting like a normal muscle strain, but honestly, I can't think of what else it could be. I can't see anything else obviously wrong. My advice would be to go as easy on that leg as you can, and just watch it. If it keeps improving, we can probably blame it on the climb. If not, well, we'll cross that bridge when we get to it I guess."

"Okay." Bo gave Dean an obviously forced smile. "Thanks for taking a look. I appreciate it."

"No problem." Dean put his flashlight back in the bag and pushed to his feet. "Okay, I'm off to mingle with the staff for a while. I'll stop back by in time for us to all walk up to Sunset Rock."

"Be careful what you say to them," Sam told him. "About me and Bo, I mean. I think Anne and Darren suspect."

"Oh, yes. Definitely." Crossing his arms over his stomach, Bo pinned Sam with a pointed stare. "Wonder why?"

Sam started to retort and was cut off by Dean. "Whoa, whoa, whoa. Do *not* start fighting about who might or might not have guessed y'all are doing it. Or at least wait till I'm gone."

Resisting the urge to hit something, Sam clasped his hands on his lap and managed to speak calmly. "We're not going to fight about that, Dean. I'm just saying, be careful. I don't think Darren will cause any trouble, but I didn't like the way Anne was looking at us on the path. She's an unknown at this point, and so are the employees we haven't met yet. We don't want to lose this job—or worse, have one of us attacked—because of mine and Bo's relationship. So just watch what you say, okay?"

"Okay. Sure." With a last thoughtful glance at Bo and Sam, Dean opened the cabin door and stepped outside. Sunlight poured in, along with a cold breeze. "See y'all later. And whether you fuck or fight after I leave, keep it down if you want to keep your business to yourselves."

The door swung shut with a squeal of hinges, and Sam and Bo were alone in the little room. Sam glanced up at Bo. Sunlight seeped in through the woven fabric of the curtains and around their edges, washing Bo in a cool blue light. The man's eyes, however, were anything but cool. They blazed with anger, frustration and the fear Sam knew Bo hadn't entirely conquered.

"I'm sorry, Bo," Sam said, breaking the uncomfortable silence. "I really didn't mean to grab you like that. You know I like to keep a low profile myself until I know someone. You never can tell how people are going to react."

"Anne knew my leg was bothering me. You were right there beside me when I tripped. It was perfectly natural for you to grab me to keep me from falling."

"So you don't think that's what gave us away?"

"No."

"What then?"

The corner of Bo's mouth twitched. "The way you looked at me. The way you held me. Your feelings were written all over your face."

A sudden surge of fury rushed through Sam's blood. He clenched his hands in the thick blankets. "And why shouldn't they be? Why should we always have to be so fucking careful to keep our feelings from showing, just to make other people comfortable? I love you, Bo. I don't want to shove it in everyone's faces, but I don't want to have to pretend I don't feel it either."

The snapping anger melted from Bo's eyes. Sliding to the edge of the chair, he took Sam's hands in his. "I hate it too, Sam. It isn't right, and it isn't fair. But it's reality. You know that better than I do."

Sam rubbed the backs of Bo's hands with his thumbs. "Yeah, I know. That's the way things are, like it or not. But I wish it wasn't like that."

"So do I." Leaning forward, Bo nuzzled Sam's cheek. "There's no one to see now. No one to be careful of. We're all alone."

The seductive tone of Bo's voice made Sam ache low in his belly. He smiled, turning his head to mouth the shell of Bo's ear. "Mmm. We are, aren't we? What should we do about that?"

"I think you should stand up and unzip your pants," Bo suggested. "Then I think you should put your cock in my mouth and let me suck it."

Bo's words, spoken in a voice husky with rising desire, sent a shudder of pleasure up Sam's spine. Hooking a hand behind Bo's head, Sam pulled him close and captured his mouth in a deep, rough kiss. Bo opened to him, soft little moans spilling from his mouth to Sam's, and Sam sank happily into it. He loved kissing Bo. Every time their lips met, every time their tongues wound together, it sent him flying.

Part of him wished he could spend the rest of eternity with his mouth fused to Bo's. But his crotch ached, his cock craving attention, and Bo wanted to go down on him. Breaking the kiss with difficulty, Sam stood between Bo's spread legs, unbuttoned his jeans and yanked the zipper down. Bo shoved Sam's jeans and underwear to his knees, grabbed his cock and wrapped his lips around the head, tongue flicking across the sensitive slit. Sam groaned. He held still with an effort, petting Bo's hair. In the past two months, Bo had gotten very, very good at sucking cock, but he didn't like having his head held still, and he hadn't gotten the hang of deep-throating.

Sam wasn't about to complain. He was lucky enough to have a lover with natural talent in fellatio, and a hunger for it that rivaled any Sam had ever seen. That was more than enough for him.

Letting Sam's prick slip from between his lips, Bo rubbed his cheek against the saliva-slick shaft. "God, I love your cock." He dipped his head to tongue Sam's balls. "I love how you smell when you're excited." Bo popped a finger into his mouth and slid it between Sam's cheeks. The wet tip pressed into Sam's hole, tearing a sharp cry from him. "I love doing this to you. Making you come." Darting a blazing look at Sam, Bo wrapped a hand around his shaft and sucked him down.

Sam wanted to answer, to tell Bo how he lived for moments like this, with Bo's enthusiastic mouth on him and Bo's inquisitive finger in his ass. But he couldn't make a sound, other than lusty moans and incoherent pleas for more. All the blood seemed to have deserted his brain and taken up residence in his prick. Whimpering, he reached up and clamped his hands onto a low-hanging rafter to keep himself from clenching them in Bo's hair and fucking his mouth.

Pushing his finger deeper to nail Sam's gland, Bo hummed around Sam's prick. The vibrations shot fire through Sam's core, making him shake. When Bo's free hand grabbed Sam's balls and tugged, squeezing just a little, it was all Sam could stand. His orgasm ripped through him, arching his spine and snapping his head back in silent ecstasy. He stood there, hanging onto the rafter for dear life and quivering from head to foot while Bo swallowed the spunk pulsing from him.

Bo eased his finger from Sam's ass and pulled back, licking his lips. He grinned up at Sam. "I love it when you come in my mouth."

Sam let out a breathless laugh. "Good, because I think I'm addicted to coming in your mouth."

Chuckling, Bo leaned forward, lifted Sam's shirt and kissed his belly. "I'm hard as a rock, Sam. You want my cock in your mouth or your ass?"

Sam considered. Sucking Bo off was tempting. But the thought of Bo fucking him made his knees weak. It always did.

Winding the long braid around his hand, Sam pulled Bo's

head back, bent and kissed him hard. "Want you to fuck me," he whispered, and bit Bo's lip. "Right here in the chair."

A soft groan escaped Bo's lips. "The lube's in my backpack. Outside pocket."

Sam kissed Bo once more, then yanked his jeans and underwear up and turned to fetch the lube from Bo's pack. They'd stopped using condoms as soon as all the tests came back negative. To Sam's surprise, Dean had gotten tested as well, and shared his negative results with them both. Just to be on the safe side, he'd said, even though he and Sam had used a condom the one time they'd been together.

With the bottle of liquid lube clutched in one hand, Sam crossed back to Bo and knelt on the floor in front of him. He laid his palms on Bo's sides, thumbs hooking beneath the elastic of Bo's underwear. "Lift up. Let me take these off you."

Bo obediently lifted his hips, allowing Sam to slide the boxer briefs over his buttocks and down his thighs. His cock sprang free, flushed and rigid, hitting his belly with a damp smack. Sam stared at Bo as he pulled the garment down and off. Bo's braid had begun to come loose, errant strands of silky black clinging to his face and neck. His breath came sharp and quick between parted lips, and his eyes burned.

Sam wanted to kneel at his feet forever and bask in the sight of him, decadent and beautiful in the grip of his need.

A dazed smile spread across Bo's face. He reached out to touch Sam's cheek. "Come up here, Sam. Come ride me."

Rising to his feet, Sam tugged off his hiking shoes and skinned out of his jeans and underwear. He stood astride Bo's lap and handed Bo the lube. "Get me ready," he ordered, tugging the rubber band off the end of Bo's braid. He started unwinding the long, heavy strands, delighting in the satin softness between his fingers.

Bo held Sam's gaze as he flipped open the lube, coated his fingers and tossed the bottle on the bed. "Take your shirt off too," he murmured, slipping a single slick digit into Sam's hole. "I want you naked."

Sam's cock twitched and started to fill, making it hard to think, hard to do anything. Thanking his lucky stars he'd worn a sweatshirt instead of something with buttons, Sam tore the shirt over his head and let it fall in an inside-out heap on the floor.

"Mmmm," Bo purred, inserting a second finger into Sam. "Mine." He wound his free arm around Sam's waist and pressed open-mouthed kisses to his bare skin.

"Yours," Sam gasped, working loose the last twist in Bo's hair and burying both hands in its dark length. "God. I want your cock in me now."

"Here it is." Removing his arm from Sam's waist, Bo grabbed his own prick and held it upright. "Sit."

Sam didn't need any more invitation than that. With Bo's free hand steadying him, he held his cheeks apart and lowered himself onto Bo's cock. They both groaned as the wide, smooth head penetrated Sam's hole. Sam moved as slowly as he could manage, wanting to savor the feel of Bo's shaft pushing relentlessly into him, filling him up and setting his world on fire.

Finally, Sam's ass rested in Bo's lap, with Bo's prick fully buried inside him. Staring into Bo's eyes, Sam gave an experimental rock of his hips. Bo's eyelids fluttered, his breath hitching. "Fuck, Sam. God, tight."

Sam moved again, trying to keep his full weight off Bo's injured leg. His thighs burned already with the strain of holding himself in this position, but he would've rather died than stop. Having Bo inside him like this felt too good. Besides, it was clear from the fine tremors shaking Bo's body that he wouldn't last long.

Panting, Sam rested his forehead against Bo's and clutched his shoulders. "Okay?"

Bo nodded, one hand curling around Sam's renewed erection. "Okay."

Tilting his head, Sam captured Bo's mouth in a slow, wet kiss. Bo growled. He gave a short, sharp thrust that zinged over Sam's gland and pulled a kiss-muffled cry from him. Fingers digging into Bo's skin, Sam began to move in a seesawing figure eight which he knew from experience brought a swift, explosive orgasm every time.

"Oh Christ," Bo breathed. His thighs spread, hips pulsing up and down to match Sam's rhythm. "Not gonna last, Sam."

"Don't try." Taking Bo's lower lip between his teeth, Sam sucked on it for a second, then let it go. "Fuck me. Come inside me."

"Uh. Yes. Love fucking you."

Hands clamped hard onto Sam's hipbones. Bo thrust up into him, the angle sharp and deep enough to hurt. Sam keened, pressed his palms to the wall behind Bo's head and forced himself down onto Bo's cock, again and again and again, until his legs shook and sweat dripped from his face and ran in rivulets down his back. Beneath him, Bo's hips snapped up and down in a brutal rhythm. Bo buried his face in Sam's neck, biting and sucking, his breath coming in harsh grunts Sam could feel against his bruising skin.

It was rough, unrefined and bordering on violent, and Sam wished it would never end. If he could halt the flow of time right here, with Bo's cock in him, Bo's lips hot on his neck and his prick rubbing against Bo's ridged belly, he could die a happy man.

The tightening of Bo's fingers on his hips and the pulse of Bo's shaft in his ass told Sam his lover was close to release. Dipping his head, Sam covered Bo's mouth with his and plunged his tongue inside. Bo responded with an equal passion, eating at Sam's mouth like it was his last meal. Snaking a hand between their bodies, Sam found one of Bo's hard little nipples, pinched and twisted it until the sweet familiar noises began to bleed from Bo's mouth. When the moment came, Bo went still, his mouth open and slack beneath Sam's, his prick moving in tiny jerks as he painted Sam's insides with thick, hot semen.

The last thing Sam wanted to do at that moment was stand up. He loved to keep Bo lodged in his ass after they fucked; the sensation of Bo's prick softening inside him made him feel an odd sort of connection between them. But the ache in his thighs was turning into a cramping pain, bad enough to keep him from coming again. And he needed to come.

Biting his lip, Sam rose carefully to his feet. His thigh muscles screamed in protest. Bo's prick slid out of him, making them both hiss at the same time.

"Want to come?" Bo asked, running his palms over Sam's abdomen and around to his back. "God, I love how you can get it up twice for me."

Sam's heart was racing, his breath coming so fast he couldn't speak. He nodded and wrapped a hand around his shaft, intent on jerking off. Bo slapped his hand away.

Sam gaped. Bo just stared at him, dark eyes gleaming with a strange light.

"Turn around," Bo said. "There's something I've been wanting to do."

Wondering what he meant, Sam shuffled around to face away from Bo. Something niggled at the back of Sam's blood-deprived brain. Before he could grasp what it was, Bo's hands pressed warm and damp to Sam's buttocks, thumbs digging in to spread him wide open.

Oh my God, Sam thought, dazed. *He's going to do it.*

Bo had been curious about it for a while, Sam knew. He loved it when Sam rimmed him, and none of the porn they'd explored together excited him quite like a man's tongue in another man's ass. But he'd never made a move to actually do it.

Until now.

Sam let out a low, ragged moan when the tip of Bo's tongue touched his stretched and sensitive hole. He reached up and grabbed the rafter to keep from falling down. "Oh fuck. Bo."

Humming, Bo licked the length of Sam's crease, then pulled back. "I can taste us both. God, this is good." He bit Sam's left cheek. "Lean against the bed. It'll be easier that way, I think."

"Uh-huh." Letting go of the rafter, Sam turned to face the bunk beds. He rested his arms on the upper bunk and leaned over, exposing himself to his lover.

Bo's appreciative growl made him grin. The smile dissolved in a wash of pure pleasure when Bo's tongue plunged into his open hole. The sensation sent him soaring, his prick jumping in the hand Bo had wrapped around it. If Sam had believed in heaven, he figured this would be it. What reward could possibly be better than Bo's tongue slithering soft and slick into his ass, which still dripped with Bo's come?

The combination of hand and tongue had Sam right on the edge in seconds. His orgasm overtook him in a rapid rush. He buried his face in the blanket to muffle the scream that tore from him when he came.

Bo's tongue withdrew. His arms went around Sam's hips, his hot cheek pressed to the spot where the sweat pooled just above the crease of Sam's ass. "Wow. Who knew licking someone's anus could be so enjoyable?"

Sam laughed, the sound hoarse and breathless. "Figured you'd like it, once you gave it a try."

"Mmm." Bo planted a tender kiss on Sam's lower back, then pulled away. "Sit down before you fall down, Sam. Your legs are shaking."

Turning around, Sam sank onto the lower bunk and flopped onto his back. He wrinkled his nose at the feel of cooling spunk on the back of his thigh where it hung over the edge of the mattress. "I always manage to get myself in the wet spot."

Bo laughed. "You could move." He stood to retrieve his underwear from the floor.

"No. Too tired." Sam yawned and stretched, watching Bo pull on his boxer briefs and jeans. "I sure hope no one notices the come on the blanket when we leave and they strip the beds."

The grin on Bo's face was pure evil. "By then there'll be a lot more spunk on the bed, and that one little spot will just blend right in."

Groaning, Sam kicked Bo's good leg with one sock-clad foot. "Quit being a smart-ass and come lie down with me. We can take a nap before sunset."

"Just a short one, though." Rising with a grimace, Bo crawled onto the bed. "We want to have time to get everything together for this evening's investigation before we go."

"I'll set the alarm on my watch." Sam raised his left arm and pressed a few buttons on his watch, squinting in the low light. "There. Half an hour. Okay?"

"That's good." Bo went into Sam's embrace and curled

against him with a sigh. "Love you."

Sam tightened his arms around Bo. "Love you too."

Lifting his face, Bo claimed a sweet, lazy kiss, then rested his head on Sam's chest. Sam kissed Bo's hair. He closed his eyes and drifted off with the feel of Bo's heart beating against his.

Chapter Five

On the way to Sunset Rock, Bo walked between Lex and Carl instead of beside Sam. Strolling along by himself behind Dean and the talkative older couple he'd befriended on the trail, Sam watched Bo in silence. Bo's faded jeans hugged the hard curves of his thighs, and his braid swung across his back as he turned to talk to first Carl, then Lex. The canvas messenger bag holding the EMF detectors, flashlights and other equipment hung at Bo's side. Sam wished Bo's red down jacket didn't hang so low. It hid his ass.

Of course, Sam reflected, not being able to see Bo's delectable rear was probably a good thing at this point. Sam already itched to push forward and claim Bo with an arm around his shoulders and a kiss to his lips. Or at least walk beside him. But Bo had thought it best for them not to pay too much attention to each other, to keep from arousing suspicion. Sam understood Bo's reasoning—even agreed with it, to some extent—but that didn't make it any easier to stay away from him. Especially not after the lovemaking they'd shared that afternoon. He flexed his buttocks, enjoying the faint soreness in his anus.

Tearing his gaze from Bo's profile, Sam glanced at the couple Dean was talking to. They looked to be upwards of seventy, both white haired with lined faces, but obviously healthy and in excellent physical condition. And, Sam noted with a twinge of jealously, openly affectionate toward one another. They walked with their hands intertwined, exchanging frequent smiles and glances full of love and heat.

It was a heartwarming sight, but it filled Sam with sadness. He and Bo could never do something as simple as holding hands in public without first assessing the situation—the environment, the people, the prevailing attitude toward gays. He envied straight couples the easy openness of their relationships. At that moment, he would've given anything to know what it was like to take his lover's hand without a second's consideration for what anyone else might think, or do.

Dean turned to frown at him. "Sam, what are you doing back there all by yourself?"

Sam shrugged. "Just zoning out. Enjoying the scenery."

"Wait till we get to the Rock," the woman said, shooting a twinkle-eyed look at Sam over her shoulder. "It's such an incredible view. Very romantic." She bumped her husband's shoulder with hers, smiling.

"Sure is," the man agreed with a nod. "We've hiked up here every year for the last seven years. We never get tired of it."

"This is their fiftieth anniversary," Dean chimed in. "Isn't that fantastic?"

"It certainly is," Sam answered, impressed. "Congratulations."

"Thank you," the two of them chorused. They looked at each other and burst into laughter. Letting go of her hand, the man slipped an arm around her waist and cuddled her close.

Dean dropped back to walk beside Sam. "Aren't they great?" he murmured, watching the couple with a dreamy look in his eyes. "Gotta say, I'm kind of jealous. I'd love to be in love like that. You know, with someone who loved me too."

Remembering what Dean had told him back in November—about the woman he'd loved, who hadn't loved him enough to put aside his past—Sam laid a hand on Dean's arm. "You'll find somebody to love you like that."

Dean glanced at him. "You think so? 'Cause I'm starting to wonder."

"I know so. You're a hell of catch, Dean. Anybody, male or female, would be lucky to have you."

Gratitude shone in Dean's eyes. "Thanks, Sam. That means a lot to me."

"It's true."

Dean smiled. They walked in silence for a little while. When the conversation resumed, it followed safer subjects than love and relationships.

The two of them were arguing about whether or not stock car racing was a sport when the trail took a sharp turn around a hulking mound of stone and spilled from the shelter of the trees into the level rays of the setting sun.

Sam stopped talking in mid-sentence and stared, awestruck.

"Oh. Oh, wow."

Dean nodded, eyes wide. "You said it."

The path opened onto an expanse of gently sloping white stone which stretched right, left and forward. Several yards in front of them, the earth abruptly ended in a vaporous white sea stained pink, orange and lavender with the sunset light. Brown and green mountaintops dusted with snow rose above the clouds, their roots hidden along with the rest of the world below. Sam felt as if they stood on an island floating in the sky. It was beautiful, serene and surreal.

Raising his camera, Dean snapped a photo of the stunning

scene. "Go over there with Bo." He nodded toward where Bo stood beside Lex and Carl, ahead and to the right of where Sam and Dean were. "I want to take some pics of y'all together."

"But Bo said we shouldn't—" Sam stopped, acutely aware of the incredulous expression blossoming on Dean's face. "Never mind. Can't we just take pictures later?"

"No. Come on."

Grabbing Sam's arm, Dean hauled him across the rock toward Bo. The determined glint in Dean's eyes told Sam he and Bo were about to be photographed whether Bo liked it or not. Sam put on what he hoped was a pleasant expression and steeled himself for one of Bo's patented silent confrontations.

"Hey, Bo!" Dean called.

Bo turned around. "Yes?"

"Stand here with Sam, I want to get y'all's picture with the sunset."

Predictably, Bo darted a hunted look at the dozen or so guests scattered across Sunset Rock before pinning Dean with a barbed glare. "I was just talking to Lex and Carl. Can't we get some pictures another time?"

"Oh, let the boy get his pictures," Carl said, slapping Bo on the back. "We'll have plenty of time to talk later. Everyone usually gathers in the common room next to the office after dinner."

Bo's eyelids fluttered closed. Sam could practically hear him counting to ten in his head. Without a word, Bo opened his eyes, stalked over to Sam and stood stiffly beside him. "Okay, Dean. Just a few."

Pursing his lips, Dean planted a hand on his hip. "Could you pretend to enjoy yourself for just a minute?"

Bo looked startled for a second, then burst into laughter.

Surprised, Sam stared at him.

"Sorry, Dean. How's this?" Slinging an arm around Sam's neck, Bo flashed a wide smile.

This close, Bo smelled like sweat and sex, with the scent of cold winter woods clinging to his black braid and red knit cap. It was all Sam could do to keep himself from pulling Bo close and nuzzling his neck. He hooked an arm around Bo's back, hoping the movement looked platonic, and smiled for the camera.

"Awesome!" Dean snapped a photo, brought it up on his camera and crowed in delight. "Oh man, this is fantastic. I'll email it to y'all once we get home and I get my pics uploaded."

"Great." Removing his arm from around Sam, Bo stepped back and stuck his hands in his pockets. He swiveled toward the west. "God, this is just gorgeous."

Turning to face the setting sun, Sam watched Bo from the corner of his eye. Bo stood so close their arms brushed. His face glowed red, orange and pink in the light of the sinking sun. Sam ached to take him in his arms and kiss him. Most of the other couples were doing just that, and it bothered Sam more than he liked to admit that he and Bo couldn't do the same.

What bothered him even more was Bo most likely wouldn't allow such contact even if there were no such thing as prejudice against gays. He simply wasn't one to cuddle in public.

You never were either, before Bo, Sam reminded himself, watching as the sun's disc sank below a bank of clouds on the horizon. *Being in love sure does change things.*

"Does it ever," Sam muttered.

Bo gave him a puzzled look. "What did you say?"

"Nothing." Pulling his scarf more snugly around his neck, Sam hunched his shoulders against a sudden blast of cold, damp wind. "So when do you want to head back?"

"You're not ready to go already, are you? It's not *that* cold."

Sam chuckled at the teasing tone in Bo's voice. "Yes it is, but I'm not ready to go back yet. Just wondering if we should leave before the sun finishes setting. You know, so we'd have the best possible chance at catching a look at this thing people are seeing."

"Hmm. Probably should." Twisting around, Bo beckoned Dean over. "Dean, Sam suggested we should go before the sunset's complete, so we'll have a better chance of witnessing the reported phenomenon."

"Sure thing." Dean snapped two more photos in rapid sequence, then turned his camera off and let it dangle from around his neck. "Why don't I run the video camera this time, Sam? That way you'd be free to do the psychic thing."

Sam nodded. "Suits me. Bo, you want notes or EMF?"

"Notes. It'll be easier for you to take EMF readings than take notes while you have your psychic senses extended."

"True. So, when do you want to go?"

"Aw, let's wait just another minute." Pushing between them, Dean slid an arm around each of them. "This is absolutely the most amazing thing I've ever seen. I don't want to miss any of it."

Bo laughed. "We can come back tomorrow."

"Yeah, but what if it snows?"

"Unless we get a full-on blizzard, we can still hike up here," Sam pointed out. "It's not a difficult trail or anything."

"That's true." With a sigh, Dean let go of Bo and Sam. "Okay, well, it's already starting to get pretty dim out. Want to head on back and get started at ground zero?"

"Yes. Just let me tell Lex and Carl what we're doing." Bo

hurried over to where their hosts stood talking with Dean's friends from the trail, spoke to Lex, then trotted back to Sam and Dean. "All right, let's go."

The three of them headed back to the path. Beneath the trees, twilight had already fallen. Bo pulled three powerful flashlights from the bag, handing one to Sam and one to Dean. He switched on the third and swung the beam in a wide arc. Branches and rocks cast weird shadows in the bright light.

As they walked, Sam let himself sink into the waking half-trance he'd come to prefer for psychic work. He felt Bo press the EMF detector into his hand and smiled when Bo's fingers brushed his.

"Here we are." Dean, who was in the lead, veered off the trail when his flashlight beam picked out the big boulder in the woods. He raised the video camera and began sweeping the woods. "Don't see anything yet."

"Neither do I." Bo glanced at Sam. "Are you picking up anything?"

"No. Nothing. Just that same dead energy." Sam shone his flashlight on the EMF detector. "EMF's three point three and steady."

Tucking his flashlight under his left arm, Bo scribbled in the notebook. "Let me know if you pick up anything different, or if the EMF reading changes."

Nodding, Sam followed Dean through the underbrush. Bo brought up the rear. They were very close to the big rock now. It glowed like a ghost in the gloom.

Dean rounded the edge of the boulder and let out a shout. "Fuck! It's here, hurry!"

Bo was moving before Dean stopped talking. He jogged to Dean's side, recording the time and location in the notebook as he went. Sam followed, switching on the backlight on the EMF detector to keep an eye on the reading. He couldn't help noticing the way Bo grimaced and kept his full weight off his right leg.

"Keep filming," Bo ordered.

"Right." Dean held the camera with a steady hand in spite of his initial shocked reaction to seeing the thing. It hadn't taken Sam or the rest of the group long to notice Dean's crisis mode was an icy calm he'd no doubt learned during his years in the emergency room. It was a good thing to have during a paranormal investigation, where things could turn strange and frightening very suddenly.

Sam rounded the corner of the rock just in time to see a nebulous black blur dart from a clump of trees not far from the boulder and scurry off into the darkness. It made no sound in the mat of plant detritus on the ground, which Sam thought was odd. Lifting the EMF detector, Sam checked the reading. It hadn't changed at all from when he'd taken the first reading.

"I'm following," Dean called, loping after the thing with the video camera still pointed at it. He thumbed his flashlight off. "Switching to infrared filter."

Beside Sam, Bo leaned against the rock, rubbing his thigh. "Sam, go with him. My leg's acting up again."

Sam didn't like leaving Bo, but the lack of any sign of aggression from the creature made him feel better about it. With a nod to acknowledge Bo's order, Sam trailed after Dean, pointing the flashlight at the ground so he could see where he was going. He couldn't see the creature anymore, and he still couldn't feel even a trace of the intelligent menace which had nearly overwhelmed him at Oleander House and South Bay High. Its absence was a relief, but felt wrong nonetheless. Sam had braced himself to face the powerful malice of another portal and its inhabitants; feeling nothing but this strange, static emptiness seemed wrong.

Ahead of him, Dean slowed to a walk, swearing under his breath. "What's wrong?" Sam asked, jogging to Dean's side.

Dean shook his head. "I lost the damn thing. It kept going, and I couldn't move fast enough to keep up."

"Well, hell, you remember how fast those things move." Sam laid a hand on Dean's shoulder. "At least you got some video."

"Yeah, let's just hope it shows up." Sighing, Dean switched off the camera. "Do you think we should keep following it? This worries me, leaving that thing running around out here."

"I agree, but I'm not sure what else to do. We're not exactly equipped for finding it, and we aren't even sure if there's an actual gateway here. Nothing's happening the way it did the other times. The other creatures came after us. This one ran away." Sam shuddered at the memories. "And the weirdest thing of all is, I couldn't feel it, or the portal."

Dean stared at him. "You couldn't?"

"No. All I felt was the same energy I picked up before. It didn't change at all when we saw that thing." Taking one more look at the EMF detector—the reading remained the same—Sam turned it off. "This is really strange. I don't know what to think of it."

"Hmm. Guess we'd better talk to the boss-man and see what he thinks." Dean looked around. "Where's Bo?"

"He stayed by the rock. Said his leg was hurting again." Sam shot a concerned glance at Bo, who was a dark blur against the pale stone. "It worries me how his leg keeps getting better then worse. You don't think the surgical incision could be coming apart or anything, do you?"

"This far out from the surgery? Doubtful. He'd have had

problems before this if the incision was going to dehisce. Come open, that is," Dean explained. He turned his flashlight on and began trudging back to the boulder. "He seems fine otherwise. Try not to worry too much, Sam. The hike up here was pretty strenuous, and the muscle and tissues in that leg are never going to be quite as strong as they used to be. It's most likely just muscle strain. Even if it's not behaving like a strain ought to, exactly."

"Yeah, I know." Sam stared at a blanket of dead ferns beneath his feet. "I mostly worry that he'll get worse and not tell either of us until it's too late. If anything happened to him, I don't think I could deal with it."

Dean pinned him with a sharp look. "Yeah, you could. Andre did it. You could too, if it came down to it."

Sam, shocked, didn't know what to say. He pressed his lips together, heart thudding painfully. Thinking of Amy's brutal death—and Andre's struggle to learn to live with it—always hurt like a knife in the gut. The fierce pain of it never lessened, and he didn't want it to. He'd learned to accept that Amy's death wasn't his fault, but she'd still died, and Sam never wanted to forget that.

Dean's hand curled around Sam's arm, fingers pressing into his skin through the thick material of his jacket. "I know you worry, Sam. And I know *why* you worry. You went through hell when Bo was in the hospital, not knowing if he'd live or die. But I don't think it'll come to that this time. Bo's stubborn as the proverbial mule, that's true, but he's not stupid. He knows better than to keep it to himself if something serious is wrong."

Lifting his head, Sam gave Dean a wan smile. "You're right, as always. Thanks, Dean. You're a good friend."

Releasing Sam's arm, Dean patted his back. "Y'all are like my family, you know? I want to take care of you."

They fell silent as they approached the boulder. Bo raised his eyebrows at them. "Well? What did you see?"

"I lost it in the woods after a little bit." Dean held up the camera. "But I got some video."

"That's great. Quick thinking, following it like that." Bo looked at Sam. "Did you pick up anything?"

Sam chewed his lip, trying to think how to explain it. "I didn't feel anything like before. Just the same static sort of energy I felt when we were up here earlier today."

Flipping the notebook open, Bo wrote a few lines. "It didn't change at all?"

"Not a bit."

"What about the EMF?"

"Stayed the same the whole time."

"Interesting." Bo stared off into the distance, sucking idly on the end of his pen in a way Sam found quite distracting. "In our previous cases, we always heard things when these beings were around. That deep, raspy sort of sound, and in Oleander House we heard its claws on the floor. I didn't hear anything this time, what about y'all?"

"Not a sound." Dean frowned. "It should've made plenty of noise. We sure do when we're walking around out here."

Bo stared off into the darkness, chewing his lower lip. "What happened to it?"

Sam and Dean exchanged a glance. "It ran off into the woods," Dean answered. "Like I said, I lost it. We thought it probably wasn't a good idea to follow it right now."

"You're right. Running off into the dark after whatever it was we saw is way too dangerous." Bo rested his hand on Sam's arm. "Sam, you've been in the minds of those things before. Do you think anyone here is in danger?"

"No, I don't." Sam twirled his flashlight in his hand, sending the beam swinging crazily around them. "Not right now, anyway. If there's a portal here, I'm not picking up on it, and I'm not sensing anything from the creature we saw. But we'll have to keep our guard up. You know things could change pretty fast."

Sounds of laughter and conversation drifted from behind them. Sam turned. The other guests were filtering in twos and threes down the trail, flashlights bobbing in front of them. Two figures stopped beside the path, their lights sweeping toward the big rock.

"Lex and Carl are looking for us," Sam said, gesturing toward the two silhouettes. "Let's go meet them. We can talk all this out later." He held one hand protectively at Bo's side. "Do you need help?"

"No, I'm fine." Bo took Sam's hand in his, shielded from sight by his body. "I promise I'll let you and Dean know if my leg gets worse. Please don't worry."

Twining his fingers with Bo's, Sam squeezed briefly then let go. "Okay, I'll try not to."

Smiling, Bo shoved the notebook and pen into his bag and turned to follow Dean, who was already making his way toward Lex and Carl. "Good. I don't want you to worry about me, when I'm just fine."

Depositing the EMF detector in the bag, Sam shoved his hands into his pockets. "I try not to, but it's hard. Watching someone you love almost die makes you kind of jumpy."

"I can imagine." Bo shot him a solemn look. "I hope I never have to find out for myself."

Sam brushed his shoulder against Bo's. "Me too."

CR

Back at the Lodge, Sam filled the bucket from the water pump—after Dean showed him how to use it—and took it back to the cabin so he and Bo could wash their hands. The water was painfully cold. Sam squealed when Bo lifted his shirt and stuck both icy palms on his lower back. Bo laughed.

After washing up, they left for the dining hall. The big dinner bell hanging outside the building clanged as they approached the office. Dean met them on the path, and the three of them headed down the steps to the dining room.

The place was simple but inviting—a large rectangular room of rough-hewn logs, with two rows of long wooden tables lined up on the plank floor. Kerosene lanterns sat on each table, bathing the room in warm lamplight. On the far side of the room, a large picture window looked out over the narrow deck. Lights from the town at the bottom of the mountain twinkled far below. The smell of plain southern cooking drifted from the kitchen, making Sam's mouth water.

A young woman with a red scarf tied over long brown braids directed them to a table in the far corner. "Oh my God," Dean moaned as they pulled the wooden chairs up to the table. "This smells soooo good. I'm starving."

"Me too." Sam contemplated the three empty chairs at the table. "Wonder if anyone else is sitting here? Other groups seem to be sitting together."

Bo shrugged. "I don't know, but I'm anxious to talk to Lex and Carl. We didn't get the chance to tell them anything much on the walk back."

"Looks like you'll get your chance." Dean nodded toward the front door, which was behind Bo. "Here they come."

Sam, sitting beside Bo across the table from Dean, turned to look. Lex and Carl waved, heading straight for their table.

"Hi, folks," Carl said, plopping into the chair beside Dean. "Hungry?"

"As a horse." Dean grinned at Lex, who'd taken the empty seat beside Bo. "What's on the menu?"

"Fried chicken, mashed potatoes, green beans, baked apples, biscuits and chocolate chip cookies for dessert." Leaning back in her chair, Lex beckoned to someone Sam couldn't see. "Everything's made fresh right here every day, and there's plenty of it. People work up a healthy appetite here."

"That's certainly true." Bo rested his elbows on the table. "I hope y'all don't mind talking about the case during dinner. We'd like to share what we learned this evening, since we didn't get a chance to talk about it on the way back here."

"Of course, that's fine." Carl glanced up and smiled at the woman with the red scarf, who'd approached the table. "Sandra, I'd like to introduce you to some very special guests. This is Dean Delapore, Sam Raintree and Dr. Bo Broussard from Bay City Paranormal Investigations. They're here to look into those things some of our guests have seen. Guys, this is Sandra Leland. She's our head cook."

Sandra held out her hand, shaking with each man in turn. "Nice to meet y'all. I saw that thing once. Creeped me right out. What'll you have to drink? We have water, iced tea and lemonade."

"You can have wine too, if you like," Lex added. "We have plenty."

Bo smiled. "I'll just have water, thank you."

"Me too," Sam told her. "Maybe another time on the wine."

"Lemonade for me, Sandra, thanks." Dean flashed his

flirtatious smile. "Is it a requirement that everyone who works here has to be incredibly attractive?"

Sandra laughed. "Oh, you're good. Too bad I don't swing that way, I might take you up on it."

Dean's eyebrows shot up. "My apologies. Far be it from me to try to turn a happily outed lesbian."

"No apologies necessary." With a wink at Dean, Sandra hurried off to the kitchen.

"Well, there's a mistake I don't usually make." Dean turned to Carl, his face the picture of innocence. "It's great that y'all are equal opportunity employers. Your other employees don't give her any trouble, I hope?"

Lex shook her head. "When we first hired Anne, she said a few derogatory things, but she apologized when we told her we don't tolerate that kind of thing here and she'd be fired if it happened again. According to Sandra, Anne hasn't given her any more trouble. They'll never be friends, I'm sure, but I doubt they would be anyway. They're very different."

"Can't see that Sandra's orientation has ever affected her cooking," Carl added. "Anybody who thinks it would, can't expect to work for us."

Smiling, Lex patted her husband's hand. "We believe in giving people a chance to correct their behavior, but there's only so much we'll put up with."

"You know what, I sort of figured that about y'all." Leaning against the backrest of his chair, Dean darted a meaningful glance at Sam and Bo.

Sam stifled a groan at Dean's smug expression. Armed with this particular tidbit of knowledge, Dean could conceivably make the next few days hell on earth by prodding Bo at every opportunity to "come out" to the staff, which Sam knew Bo very much did not want to do. Sam didn't either, actually. Rather than convincing Sam that he and Bo could safely tell Lex and Carl about their relationship, Lex's revelation about Anne just made him more determined not to. Clearly, Lex and Carl didn't know their employees quite as well as they thought, which made Sam feel less than safe confiding in them.

Not that explaining his reasoning would stop Dean from pestering him and Bo both about it. Which would make Bo far pricklier than normal, thus possibly putting a temporary halt to Sam's sex life. That was the last thing Sam wanted, when he and Bo had a few nights to themselves in this lovely, romantic place.

He resolved to beg Dean's mercy later, then put the matter to the back of his mind when Sandra and a man Sam hadn't yet met arrived bearing huge bowls of steaming, heavenly smelling food.

Lex introduced the young man as Jerome Van Dyke, a student taking a year off between high school and college. Sam liked him right away. He was almost as outgoing as Dean, with a wide gap-toothed smile and a thatch of sandy brown hair that flopped over a pair of dark blue eyes and crooked wire-rimmed glasses. The way he talked about his girlfriend back in Chattanooga left Sam with no doubt the boy was straight, but he seemed to have no problem working with Sandra, and Dean's not-so-subtle flirting didn't appear to bother him. Sam found that encouraging. Maybe he and Bo wouldn't have to be quite as careful as he'd previously thought.

Not that Bo would see it that way, especially since others of the staff—namely Anne—evidently didn't share Jerome's easygoing attitude.

"So tell us about what you found tonight," Carl said when Jerome excused himself to help serve the other tables. "Anything helpful?"

Bo spooned mashed potatoes onto his plate and handed the bowl to Sam. "We saw the thing your guests have seen. And it certainly looked like what we've seen in the past, associated with the portals."

Lex paled. "Oh my God. Are our guests in danger?"

Bo glanced at Sam, who shrugged as he heaped potatoes onto his own plate. "It didn't act threatening the way the ones we've encountered before did," Sam answered, handing the bowl across the table to Dean. "And I know not everyone sets any stock in psychic phenomena, but with the creatures we've run across in the past, I've always felt a very strong, very malevolent energy. I didn't feel that with this one."

"We think there is probably not any danger," Bo continued, cutting a biscuit in half. "But the possibility certainly exists."

Carl set his fork down and leaned forward. "What do you think we should do? Is it necessary to evacuate our guests?"

"Not tonight. Sending people down the mountain in the dark would be far more dangerous than keeping them here, whether the thing is out there or not." With his fork, Bo speared a chicken breast from the platter in the middle of the table. "Are any of tonight's guests staying another night?"

"No. And we've already had two cancellations for tomorrow night. Altogether, there are..." Lex tapped a finger on the table, her lips moving as she counted under her breath. "Fifteen people scheduled for tomorrow, in seven cabins. Should I call and tell them they shouldn't come?"

Bo forked green beans into his mouth, chewed and swallowed. "I hate to say it, Lex, but that might be best. Just in case."

"Better safe than sorry," Dean added, reaching over to pat Lex's hand. "Is the forecast still calling for snow? 'Cause they might not make it anyhow if it snows enough."

Lex gave him a wan smile. "Yes, it is, actually. We're predicted to get up to eight inches by tomorrow night."

"Wow." Dean winked at Sam, eyes twinkling. "Bet you're looking forward to getting eight inches tomorrow night."

The memory of that afternoon popped into Sam's head, heating his cheeks. He glared daggers at Dean, who batted his eyelashes and turned his attention to heaping food onto his plate.

"Parts of the trails up here become almost impassable in the snow." Carl tore a strip of chicken off the bone and popped it into his mouth. "Lex, honey, I know it's bad for business, but I think we should cancel our remaining reservations until this is resolved."

With a deep sigh, Lex nodded. "Yes, you're right. Okay, as soon as dinner's done I'll radio the main office and have them cancel all reservations for tomorrow night and Tuesday night. We'll reevaluate tomorrow evening. I don't want to cancel too far ahead."

"Sounds good." Taking her hand, Carl kissed her knuckles. "Don't worry, honey. I'm sure everything will work out."

Lex nodded, but her expression was grave. Canceling reservations could mean real trouble for Sunset Lodge. But if there was an active portal here, lives could be in danger. Sam's heart went out to her.

A loud moan from Dean broke through Sam's thoughts. "Oh, man, this is amazing," Dean declared through a mouthful of baked apples. "I swear, y'all, if we stayed here too long I'd get too fat to move."

Sam smiled. Dean could always be counted on to lighten the mood.

"Why do you think we don't live here all the time?" Picking up the bowl of green beans, Carl spooned more onto his plate.

"Who wants seconds?"

⌘

After dinner, Lex and Carl went to radio their reservation office, which was located in the town of Jones Mill in the valley below. Dean learned there was a Clue set in the common room and headed inside to get a game together. Most of the other guests followed him. The rest went back to their cabins, leaving Sam and Bo alone in the frigid night.

Bo let out a contented sigh and patted his stomach. "God, I'm stuffed. That was a wonderful dinner."

"It was." Wandering toward the edge of the precipice where the dining hall perched, Sam gazed out at the cluster of lights marking the town. His breath puffed white in the cold. "It's so peaceful up here. I really hope this isn't a portal we're dealing with."

"Me too." Footsteps crunched the frozen grass at Sam's back. Bo's chin rested on his shoulder, Bo's hand brushing his hip for a moment before he restored the distance between them. "I'm tired, Sam. Why don't we go back to the cabin and go to bed?"

The suggestion threading through Bo's voice told Sam he wasn't talking about sleeping. Following a sudden impulse, Sam took Bo's hand and pulled him into the dense shadows under the deck outside the office. There in the darkness, Sam cradled Bo's head in his hand and kissed him.

Bo made a needy little sound in the back of his throat. One of his hands fisted into Sam's hair, the other clamping onto Sam's ass. His tongue stroked soft and slick along Sam's. Groaning, Sam clutched Bo closer, slipping a hand under his jacket and sweatshirt to find warm, bare skin.

"Oh Christ," Bo gasped, breaking the kiss. "Sam. Not here."

"Cabin," Sam growled.

Nodding, Bo grabbed Sam's wrist and dragged him toward the pathway to the cabins.

They'd just passed the bottom of the stairs to the office when a door banged open somewhere above and Dean's voice floated down to them. "Hey, guys, y'all out here?"

Bo's fingers tightened around Sam's wrist. "Down here," he called.

Dean appeared at the porch rail. He leaned over the railing, grinning. "Going to bed?"

"Yes," Sam answered. "Good night."

Laughing, Dean waved at them. "'Night. Try to get some actual sleep, huh? And keep it quiet!"

Shaking his head, Bo started walking again as Dean hurried back into the common room. "I swear, that man is crazy."

"Yeah, but I think we can forgive him, since we might not be together right now if it wasn't for him."

Bo slid his hand down to lace his fingers through Sam's, squeezing gently. He didn't say anything, but Sam understood him just fine. They'd come so close to losing one another during the South Bay High investigation. Sam went to sleep each night and woke every morning desperately grateful for Bo's presence in his life, and he knew Bo felt the same.

So what if we have to watch ourselves around other people? We're together, and that's what's important. Anything else is just details.

Sam hoped he could remember that next time he saw the familiar revulsion in a stranger's eyes.

Chapter Six

The next morning, Sam woke feeling stiff in more places than usual. His back and shoulders ached, and his thighs protested violently at the slightest movement. Even his calves, strong and muscular from years of regular running, were sore. In fact, his whole body felt like a giant toothache.

"When we get home, I'm joining a gym," he declared, picking his slow, careful way down the slate steps to the dining hall for breakfast. "I'm obviously not keeping all my muscles in shape. I hurt all over."

Bo grinned, dark eyes full of mischief. "Hey, I did guarantee you'd be sore after I got done with you."

"Yeah, well, *those* parts of me aren't the worst of it," Sam shot back, returning Bo's smile. "They're used to your abuse. It's my legs and back that're killing me."

Snickering, Bo elbowed him in the ribs. "You can blame the sore thighs on me too, I believe. The chair? Remember?"

"Like I could forget. We're definitely doing that again sometime." Sam stepped onto relatively level ground with a sigh of relief. "How's your leg today? Is it still hurting?"

Bo shrugged. "It's like yesterday afternoon after we got up here. It feels strange, sort of overly sensitive and jumpy, but not really painful. Both my legs are a little sore from the hike up here, though, so I'm leaning toward blaming it on unaccustomed strain."

"Well, at least it's not worse. And I know you know to tell me and Dean if it *does* get worse."

"Absolutely. It's a long way to civilization. This isn't the time or place to keep something like that to myself."

"Good."

"Sam?"

"Hmm?"

"Good idea about joining a gym. I think I will too." Bo rubbed at his lower back, a grimace twisting his features.

Sam bit his lip, trying not to laugh. He knew exactly how loudly Bo's overworked muscles were screaming, because his own were doing the same.

Tilting his head back, Sam squinted up at the sky. Heavy gray clouds shrouded the mountaintop, completely obscuring the view of the valley. The air was still, cold and breathless. Sam could practically feel the weight of the snow ready to fall. The other guests drifting in twos and threes from their cabins watched the sky with apprehension on their faces. Sam didn't blame them. The idea of hiking down the steep, narrow trails in a snowstorm was not appealing.

Dean was already in the dining hall when Sam and Bo entered. Spotting them, he jumped up from the table where he was talking to Anne and Jerome and bounced over to Sam and Bo.

"Hey, y'all," he said, taking them each by an arm and leading them to the table where they'd sat the night before. "How'd you sleep? Or *did* you sleep? You both look kind of tired."

Sam blushed. He and Bo had indeed stayed awake long into the night, making slow, lazy love. "Dean..."

"Yeah, I know, I know." With a dramatic sigh, Dean flopped into his chair. "At least y'all got some. Nobody here'll have me."

Bo quirked an eyebrow at him. "You don't have enough people lined up to have you back home? You're collecting lovers in other states now?"

"I would be, but like I said, nobody's interested."

Glancing at Anne, who'd gotten up and was heading for the kitchen, Sam sat across from Dean and leaned his elbows on the table. "Anne seemed pretty interested yesterday. You still interested in her, knowing how she acted toward Sandra?"

"Well, I wouldn't want to get serious with her, but I'm not about to let one little incident keep me from getting laid." A frown curved Dean's lips. "She's playing hard to get, though."

Sam chuckled at the pout in Dean's voice. "Come on, you know as well as I do that *hard to get* is just *interested* in a different outfit."

"Yeah, but we're not gonna be here long. I don't have much time."

Bo shook his head. "Give your libido a rest for a few days, huh? We're not here for you to pick up yet another bed partner anyway. We're here to work."

"Speaking of which, I watched the video I took last night." Dean took the carafe of coffee Sandra had set on the table and started filling three mugs. "And what do you mean, 'yet another bed partner'? I'll have you know I've only slept with four guys and two girls in the last couple of months." He stopped talking and frowned at the ceiling. "Okay, that is kind of a lot."

Biting back a laugh, Sam mixed sugar and creamer into his coffee and took a cautious sip. It was good, hot and fresh and fragrant. "What was on the video? Did it pick up the thing?"

"It did, yeah. But it was very indistinct. I couldn't see it at all on the night vision, so I guess its heat signature is the same as the surrounding environment." Dean stirred three sugars and a generous amount of cream into his coffee. "I wish we had video of the ones y'all saw before, so I could compare. So far, everything points to this one being different from the others, but I have no idea *why* or *how*."

"I think you're right. The damn thing looks the same as the others we've seen, but it acts all wrong, and feels wrong. It feels…" Sam stopped, trying to find the right words. "Absent. Like it's not even there."

Bo gave him a thoughtful look over the rim of his coffee mug. "Sam, do you feel up to going out there again this morning? I'd like to have a look around in those woods before it snows."

"Sure. What equipment do you want to bring?"

"EMF and video, and the notepad. Frankly, I don't think there's much point in more than that. It's too cold out here to notice if there's much of a temperature drop, and there's only three of us anyway. You can carry the still camera in case we need it, but I mainly want you to feel out the area again psychically."

"Okay." Glancing up, Sam saw Sandra and Jerome heading toward them carrying platters stacked high with pancakes. His stomach rumbled. "Oh, man, that smells great."

Dean grinned at him. "Yeah, I guess y'all probably worked up an appetite last night, huh?"

Bo shot him a warning look, but didn't have time to say anything before the two Lodge employees arrived at their table. "Good morning," he greeted them, ignoring Dean's snicker. "Those pancakes look wonderful."

"Yeah, Sandra's the *queen* of pancakes," Jerome declared, setting a platter laden with pancakes and bacon and a pitcher of warm syrup in the middle of the table. "Y'all enjoy."

Talk subsided as the group dug in. The first mouthful of hot, buttery pancakes dripping with syrup hit Sam's tongue, and he moaned loud enough to garner a few strange looks from the other tables. He blushed while Dean laughed so hard he nearly choked on his bacon.

They didn't see Lex or Carl. Sandra told them the Lodge owners were busy doing damage control after having canceled all the remaining reservations for the next two nights. After breakfast, Sam and Bo waited on the path while Dean went to fetch the video camera from the staff quarters.

After a brief discussion, they decided to go ahead and investigate the area of the sightings before the threatening snowstorm broke. They could upload last night's video to the laptop later, along with any video from this morning. The heavy gray sky told them they had a limited amount of time to look around before the snow began.

The three of them stopped at Sam and Bo's cabin to gather the rest of the equipment, then set off down the path. Bo switched on the EMF detector, saying he wanted to take readings of other areas for comparison's sake. The reading was roughly the same as it had been in the woods. They passed several familiar faces going the other way as last night's Lodge guests hurried to descend the mountain before the trails became too treacherous. The older couple from the previous night called goodbyes to them as they passed.

The trail was empty and silent when they reached their destination. They turned off the path and tramped toward the big boulder. Frost-coated pine needles and twigs crackled underfoot, the sound unnaturally loud in the breathless quiet.

When they reached the rock, Bo studied the EMF detector. "Three point four," he announced. "Just a hair higher than last night. I think we can safely say that's about baseline for this whole area. We'll need to get readings around the rest of the Lodge to be sure, but so far baseline EMF's been a bit high everywhere."

Just like at Oleander House. Suppressing a shudder of fear, Sam wrote down Bo's reading. He reached out with his psychic senses, easily finding and latching onto the fine thread of strange energy lingering around the boulder. "Still picking up the exact same thing as I did before. No stronger, no different."

Dean pursed his lips. "Y'all, this whole thing gets weirder by the second."

Winding the end of his braid around two fingers of his free hand, Bo gazed into the dense forest with a thoughtful expression. "I wonder..."

Sam glanced at him. "What?"

"Nothing. Just..." Bo shook his head, his brow furrowing. "I don't want to say anything yet. Let's just see what we find today."

Curiosity burned in Sam's gut, but he knew better than to press the issue. If Bo didn't want to explain himself yet, nothing short of torture would make him do it. Maybe not even that.

"You want to hike out into the woods, where that thing went last night?" Dean asked, thumbing the video camera on for a quick pan of the area.

"Yes. We need to do that before—" Bo broke off, eyes widening. "There it is. Video and stills, right now."

Shoving the notebook and pen into his jeans pocket, Sam whipped around, turning the camera on and raising it as he moved. A few feet behind the boulder, something black and shadowy emerged from thin air, paused a second, and scuttled off into the trees. Forcing back the urge to drop everything and run like hell, Sam snapped two photos back to back. His heart pounded in his throat, the rush of blood loud in his ears. His knees shook.

"It's not coming after us," Dean whispered, keeping the video camera trained on the thing plunging through the forest. "I'm following it."

Before Sam or Bo could say anything, Dean bounded after the creature, camera held as steady as possible in front of him. With a swift glance at each other, Sam and Bo followed.

"No change in EMF," Bo called. "Sam?"

"Energy's the same too." Sam darted a concerned look at Bo. "You're limping again."

"I know." Bo stumbled, his features twisting in a grimace. "Fuck. Stay with Dean."

"I'd rather not leave you alone."

An odd look came over Bo's face. "I don't think it'll hurt us. Just stay with Dean. Hurry, he's almost out of sight."

"But—"

"Trust me, Sam." Bo shoved his shoulder. "Go!"

Despite his irritation at Bo for insisting he leave him, instinct told Sam Bo was right. He picked up his pace, darting through the trees as fast as he could. Within seconds, he'd caught up to Dean. Bo limped along several yards behind them.

"It's just ahead," Dean panted, leaping over a fallen tree. "See?"

Sam looked in the direction Dean pointed. A translucent black mass moved from tree to tree before them. Fear curled in Sam's belly.

"I still can't feel it," Sam said. "But there it is. Looks just like the others."

Beside him, Dean slowed to a jog. "It's stopping."

Indeed it was. As Sam watched, the thing came to a halt, one black claw poised in front of its body. The level of energy in Sam's head didn't change. Feeling reassured by this, Sam raised the camera and took three more stills while Dean filmed it.

An uneven crunch of pine needles under hiking boots announced Bo's arrival. "What's it doing?" Bo murmured, laying a hand on Sam's shoulder.

Dean shook his head. "Nothing. Just standing there."

In a clump of rhododendrons not far from the creature, something moved. Sam squinted, trying to make it out. A flash of dull orange peeked from between the close-packed branches. Adrenaline jolted through Sam's blood as he realized what it was. He dropped the camera, letting the strap around his neck catch it.

"Shit!" Without stopping to think about what he was doing, Sam sprinted toward the alien thing and the person it had trapped in the rhododendron thicket.

A string of colorful curses and pounding footsteps behind him told him Bo and Dean were following him. He wanted to order them both to stay back, but knew there was no point. Neither of them would listen.

"There's a person there," Sam called as he ran. "I'll try to send the thing back if I can. Be ready to help whoever this is."

He didn't wait for an answer. The creature loomed mere feet in front of him. Focusing his mind on it, Sam searched for the fiery string of energy connecting it to the portal he was now sure must be here.

He couldn't find it. The weird, blank feeling which had been there all along remained static and unchanged.

Panicking now, Sam opened his mouth to tell the trapped person to run for it. Before he could say anything, the creature flowed like smoke into the cluster of bushes and sliced the person's head off.

A horrified cry from behind him told him Dean, at least, had seen the same thing he had. Frozen, Sam watched helplessly as the creature tore its victim apart. He couldn't find the thing in his head, couldn't connect with its mind, and he didn't know what to do.

Bo's arm snaked around his waist, pulling him away, but Sam barely felt it. All he could think was, *I've failed again. Another person's dead because I couldn't send that fucking thing away fast enough.*

Icy hands framed Sam's face, forcing him to turn. He stared into Bo's worried eyes, feeling sick. "It happened again," he said, his voice shaking. "Did you see?"

"Yes, I did." Holding his gaze, Bo leaned closer. "Did you feel anything this time?"

Sam shook his head. He swallowed, throat aching.

Brushing a kiss across his forehead, Bo pulled Sam into his arms. "It's gone," Bo murmured against Sam's ear. "It disappeared. Did you send it away?"

Surprised, Sam pulled back and looked at the spot where he'd seen the thing kill someone. The woods were bare and undisturbed, just like nothing had happened.

"No. I tried to send it back, but I couldn't find it." Sam drew a deep breath, feeling calmness return. "Where did it go?"

"Don't know. It just vanished." Dean tramped over to stand beside them. "Did y'all notice there was no sound? No freaky-ass noise like at South Bay, no screams, not even the sound of bushes being moved around. Nothing. Quiet as the fucking grave."

Startled, Sam thought about it. "You're right. I didn't notice at the time, but yeah. No sound at all. Just like earlier."

Bo gave them both a solemn look. "Let's go take a look. We need to find out if someone really did just die here, because if they did we'll need to radio the police."

"What do you mean, 'if'?" Sam demanded. "We all saw it!"

"And I got it on video," Dean added, holding up the camera.

"Okay, maybe 'if' is the wrong word, but..." Shaking his head, Bo moved off toward the spot where they'd just seen a person die. "Come on."

Confused, Sam glanced at Dean, who shrugged. With a deep sigh, Sam turned to follow Bo. Dean fell into step beside him.

The three of them stopped just outside the rhododendron thicket and silently scanned the ground inside. To Sam's relief, he didn't see a trace of blood. Puzzling as it was, he was glad to know he hadn't actually seen what he thought he had. They could figure out why they'd all imagined the same thing at the same time later. Right now, he was just glad they didn't have a dead body to deal with.

Then he saw the fingers sticking up from the thick carpet of dead rhododendron leaves. Fingers attached to a curled, bloody hand, ending in a ragged stump of a wrist.

"Oh fuck," Sam breathed, stumbling backward. "There. A hand, in the leaves."

Bo and Dean both leaned over to look. Bo drew back with a hiss. "Oh, Jesus. I see." He turned his back to the spot, throat working.

Dean crouched on the ground, peering into the bushes. "I can see the rest of the body now. Except for that one hand, it's pretty far back and scattered around, which is probably why we didn't see it at first." He turned to Sam with a frown. "It's weird that there's no blood on the ground, though. We just saw this, right? So why isn't there blood?"

Bile rose in Sam's throat. "I'm gonna be sick."

He stumbled toward a space in the trees to his left, searching for open air. Something rolled under his foot, causing him to lose his balance and stumble forward. Both hands came up instinctively to break his fall. One palm slid on the leaves and into open space, and he found himself flat on his stomach on the ground, staring down over a sheer drop-off.

Behind him, Bo let out a gasp. "Sam, for God's sake. You almost—"

"I know." Moving carefully, Sam scooted backward away from the edge and sat up on his knees. He took the hand Bo held out for him and rose to his feet, shaking all over. "I stepped on something round, and lost my balance. Shit."

"Is this what you stepped on?"

Sam turned toward Dean's voice. Dean squatted on the ground a few feet away, staring at something half-hidden by pine needles and rhododendron leaves.

"I don't know." Keeping hold of Bo's hand, Sam moved closer to Dean. At Dean's feet was a small white paper bag, and beside it a prescription bottle. "Maybe. Was that on the ground?"

"Yes. The cap's cracked, and there's a fresh shoe mark on the bag. Looks like it was maybe buried in the leaves, and you slipping on it shoved the leaves off it." Glancing up, Dean beckoned them down to look. "Check out the label on this, y'all."

Sam and Bo crouched beside Dean, Bo keeping a hand on Sam's shoulder and grimacing as his injured leg bent. Sam squinted at the tiny print on the label. His eyes went wide. Beside him, Bo let out a small, shocked sound.

The name on the label read "Norton, Harry". The prescription, lying abandoned in the forest next to the spot where they'd just witnessed a brutal slaying, belonged to Sunset Lodge's missing employee.

Chapter Seven

By the time the police arrived on the scene, the snow had been falling for nearly three hours. It crunched under Sam's boots as he, Bo and Dean followed the two detectives and two uniformed officers to the spot where they'd found the body and the prescription. All around, the deep green of the pines and firs was frosted with white, giving the forest a fairy-tale quality.

Gloved hands in his pockets, Sam turned his face up to the glowering gray sky. Fat white flakes drifted down in slow motion, catching on his lips and eyelashes. The only sound was the crackle of their footsteps and the occasional hiss and rustle when a clump of snow fell from a branch. If it weren't for the horrific circumstances, it would've been a wonderfully peaceful scene.

Detective Parsons stopped when they drew parallel to the big boulder in the woods. "This the place?"

Bo nodded. "Yes. We ran probably fifty yards or so through the woods before we found the thicket where we saw the body."

"Can you find the spot again?"

"We can find it," Dean told her.

"All right. Lead the way." Tucking a strand of dark blonde hair behind her ear, she glanced at her colleagues. "Ramirez, get ready with the camera."

The tall, hulking man gave a curt nod. One of the uniformed officers, Boone, tightened her grip on the large cooler she carried. No one but Parsons had spoken more than two words since Sam, Bo and Dean had first met them in the Sunset Lodge office. Their watchful silence made Sam nervous.

Dean moved to Detective Parsons' side, to lead the way. The group walked in silence for a few minutes, until the rhododendron thicket came into view. Dean and the police approached the clump of shrubs. Sam hung back, hoping he wouldn't be required to go any closer. He didn't want to see the body again.

"That's where the body is," Dean said, pointing into the depths of the bushes. He turned and gestured at the drug store bag, the edge of which barely stuck up above the mounting snow. "And there's the bag and prescription bottle. We left everything right where we found it."

"We searched out here before, when Harry Norton went missing," Boone spoke up. "Not this exact spot, maybe, but I know we were in this general area. Didn't find anything at that time."

"It was snowing then," said the other uniformed officer, a tall, fidgety young man whose name Sam couldn't remember. "Five inches by the time we got up here. That's probably why we didn't see the body or prescription then."

"It's snowing now," Boone pointed out.

The younger officer shrugged. "Yeah, but it wasn't snowing when these guys found the body and prescription bottle. Makes it a lot easier to spot things if they're not covered with snow."

Boone nodded. "True. Of course, whatever happened might've happened since we were out here."

"All right, that's enough." Parsons reached into her pocket and pulled on a pair of latex gloves as Ramirez began snapping

119

photos of the bag and bottle and surrounding area. She turned a keen gaze to Bo. "Did any of you touch anything?"

"No." Bo moved closer to Sam, shoulders hunched. "Sam stepped on the bottle, which is how we found it in the first place, but no one touched it after that."

Crouching on the ground, Parsons carefully brushed the snow away from the bottle. "And how exactly did the three of you come to be out here? This is a pretty long way off the trail."

Sam, Bo and Dean exchanged nervous looks. They'd dreaded this question. Telling law enforcement personnel that they'd followed a creature from another dimension into the woods and saw it kill someone wasn't likely to go over well. Nevertheless, a brief discussion after Carl had radioed the police resulted in the unanimous decision to tell the truth. After all, they'd done nothing wrong and had nothing to hide.

Bo cleared his throat. "I believe the Bledsoes told you why Sam, Dean and I are here."

"Yes, they did." Parsons held out a hand. The other officer—Torrence, Sam suddenly remembered—took two Ziploc bags from the cooler and gave them to her. "I did a quick Google search before we left to come up here. You've made quite a name for yourselves investigating these so-called interdimensional gateways. Is that what you think you've found here?"

The detective's expression didn't change, nor did the neutral tone of her voice, but Sam felt her skepticism and suspicion all the same. "We're not sure yet what exactly the guests here have seen."

"But you've seen it too, yes?" Fishing a pencil out of her purse, Parsons slipped the point under the edge of the prescription bottle's cap, lifted it from its nest of snow and pine needles and dropped it into a baggie. She met Sam's gaze, one eyebrow arched. "You saw this...thing, you followed it into the woods, and it led you straight to a body which just might be a missing Sunset Lodge employee. That's what you're about to tell me, isn't it?"

A muscle twitched in Bo's jaw. "Yes, it is. We were hired to investigate these sightings, so when all three of us witnessed this being—whatever it may be—manifest and run into the woods, we followed it."

Bo's clipped, careful tone told Sam how angry he was, and how hard he was suppressing it. Sam felt the same way. Even though he knew suspicion and close questioning were essential for a detective to solve a case, he hated having that suspicion aimed at himself and his friends when they'd done nothing wrong.

"I thought I saw someone in those bushes," Sam continued. "I was afraid the...the thing was going to hurt the person, so I ran closer to try and make it go away. Bo and Dean followed me. We all saw the thing go into the bushes and kill the person it had trapped."

"It just disappeared after that," Dean added. "And we looked in the thicket and spotted the body."

Parsons glanced at Ramirez, who'd taken out a notebook and was writing in it. "You getting this, Ramirez?"

He nodded without looking up.

"And then you found the prescription bottle how?" Parsons asked, extracting the paper bag from the snow with a pair of tweezers from her case. She deposited it in another Ziploc bag handed to her by Torrence.

"I stepped on it when I walked away from the thicket," Sam explained. "It rolled under my foot and made me lose my balance. Dean found it when he went to see what it was I stepped on."

"I see." Rising to her feet, Parsons turned a cool gray-eyed gaze to each of them in turn. "Ramirez, keep an eye on them while Boone and I take a look at the body."

Ramirez stuck his notebook and pen in his coat pocket. He crossed his arms loosely over his chest. The movement looked casual, but Sam knew better. He'd seen the shoulder holster earlier. Ramirez had them covered and wouldn't hesitate to shoot them if he felt it necessary.

Sam glanced at Bo and Dean. Their expressions said they'd both noticed as well, and neither was any happier than Sam about being considered possible suspects.

The three of them stood still and silent under Ramirez's watchful eye while Boone, Torrence and Parsons photographed, measured, jotted notes and finally put each of the scattered body parts in its own large Ziploc bag. By the time they were finished, the soft sides of the collapsible cooler bulged outward.

The trek back to the Lodge was silent and tense. Sam, Bo and Dean walked side by side behind Boone and Parsons. Boone had extended the handle on the large, wheeled cooler and was pulling it behind her. The wheels made two sharp parallel tracks in the snow.

Sam stared at the back of Parsons' head as they plodded along. He didn't know whether her silence was a good thing or a bad thing. In his limited experience, police detectives were a pretty tight-lipped lot, but they'd never had this little to say to him before. It made him anxious, wondering whether he, Bo and Dean were about to be dragged back down the mountain in handcuffs.

When they reached the Lodge, Boone and Torrence hurried to collect the horses, so they could get back down the mountain with the body and other evidence while the trail was still passable. The rest of the group followed Parsons into Lex and

Carl's office.

Lex looked up from a pile of papers. Anxiety was etched into every line of her face. "You're back. Was the body...? Was it Harry?"

Parsons' expression didn't change, but the hardness in her eyes melted into sympathy. "We can't be sure until we run some tests, Mrs. Bledsoe. But we'll let you know as soon as we know anything."

"I...I can identify him," Lex quavered, twisting her fingers together. "If you need me to, that is."

"I think that might be impossible," Parsons said, her voice gentle. "The body isn't intact. There isn't enough of the face left to allow positive identification."

Lex paled. "Oh."

"Whoever this is," Parsons continued, all business again, "they have been dead at least a few days. Possibly as long as two or three weeks. Again, it's difficult to know for sure until we're able to run some tests."

Two or three weeks? But we just saw it happen, how can it have happened that long ago?

Sam glanced at his coworkers. Dean looked just as startled as Sam felt. Bo merely looked thoughtful, and Sam wondered what he knew, or suspected.

A loud sniff from Lex brought Sam out of his thoughts. Lex blinked, clearly fighting tears. Sam felt terrible for her. He wished he could go give her a hug, but he didn't dare. It was irrational, Sam knew, but he felt that everything he said or did was under scrutiny by Parsons and the silent Ramirez, and he didn't want to draw undue attention to himself.

Evidently Bo didn't feel the same. He limped forward and leaned against Lex's desk. "What about my employees and myself, Detective Parsons? Do you have any more questions for us?"

Parsons glanced at Sam and Dean before settling her calm gaze on Bo. "Actually, Mr. Broussard, I do have more questions for you. You and your friends may wait in the common room for me. I need to speak with Lex privately before I question you."

The muscle in Bo's jaw twitched, announcing his anger to anyone who knew what to look for. "That's *Doctor* Broussard, Detective. And unless you have a very good reason to tell me where I'm allowed to go, I will be in my cabin, resting. You can find me in cabin four when you're ready to question me."

If Bo's declaration fazed Parsons at all, she didn't show it. She nodded. "Very well. Now, if you'll all excuse us?"

Without another word, Bo turned on his heel and strode out of the office. Sam and Dean followed. As he pulled the door shut behind him, Sam caught Lex's eye. She gave him a wan smile.

In the empty common room, Bo fell into one of the rocking chairs gathered around the woodstove and shut his eyes. His expression was blank and calm, but the crease between his brows spoke volumes.

Easing himself into the chair beside Bo's, Sam leaned as close as he dared. "You okay?"

"No. I'm tired, and angry, and my leg's bothering me again." Bo opened his eyes and met Sam's gaze. "I probably shouldn't have let her get to me, but damn. She was acting like we were suspects. Wasn't she?"

"I'd say." Plopping into the chair on the other side of Bo, Dean picked up a book lying on a nearby table and scanned the back cover. "Don't worry about it, Bo. It'll only take a few minutes for her to find out we weren't even here when that person was killed."

"If she's right about the body being there for several days, that is," Sam pointed out. "What if she's wrong? What if that person was killed after we got here?"

Dean shook his head. "There's no way. There was no blood on the ground, remember? If it had happened in the last two days, there would've been blood. So it had to have happened before we got here."

"How?" Sam wondered. "We were all there. We saw it happen. How is it possible that it actually happened up to three weeks before we saw it?"

Bo's brow furrowed. "I have an idea—"

"What?" Dean interrupted.

Bo let out a soft laugh. "I don't want to say anything just yet, in case I'm wrong."

"Fine, be that way." Setting the book down again, Dean leaned back in his chair to peruse a nearby shelf. "Oh man, they have Jenga! We should totally play later."

Sam smiled. "Yeah. Tomorrow, maybe. Bo, you want to go back to the cabin now?"

"I do, yes." Wincing, Bo rose to his feet. "Sam, you don't have to come with me if you don't want to. I'll be fine."

Sam gave Bo a narrow look. "In other words, you'd rather I didn't stay in the cabin with you."

Bo's cheeks went pink. "Sam—"

"It's okay, I know what you're thinking. If we're alone in the cabin, Parsons might get more than she expects when she shows up to question us. I don't think anybody wants that." Sam stood, one hand on Bo's arm. "Okay if I walk you to the cabin?"

Bo's gaze softened, and he smiled. "I'd like that."

"I'll just wait here," Dean said, slouching in his chair and stretching his feet toward the warmth of the woodstove. "Bo, you want to meet me and Sam back here later and hike up for the sunset?"

"If Parsons will let us, yes." Bo scowled at the closed door to Lex's office. "I hope we don't have to stay inside. I'd like to see if we can gather more information about whatever's going on in those woods."

Sam's stomach clenched. "I guess we should do that. I'd still like to know why we witnessed a death that most likely happened days or weeks ago. But I have to say, I don't want to see it again."

"Amen, brother," Dean agreed.

Bo rubbed his chin, a thoughtful look in his eyes. "Like I said, I have a theory about what's going on. I just want to see what happens tonight before I say anything."

Dean gave him a sour look. "Tease."

A wide grin smoothed the lines of anger and frustration from Bo's face. "Call it what you want. I'm not talking until I have something to back me up."

"Why not?" Sam asked, moving toward the door.

"Because I don't want to influence yours or Dean's observations." Bo followed Sam to the door, giving Dean a wave. "I'll see you in a couple of hours, Dean. You and Sam talk to some of the staff, if you get a chance. Find out precisely what they've seen, and precisely what days and times, if possible. I'd like to know if there's any consistency in the timing of the sightings."

Dean nodded. "Will do, boss."

"Great, thank you." Pulling the front door open, Bo walked out onto the deck, with Sam close behind.

Outside, the snow continued to fall, veiling the day in a still white silence. With no one around to see, Sam slipped his arm around Bo as they made their way down the steps.

"You're still limping a little," he explained in answer to Bo's raised eyebrow. "Don't want you to slip in the snow."

Chuckling, Bo stepped off the last stair and into the snow covering the path. "In that case, I'm glad my leg's still acting up, because I like your arm around me like this."

Sam smiled, warmed by Bo's words. "Me too. Though I'm still sort of worried about your leg."

Bo was quiet for several seconds. "I'm worried too. It still isn't hurting, exactly. But every time we go out to the woods, that weird jumpy feeling comes back. And this time it hasn't entirely gone away. It still feels overly sensitive, though not as much as it did in the woods."

Frowning, Sam pulled Bo closer. "I don't like that at all, Bo. It sounds like what you're feeling might be related to that bite after all."

"I know." Bo glanced sidelong at Sam. "I can't help but think that something about the bite is reacting to the presence of a portal."

Fear spiked cold and sharp through Sam's bones. "So you think there really is a portal here?"

"Is, or was." Bo's arm slid around Sam's waist as they neared their cabin. "Let's not jump to conclusions, though. We're still investigating. Let's finish collecting evidence, then see what we have and draw our conclusions from that."

"You're right." Forcing his worry to the back of his mind, Sam pulled the cabin key out of his jeans pocket. "We should probably sit down as a group tonight and go over what we have so far."

"Good idea."

Sam unlocked the cabin and pulled the door open. Leaning against the doorframe, Bo dragged Sam to him by the front of his jacket and planted a hard kiss on his mouth. Surprised, Sam let out a squeak. Bo laughed, slid a hand into Sam's hair and kissed him again, taking it deep this time. Sam opened to him, enjoying the possibility of discovery nearly as much as the slide of Bo's tongue against his. Contradictory, but true.

"Don't think I'm complaining," Sam murmured as they pulled apart, "but what was that for?"

Bo smiled, his thumb caressing Sam's cheek. "Because I love you. And because that detective made me feel rebellious."

"Someone might see us."

"Who? We didn't pass any of the staff on the way here, and all the guests are gone." Bo thrust his hips against Sam's. His eyes gleamed with a rare mischief which always managed to take Sam by surprise. "I wish I could bend you over the bed and fuck you blind right now. But those damn detectives might walk in on us." Latching his mouth onto Sam's neck, Bo sucked very gently for a second. "Of course, it'd be interesting to see whether or not Parsons' expression changed."

Sam laughed out loud. "Oh, I see. Detectives giving you attitude makes you feel rebellious, and feeling rebellious makes you horny. I'm going to have to remember that."

"See that you do." Bo licked the corner of Sam's mouth. "Go on back and help Dean interview the staff. I'm going to organize our notes so far and plan out what to do next."

"Okay." Sam picked up Bo's braid and let it run across his palm like a glossy black rope. He met Bo's gaze. "I love you."

The joyful shine in Bo's eyes made Sam's spirit sing. With one last swift press of lips, Bo stepped into the cabin and shut the door.

Hands in his pockets, Sam jumped back down the steps

onto the path. He smiled up at the threatening gray sky. Snowflakes pelted his face, their icy sting melting into liquid cold in the heat of his skin. The trees, the ground and the roofs of the cabins were all covered in white. The snow was falling so fast Sam couldn't see more than twenty feet or so. At this rate, he figured, they'd definitely have eight inches by that night.

So will I. Sam snickered. Dean was a bad influence.

He hadn't gone more than a few steps when he saw Anne and Darren standing beside the cabin next door. Both were eyeing him with a wary sort of look. The happy afterglow of kissing Bo faded away, leaving Sam feeling cold inside. Forcing his feet to move, he walked up to them with a smile. He and Dean were charged with interviewing the staff about the sightings. Now was as good a time as any to start.

"Hi," he said. "Do y'all have a few minutes to talk?"

They glanced at each other. "Um, sure," Darren answered, sounding anything but. "Common room okay?"

"That's great, actually. Dean's already up there, he and I wanted to ask you guys about the sightings out in the woods." Sam turned to Anne. "What about it, Anne? Can you talk?"

"Not right now. I have things to do." Her voice was distinctly cool, and she wouldn't meet Sam's eyes. "See you later, Darren."

"Yeah, see you." Darren gave Sam a nervous smile. "Let's get inside."

Sam nodded. He watched Anne's tense back as she hurried toward the staff quarters. Instinct told him she and Darren had seen him and Bo kissing, and both of them now knew the true nature of his and Bo's relationship.

Having Anne of all people know about him and Bo gave Sam a sick feeling in the pit of his stomach. *Lex and Carl won't hold it against us,* he reminded himself. *They hired Sandra*

129

knowing she was a lesbian, why would it make any difference to them that Bo and I are together?

Sam wished he felt more reassured than he did. Vowing to break it to Bo before Anne could confront him—or prod Lex or Carl into it—Sam followed Darren toward the common room.

Chapter Eight

The uncomfortable looks Darren kept darting at Sam from the corner of his eye cemented Sam's certainty that he and Bo had been seen. To his relief, Darren didn't mention it. Sam's gut told him Darren wouldn't say anything to anyone else either. If only Anne could keep it to herself, they'd have nothing to worry about.

You don't have anything to worry about anyway, he told himself as he and Darren climbed the steps to the office and common room. *There aren't any guests here, and Lex and Carl aren't the sort to kick us off the job for something like this.*

He dismissed the little voice in the back of his head warning him that Anne was a wild card, and he and Bo should be careful. The worst she could do was tell the others here at Sunset Lodge, and no harm could come of that. Not really.

When they entered the common room, Dean wasn't there. Sam frowned. "Wonder where Dean went? He was supposed to wait here."

"He may have gone down to the staff quarters with Anne." Darren gave Sam a cautious smile. "They've been flirting back and forth like crazy."

"Yeah, I noticed." Relieved that Darren seemed to have regained his normal comfort level with him, Sam crossed the room and sat in one of the chairs beside the window. He

131

motioned Darren to join him. "Hopefully, Dean's asking her about the sightings instead of trying to get in her pants."

Darren let out a startled laugh. "So what is it you'd like to know?" he asked, settling in the chair beside Sam's.

"Have you seen the creature some of the guests claim to have seen?"

Grimacing, Darren nodded. "Yes, I did. Once."

Sam turned in his chair and leaned forward. "Tell me what you saw, if you don't mind."

"It was the day after Harry went missing. I'd walked up to Sunset Rock to watch the sunset. Hoping I'd run into Harry, I have to admit, even though we all kind of figured even then that he wasn't coming back." Darren sighed, his dark eyes filling with sadness. "Anyway, I started back a little ahead of the crowd. When I drew even with that big boulder, I caught a movement on the edge of my vision. I turned to look, and I thought I saw something like a black shadow move off into the woods. It moved incredibly fast. I thought it was my imagination, until two guests saw it the next evening."

"So you saw it at twilight, just like the other people did."

"Yes."

"Has anyone seen it in the daytime?" He kept quiet about what he, Bo and Dean had witnessed. The goal here was to find out if anyone besides the three of them had seen the thing any time other than twilight.

"Not that I know of. Of course very few people go by there in the daytime, except when we have to go down the mountain for something. Even then, not everyone uses the staff trail all the time. It's shorter, but it's also steeper and more difficult, so we sometimes use the guest trails, and you don't pass that area to get to those trails."

Pursing his lips, Sam considered asking if anyone had ever witnessed the creature killing someone. He decided against it. If anyone had seen such a thing, surely they would have told Lex or Carl, and the information would have been passed on to BCPI. Besides, he wasn't sure if he was allowed to talk about an active police investigation, never mind that the staff would eventually find out anyway.

"Has anyone followed it?" he asked after a moment's thought.

Looking puzzled, Darren shook his head. "Not that I'm aware of. I sure as hell didn't."

"And no one's seen it...do anything?"

Darren frowned. "Like what?"

"Anything at all," Sam hedged. "Other than run into the woods, that is."

"Not that I've heard." With a quick glance toward the closed office door, Darren leaned an elbow on the arm of his chair and lowered his voice. "Does this have anything to do with the police officers and the detectives who came up here on horseback earlier? The two uniforms went back down, carrying what looked like a very full cooler, but I didn't see the detectives with them that time, so they must still be here."

Sam smiled. Darren was too smart for his own good, or anyone else's. "It does, yes. But I can't tell you what. Sorry."

"It's okay. I'm sure Lex and Carl will tell us as much as they can tonight." An apprehensive expression crossed Darren's face. "I know you can't say anything, but I really hope the cops aren't here because... Because of Harry. Everybody here is crazy about him. And he's one of the most hard-working and reliable employees here, in spite of his condition."

Instantly, Sam thought of the prescription bottle he'd stepped on in the woods. He'd seen the name of the drug—

Dilantin—but he had no idea what it did, and he hadn't thought to ask Dean or Bo. Maybe it had nothing to do with the dismembered body or the thing they'd seen in the woods, but it never hurt to have as much information as possible.

"What condition was that?" Sam darted a swift glance at the office door. It was still shut. "Was he sick? Is it possible his disappearance had something to do with that?"

"He had—has—epilepsy. It's always been well controlled, though. I've never seen him have a seizure, and I don't think anyone else has either." Darren dropped his gaze to his lap. "He ran out of Dilantin. That's why he went into town that day. He usually got three months worth of drug, but he'd had to switch pharmacies on the last refill, and they screwed it up and only gave him two months worth. We had a huge ice storm up here, and it kept him on the mountain long enough for him to run out of his medicine."

In his mind, Sam saw the pharmacy bag and prescription bottle buried in the leaves mere feet from the spot where the mountain dropped into empty space. "Oh, my God. Do you think he could've had a seizure or something? He could've fallen off the mountain."

Darren gave him an odd look, but before he could say anything the office door swung open. Lex walked out, looking pale and dazed. Parsons and Ramirez followed in her wake.

Leaping to his feet, Darren hurried over and put an arm around Lex's shoulders. "Lex? Are you okay?"

She patted his hand and gave him a watery smile. "I'll be all right. I'll tell you and the others all about it as soon as Detective Parsons says it's okay."

Parsons glanced up from the notebook in which she was writing. "Actually, Mrs. Bledsoe, I think it's okay to go ahead and talk to your employees about what's happened. Ramirez and I will be staying here, and we will be questioning each of them anyway. They might as well know why, and they'll probably take it better from you."

Darren's eyes narrowed, but he kept quiet. Rising slowly to his feet, Sam walked over to the group outside the office door. "Detective Parsons, what about Bo, Dean and myself? Are... Are we..."

He didn't know quite how to phrase what he wanted to ask, but Parsons seemed to know. She gave him a cool look. "You and your coworkers are under no suspicion at this time, Mr. Raintree. However, I will ask that you not leave here until we've had a chance to question you all and take your official statements."

Sam nodded. At the rate the snow was falling, they wouldn't have been able to get down the mountain even if they'd wanted to. And they certainly weren't ready to leave. Not with their own investigation still in progress.

"Darren, would you mind finding Anne and Jerome and having them meet us in the dining hall? Sandra should already be there. I'll explain the whole thing to all of you at once." Lex gave Detective Parsons a nervous look. "Will you and Detective Ramirez be coming to help me speak with the staff, or are you going to go ahead and start questioning Sam, Bo and Dean?"

Parsons raised her eyebrows at Ramirez, who shrugged. "We'll come with you," she said. "I want to set up a schedule for questioning your staff while we're there. I think talking to them is the priority, since it seems the event in question most likely occurred before the team from Bay City Paranormal arrived here."

It was all Sam could do to keep from whooping out loud in relief. Parsons must be fairly certain the person in the woods had been killed many days past, or she wouldn't have said that.

If she wondered why Sam, Bo and Dean had witnessed a slaying which happened before they arrived at the Lodge, she kept it to herself.

A suspicion had begun to worm itself into Sam's brain regarding what they'd seen. Afraid to look at it too hard in case he was wrong, Sam pushed it to the back of his mind. If he was right, their observations tonight would hopefully tell the tale.

Sam fell into step with Darren as they left the common room. To his relief, the young man's expression had lost its guarded look. It was good to know his first impression of Darren had evidently been right. He might not be comfortable with Sam and Bo being gay, but that fact would have minimal impact on his treatment of them.

"I'm heading down to the staff quarters to get Anne," Darren said as they clumped down the steps behind Lex and the detectives. "You might as well come with me. Dean's probably down there with her."

"Yeah, probably." Sam hunched his shoulders against a sudden gust of cold, damp wind. "Listen, I expect we'll be up here another two or three days, so let one of us know if you think of anything that might be helpful to us."

Darren grinned. "You'd make a good cop, Sam. You've got the lingo down."

Sam laughed. "Thanks, I think."

"Are you going out to Sunset Rock tonight?"

"Yeah. We want to try to see the phenomenon again, and see if it's the same as before or if there are differences."

"And that'll help you determine whether or not it's a portal?"

"Hopefully." Hesitating, Sam tried to think of a succinct way to explain the process. He couldn't come up with one. "I don't know. We've only dealt with two portals before. We're still learning the rules."

"I hear you." They reached the door to the staff quarters. Darren fished a key out of his jeans pocket. "What are the common factors you've found so far between the other portals?"

"Not many. In both of the other cases, the baseline electromagnetic field of the entire area was high. Not dangerously so, but higher than you'd normally expect. Around two and a half to three."

Looking thoughtful, Darren turned the key and pushed the door open. He let out a surprised sound and promptly turned his back to the room, his eyes wide and startled. "Good grief."

Darren was blocking Sam's view of the room beyond the door. Leaning sideways, he caught a brief glimpse of what had startled Darren. On the other side of the narrow, wood-panelled room, Dean and Anne lay tangled together on a sagging red paisley sofa. Dean's shirt was draped over the back of the couch. Anne's sweater was hiked up to her armpits, revealing her bare breasts, one of which was covered by Dean's hand. One of her hands was shoved down the back of Dean's undone jeans, the other buried in his hair as they kissed. The scene revealed in the dim glow of the single beige-shaded lamp burned itself into Sam's retinas in the split second before Darren slammed the door shut.

Still looking stunned, Darren leaned against the door. "Okay, I really didn't expect to walk in on *that*."

Sam stifled a smirk. "Honestly, I'm not surprised. Dean's been interested in her since they first met, and he usually gets who he wants."

Darren let out a sigh. "So does Anne. I guess it was bound to happen."

At that moment the door flew opened, sending Darren

stumbling backward into Dean, who stood grinning on the other side. He'd pulled his sweatshirt back on. "Sorry about that," he said, sounding not the least bit sorry. "We didn't figure anybody would be back down here this soon."

"It's okay." Darren glanced behind Dean as if afraid of what he might see. "Is Anne...um, decent? Lex wants us in the dining hall."

"I'm right here." Anne slipped through the door, clothes back in place and jacket zipped to her chin. Her face was flaming red. "What does Lex want?"

"She's going to tell us why the cops are here," Darren answered.

A look of smug satisfaction crossed Anne's face. "Good. I need to talk to her after she gets done."

"Okay, well, I guess we're off. See you guys later." With a nod at Sam and Dean, Darren headed in the direction of the dining hall with Anne beside him.

As they left, Anne shot a glare at Sam. The pure hatred in her eyes made his blood run cold. He stood beside Dean in the open doorway, watching Anne and Darren and wondering if he ought to keep a closer eye on her.

Dean's warm palm closed over Sam's wrist. "Let's go to your cabin. I need to tell you and Bo something."

Curious, Sam followed Dean inside while he gathered his jacket and cameras. "What is it?"

"Not yet." Dean pulled his knit cap onto his head and led Sam back out into the dim afternoon. "Y'all both need to hear this."

Sam studied Dean's profile as the two of them trudged through the fast-mounting snow. Dean's expression was unusually grim, his stride full of purpose in a way Sam rarely saw when they weren't actively investigating. He wondered what had his friend so worried.

When they reached the cabin, Dean bounded up the steps and rapped hard on the door. "Bo, it's me and Sam, can we come in?"

"Yeah, it's open," Bo called from inside.

Dean opened the door, dragged Sam inside and shut the door behind them. Bo lay on the bottom bunk, a pillow folded double beneath his head and a notebook resting on his bent knees. His hiking boots and jacket lay on the floor. He set his pen on the bed beside him and gave them a curious look.

"Anne and Darren saw you," Dean blurted out before Bo could speak. "They were cleaning the cabin next door, and when they came out they saw you and Sam standing in the doorway here, kissing."

Putting his notebook down, Bo covered his face with both hands. "Wonderful."

"How did you know that?" Sam stared at Dean, his eyes widening. "Oh, my God. Anne told you."

Dean nodded. "I'd gone down to the staff quarters to get my camera so I could take some pictures of the snow. She came busting in, and asked me did I know y'all were 'fucking queers', as she put it."

"What did you say?" Taking his jacket off and hanging it over the back of the chair, Sam sat on the bed at Bo's feet and rested a hand on Bo's knee. To his relief, Bo didn't move away. He needed to touch Bo right now.

"Nothing. She kept on ranting about the evils of being gay for like ten minutes before I could get a word in edgewise. I just let her talk. I figured as long as she was yacking my ear off, she couldn't be spilling the beans to anyone else." Dean plopped into the chair. "When she finally settled down some, she said she was gonna go tell Lex and Carl about your quote-unquote unprofessional behavior. So I distracted her."

Sam's mouth fell open. "You *distracted* her? Jesus, Dean, you two were practically fucking on the couch."

Bo let his hands drop. His face radiated shock. "What?"

"Sam and Darren walked in on me and Anne making out." Grimacing, Dean ran a hand through his hair, making it stick up in all directions. "I'm glad it didn't go any further than that, 'cause there's no way I could've gotten it up after what all she said."

"You mean to say that even though you've been flirting with her since the second you met her, you didn't want to fuck her?" Sam shook his head. "Fickle, Dean. Very fickle."

"Well excuse me if I stop finding people attractive when they go all homophobic on me." Propping one foot on the bedframe, Dean crossed his arms and arched an eyebrow at Sam and Bo. "I made damn sure she wouldn't be able to tell anyone else about what she saw before I could warn y'all. I totally took one for the team. I hope you appreciate my sacrifice."

Sam laughed. "We do. Even though I find it hard to believe you didn't enjoy it at all."

"She has really nice tits, so I did kind of like that part, but she can't kiss for shit." Dean grinned. "Call me spoiled, but if I'm going to get horizontal with someone, they *have* to be a good kisser."

"You didn't tell her you're bisexual?" Bo asked, breaking his silence.

Dean sobered instantly. "No. Something tells me she wouldn't have stayed and let me distract her if I had."

"You're probably right." Taking Sam's hand, Bo laced their

fingers together. "Thank you, Dean. For watching out for us, and for wanting to protect us."

"Y'all are some of my best friends. I love you." To Sam's amusement, Dean leapt from the chair and bent to hug first him, then Bo. "Anne's a bitch. Hot, yeah, but a bitch."

"I think you're right," Sam said as Dean pulled away. "Do you think she'll cause any real trouble for us?"

"I think she'll try." Insinuating himself between Bo and Sam, Dean turned a somber look to first one, then the other. "And honestly, I don't think I can keep distracting her with groping. Even if I could stand to do it again, which I'm not sure I can, she'd eventually notice I wasn't really into it."

Smiling, Bo patted Dean's hand. "There's no need for that, Dean. I believe she *will* try to make trouble for us. But really, there's not much she can do. Lex and Carl are the ones in charge here, and neither of them is homophobic. I'm sure we'll be fine."

"Yeah, you're probably right." Dean drew a deep breath and blew it out. "So what do you want to do now? It's not time to head out for the sunset yet, and Lex has the whole staff in the dining hall right now explaining what's been happening. We could go over evidence, or we could just have a rest before heading up to Sunset Rock."

Glancing at Bo, Sam frowned at the odd mix of fury and melancholy on his face. "I'd like a little rest, personally."

Dean gave him a knowing look. "I figured you might." He squeezed Sam's hand, then Bo's, and stood up. "I think I'll go over to the dining hall and see what all Lex and the good detective are telling everyone. Should I come back around five, so we can get our stuff together and hike up to Sunset Rock?"

"Yes, that's fine," Bo answered with a strained smile. "See you then."

"Yeah, see you. Oh, and make sure you lock the door, just in case." With a suggestive grin, Dean opened the cabin door and slipped outside.

Sam stood, walked over and locked the door. When he turned around again, Bo held out a hand. "Come here."

Sam obediently crossed the room, took Bo's hand and sat beside him. The fire in Bo's dark eyes made his head whirl. Without a word, Sam leaned down and captured Bo's mouth with his.

Bo moaned, the sound low and rough. His arms went around Sam's back, pulling Sam on top of him. His kiss tasted of need and desperation. Sam rose up on one elbow, breaking the kiss to search Bo's eyes.

"Bo, is something wrong?" He laid a hand on Bo's cheek. "You seem upset."

Bo stared into his eyes, fingertips trailing up and down his back. "Is this what you've faced all your life? This unreasoning hate from other people, all because of something you have no control over?"

A humorless smile curved Sam's mouth. "Pretty much, yeah. But the worst thing I've personally experienced is being verbally harassed now and then. Most people really don't care one way or the other, and the majority of those who disapprove don't get violent about it, thank God. In fact, of all the people who think we're pure evil—or at least making a wrong choice— most people never say anything."

"They're still thinking it, though. Every time I see an openly gay couple, I also see people glaring at them behind their backs, and I've heard some of the things they whisper about them." Bo wrinkled his nose. "Bastards. Why can't they just let other people be who they are, and leave them alone?"

Bo's voice dripped with anger, and his eyes shot sparks,

but Sam saw the sadness and fear underneath the fury. Kicking off his shoes, Sam rested his head on Bo's chest and curled his body around Bo. "I don't know," he answered softly. "I just tell myself it doesn't matter what those people think."

He didn't voice the fact that sometimes it *did* matter, when some of the worst homophobes held positions of power over your life. Or when you're walking down the street and a crowd of those whose opinions shouldn't matter follow you, laughing and calling you "fag" or worse, making you feel vulnerable and angry and afraid. It wouldn't help to remind Bo of things he already knew.

Tucking a hand beneath Sam's chin, Bo tilted his face up and brushed a soft kiss across his mouth. "Do you think we have time?"

The need in Bo's whispered voice sent Sam's pulse racing. "I hope so, because I really want you right now."

Bo didn't say anything, but he didn't need to. The way he attacked Sam's mouth, with teeth and tongue and open, hungry lips, expressed his desire with perfect clarity. His hand clamped onto the back of Sam's head, fisting in his hair to hold him in place.

Sam would've smiled at that if his mouth hadn't been otherwise occupied. An army couldn't have dragged him away from Bo's kiss.

The kiss went on for long, wonderful minutes. Sam only broke it when his cock began to scream for relief he couldn't obtain through rubbing his denim-entrapped crotch against Bo's similarly clothed thigh. Nuzzling Bo's chin up, Sam licked a wet line up his throat. The tastes of sweat, skin and lust shot fire through his blood, and he growled.

The sound seemed to ramp up Bo's excitement. He whimpered, thighs spreading so he could hook a leg around

Sam's hips. "God, Sam. Suck me?"

At that moment, Sam was convinced a better idea had never been conceived in the entire history of the world. However, he knew without a doubt that he was far too close to release himself to be able to hold out. With Bo's taste and scent and the texture of his skin filling Sam's senses, he would shoot all over the bed without so much as a touch from Bo. And he desperately wanted Bo to touch him.

Pushing up on one hand, Sam stared down into Bo's eyes. "Sixty-nine?"

A visible shudder ran through Bo's body. His eyelids fluttered closed. He took three slow, deep breaths, opened his eyes again and pinned Sam with a smoldering stare. "That would be nice."

Sam had to laugh. Of all the things they'd tried in bed, simultaneously sucking each other off was Bo's number one favorite. So much so that he rarely allowed it, claiming it was special and therefore shouldn't be overused.

The corners of Bo's mouth turned up in a sly smile. "Stop laughing and start sucking."

Still snickering, Sam pulled off Bo's shirt, then his own. He bent and took Bo's right nipple into his mouth, sucking gently and rolling the little bud with his tongue. Bo moaned, one hand kneading Sam's back, the other buried in his hair. Closing his teeth around the hardened nub of flesh, Sam tugged until Bo let out a hiss, then let go and turned his attention to the other nipple.

When he had Bo squirming beneath him, reduced to incoherent babble, Sam climbed off the bed and skinned out of his jeans and underwear. Bo watched, panting, one palm rubbing his crotch. He made no move to remove his own pants, Sam noted with satisfaction. Bo knew how much Sam loved to undress him.

Naked, Sam knelt over Bo's knees. He flipped open the button of Bo's jeans and tugged the zipper down, watching Bo's face the whole time. Bo stared straight into his eyes, as he often did. Sam loved it. He'd never before had a lover who didn't shut his eyes or look away during sex, and he found the incredible intensity of unbroken eye contact addictive.

Grasping the waistband of Bo's jeans, Sam worked the garment down over Bo's hips. He scooted backward to pull the pants off Bo's legs and toss them on the floor. With the jeans out of the way, Sam pushed Bo's legs apart and bent to nuzzle his crotch through his underwear. The smell of cock, precome and unwashed man set Sam's mind and body on fire. He mouthed Bo's balls through the thin Jersey knit.

"Oh God," Bo gasped, hips lifting and hands winding into Sam's hair. "Sam."

Humming, Sam pressed the flat of his tongue to the base of Bo's shaft. The fabric of Bo's underwear felt slightly rough on his tongue, and tasted of dried sweat. Sam licked and sucked, gathering as much of the sharp, salty flavor as he could.

Bo whimpered, his prick twitching against Sam's lips. The whimper turned into a rough moan when Sam hooked his fingers into the waistband of Bo's boxer-briefs and pulled them down just enough to expose his erection.

Burying his face in Bo's groin, Sam breathed deep. "You smell so good," he murmured, caressing Bo's trembling thighs.

Bo let out a breathless laugh. "Sweaty and dirty is good?"

"Yes." Swiping his tongue the length of Bo's shaft, Sam crawled up for a hard, deep kiss. "I can't wait to suck your cock. I bet two days worth of not bathing makes you taste better than ever."

Bo's groan was answer enough. Grinning, Sam pushed up

onto his hands and knees and turned around to straddle Bo's head. Immediately, Bo's fingers dug into his hips, pulling his cock down into a warm, wet, enthusiastic mouth.

With Bo's lips and tongue working his prick, it took every ounce of concentration Sam could summon to get Bo's underwear off. He managed to shove the garment down past Bo's knees. Bo pulled one leg free and opened his thighs wide, and Sam downed his cock in one gulp, savoring the explosion of rich male flavor on his tongue.

A sharp thrust of hips and the feel of fingers digging into his ass announced Bo's pleasure more clearly than any words could. Bo swallowed Sam's cock deeper, his muffled moans vibrating through Sam's shaft and up his spine.

Pulling off long enough to wet a finger in his mouth, Sam wormed the single digit into Bo's ass as he wrapped his lips once more around the head of his prick. Bo keened and shoved himself hard into Sam's throat.

God, yes. Yes. Relaxing the muscles in his throat, Sam shut his eyes and let Bo's cock stretch his jaw wide.

Outside, the rising wind sighed around the corners of the cabin and pelted the window with tiny crystals which pattered like sand against the glass. The only other sounds were muffled moans and the wet slurp of mouths on cocks. Snow falling thick and fast muted the late afternoon sun to a dim gray glow, shaded blue by the drawn curtains. The little room felt like a warm, sex-scented sanctuary, sheltering Sam and Bo from the icy white storm beyond its walls.

Sam was so lost in sheer sensual joy, he almost didn't notice Bo's mouth inching further up his shaft with each stroke. The sensation crept into his brain by degrees, until Bo's nose dug into his balls and he abruptly realized his entire dick was inside Bo's mouth. Bo was deep-throating him, something he'd never managed before.

Sam's eyes flew open. Bo swallowed, his muscles undulating around the head of Sam's cock. The feel of it, so unexpected and so very delicious, was more than Sam could take. Orgasm roared through him, and he was helpless in its grip. He came with his prick fully buried in Bo's throat. His hands spasmed, the finger still inside Bo's ass crooking. Bo grunted, his hips jerked, and the taste of semen flooded Sam's mouth. Sam gulped it down, feeling like the luckiest man in the world.

Sam didn't stop sucking until he'd swallowed every drop. When Bo's cock began to soften, he finally drew back, letting his hips rise to pull his spent prick from Bo's mouth. He nuzzled Bo's balls, smiling at the way Bo squealed and tried to wriggle away. For some reason, Bo was horribly ticklish after he came.

"Sam..."

Bo's voice was sex-roughened and breathless, but Sam knew what he wanted. Taking care not to hit Bo as he moved, Sam rose onto hands and knees and turned around. Bo smiled, eyes dazed and shining. His lips were red and swollen, a glaze of semen making them gleam in the dim light. Silky black strands had come loose from his braid to tangle around his face and neck. To Sam, he'd never looked more beautiful.

Lying on his side, Sam pulled Bo to him and buried his face in the crook of Bo's neck. Bo's heart thudded hard and fast against Sam's chest, his warm breath tickling Sam's ear. A long, sweat-dewed leg slung over Sam's hip. Bo wound his arms around Sam, caressing his back in slow, lazy strokes.

"Mmmm," Sam hummed, clutching Bo's damp body closer. "I swear, there's nothing better in this world than coming down someone's throat while you've got a mouth full of cock."

Bo's soft chuckle vibrated against Sam's lips where they nuzzled his neck. "What do I keep telling you? It's special."

"When you're right, you're right." Sam drew back enough to look into Bo's eyes. Laying a hand on Bo's cheek, he kissed the end of his nose. "It's never been this good for me, Bo. Not with anyone else, ever. And I don't just mean sucking each other off. The sex is amazing, but it's everything else that makes us so good together. I just...I feel like we belong with each other. Does that make sense?"

"It does. I feel the same way." A fierce, dead-serious expression came over Bo's face. "This isn't wrong. What we have together. How can anyone else say it is? How dare they make that judgment?" He rested his forehead against Sam's. "I love you, Sam. And you love me. Isn't that what everyone wants? How can anyone believe that's wrong?"

A familiar mix of affection, sadness and helpless anger curled in Sam's chest. Not knowing what to say, he tilted his head and covered Bo's mouth with his. Bo's lips opened to him with a soft sigh. He plunged his tongue inside, drinking in the taste of salt, skin and their combined seed.

No, something this good could never be wrong. They both knew it, even if the rest of the world didn't. After all they'd been through to get to this point, that was good enough for Sam.

Chapter Nine

Dean returned at five o'clock on the dot, camera in hand. Detectives Parsons and Ramirez, he said, were interviewing staff and had given their permission for Sam, Bo and Dean to continue their investigation in the woods, provided they did not cross the line of police tape the uniformed officers had put up. The three of them gathered the equipment, donned jackets and hats, and headed out.

The snow was still falling, but had tapered off. *Not quite eight inches,* Sam thought with a smile. Nevertheless, it was deep enough to trickle over the tops of his boots as they tramped up the path and onto the trail. The wind had died down, and the evening smelled of evergreens and biting cold.

"We're going up to Sunset Rock, right?" Dean asked, stopping on the path when they drew even with the boulder.

Bo pursed his lips. "I'd like to, yes. Not just to watch the sunset, though. I think we need to document the EMF level at the rock, and let Sam feel it out psychically. We haven't done that yet, and I think we should have the comparison between the rock and the woods."

"Sounds good." Sam frowned when he noticed Bo favoring his right leg. "Is your leg worse again?"

"Yes, it is." With no one around to see, Bo slid an arm around Sam's waist and leaned against him. "That's another good reason to go out to Sunset Rock, I think. The discomfort settles down when I'm at the lodge, but flares up every time I get close to this area. I'd like to consciously compare how it feels at Sunset Rock and other areas as opposed to the Lodge and the area where we saw the thing yesterday."

"Even your injuries are subject to the scientific method." Dean grinned. "You're so hardcore."

Bo laughed. "It's a lifestyle."

Sam took the notebook and pen out of his pocket. "Okay, we already have EMF levels from around the boulder and the place where we found the body. And, Bo, we've documented how your leg felt as well. Let's document those same things right now for this spot, then at intervals as we're walking to Sunset Rock, and at the Rock itself."

"Good idea." Bo gave Sam a smile which warmed him right through. "We'll check about every twenty-five feet. It's pretty often, but I'd rather have too much information than not enough."

Dean plucked the EMF detector from the equipment bag he carried and turned it on. "EMF's three point two here."

Sam dated and timed a fresh page in the notebook and wrote down the number, then shut his eyes and let his mind float. Bo and Dean stood quietly waiting. The sound of some small animal scampering through the snow was the only thing to break the silence. He found only a faint trace of the energy he'd felt at the boulder, like the fading remains of an unpleasant odor. The sense of malevolent purpose he'd experienced with the portals remained absent.

"I'm picking up the same thing as before, only weaker." Opening his eyes again, Sam scribbled down what he'd felt. "Bo? What about your leg?"

"The skin feels overly sensitive, similar to a developing

bruise, or the way it feels when you have a fever. The muscle feels twitchy and a bit weak." Bo rubbed a palm over his thigh. "Very much like it felt before at the boulder, actually. Not quite as bad, but close. Definitely worse than it felt at the Lodge, though it seems that every time we come out here the sensations intensify and hang around longer."

Biting his lip, Dean tapped a finger on the side of the EMF detector. "That's not really consistent with muscle strain, Bo. I don't like it."

"That's exactly what Sam said." Bo wrinkled his nose. "We were speculating earlier that the old bite might be reacting in some way to the presence—or former presence—of a portal, though I have no idea how or why that would happen."

"Hmm. The pattern of symptoms fits." Bending down, Dean peered at Bo's thigh, then pressed it gently with his fingers. "There's no swelling that I can see, no lumps or anything like that. Still no redness? No opening or drainage of the incision?"

"Not a bit."

Dean straightened up and stood staring thoughtfully at Bo's leg while Sam recorded the information. "I hate to say it, but it sure is looking like it might be reacting to something in this area, whether a portal or something else."

"We'll do as we discussed and record the information at intervals. Then we can analyze what we have and see what shows up." Bo drew away from Sam, reached over and took the video camera from the bag. "Let's go."

What with stopping every few minutes to take EMF readings and documenting information on Sam's psychic senses and Bo's leg, it took them much longer than usual to reach Sunset Rock. They arrived just as the sun's disc met the bank of ominous faery clouds hovering just below the mountaintops. Swirls of tiny snowflakes glinted in the sunset light. The sky blazed angry red, making the rounded tops of clouds look like they'd been dipped in blood.

"EMF's zero point two all over," Dean announced after pacing off the entire rock. "No spikes or dips, it's rock steady. Pun intended."

As he noted the figure, Sam shot Dean an amused look. "You just can't help yourself, can you?"

"Nope."

Bo shook his head. "The discomfort in my leg has eased a little, but hasn't entirely gone away. Just like last time, Sam."

Nodding, Sam wrote down the information. "It's gotten a little weaker at every checkpoint."

"Just as the EMF level's gone down," Bo agreed, rubbing his thigh. "Though it dropped kind of suddenly, didn't it?"

Sam consulted his notebook. "Yeah. It went from three point oh at twenty-five feet from the start point to zero point five at fifty feet."

"But your leg's felt a little better at each stop. The change has been more gradual." Dean frowned. "So it seems that it's not related to the EMF level."

Bo glanced at Sam. "Sam? What do you feel this time?"

Sam hadn't felt anything other than the normal psychic energy of the living forest since the first check. Letting his eyelids flutter shut, he relaxed his mind to search for what he'd sensed beside the boulder. As before, he found no trace.

"Nothing that doesn't belong here," Sam answered, opening his eyes. "The level of abnormal energy doesn't correlate exactly with your leg, Bo, but it's close."

Bo grimaced. "I know. Damn it."

Brow furrowed, Dean walked over to stand beside Bo. "I wonder if it has anything to do with that chemical they found in your tissues after that thing bit you."

"I'm wondering the same thing." Bo tugged on his braid. "The chemical never was identified, and its properties never were defined. No one's sure what else it might do."

Bo's expression was tight and blank. Sam knew that look well. It hid Bo's worry and fear when he didn't want anyone to know he was worried or afraid. Moving closer, Sam slipped an arm around Bo's shoulders and pulled him close. Bo leaned against him and rested their heads together. Neither said anything, but Sam felt better with the contact, and he could tell Bo did too.

The creature which had bitten Bo in the tunnels beneath South Bay High School had injected an unknown organism and an unidentified chemical into Bo's leg with the bite. Testing had shown that the chemical appeared to activate the organism for a limited amount of time, but after a few days the chemical had become dormant and the organism had died in culture. Nothing more had been discovered from either, and neither the chemical nor the organism had ever been identified.

Sam had begun to hope the alien chemical would cause Bo no further trouble. The possibility of it reacting to the portals made his stomach clench.

Dean glanced at his watch. "We'd better head back to the boulder. It's getting close to the time we saw the thing before, and I know we want to see if it shows at the same time or not."

"Absolutely." Bo drew back enough to look into Sam's eyes. "Is it okay if I hang onto you, Sam?"

Smiling, Sam let his arm fall from Bo's shoulders to his waist. "You know it is."

Laughing, Dean turned and started back down the path. "I'll just give y'all a little privacy."

"You don't have to do—"

"Shut up," Sam murmured, cutting Bo off.

To his surprise, Bo did. He stood staring silently at Sam, eyes wide and solemn. This time, the apprehension was clear on his face. Shoving his notebook and pen in his pocket, Sam cupped Bo's cheek with his free hand and kissed him.

When they drew apart, Bo gave him a tiny smile which made Sam's heart thump. They started down the path with their arms around each other, Bo letting Sam help support his weight. Bo's gait hitched with each step, the limp less noticeable than it had been near the boulder but still there. Sam only hoped he wouldn't have to endure anything worse.

A few minutes later, the three of them veered off the trail and plowed through the snow toward the boulder. Dean pulled a flashlight out of the bag and switched it on. The mounded snow sparkled in the light.

"EMF's three point four," Dean said as they drew even with the large rock.

Slipping from Sam's embrace, Bo took several slow steps. "The sensations in my leg are the same, but more intense than they were on the path."

Sam took the notebook and pen out. "Dean, shine the flashlight over here so I can write this down."

"Sure thing." Moving closer, Dean shone the beam on Sam's notebook.

Sam scribbled down the information from Dean and Bo. "Thanks. Now let me see what I can feel this time."

Closing his eyes, Sam drew a few slow, deep breaths, letting his mind relax and his consciousness expand. He caught the thread of alien energy right away. It was just as blank and empty as before.

"No change from last time," Sam said, opening his eyes

again. "It's no stronger than it is on the path, really. And it still doesn't feel like an active portal."

Silence. Dean opened his mouth as if to speak, shook his head and closed it again. Bo moved back to Sam's side, his hand resting on Sam's shoulder. Sam had a feeling they were all thinking the same thing. He hoped they were right.

A sharp indrawn breath from Dean and the sudden tension in Bo's body told Sam the moment they'd come here for had arrived. He glanced up just in time to see a nebulous black shape flow from behind the boulder into the trees.

Without a word, the three men darted after it. Sam kept his arm around Bo and his psychic senses extended. With Sam supporting him, Bo managed to move fast enough for him and Sam to keep the thing in sight. As before, Dean was farther ahead, the video camera trained on the creature. The twilight echoed with the noise of three grown men crashing through the forest, but not a sound could be heard from their quarry. It moved with an eerie silence, the trees and bushes utterly undisturbed by its passing.

Sam wasn't surprised when the thing passed like smoke through the police tape, the bright yellow material not even fluttering in its wake. He, Bo and Dean stood still and quiet, watching the scene play out before them exactly as it had before. Sam couldn't see into the rhododendron thicket as well as he had the last time, but he saw enough. By the time the creature vanished, with no sign it had ever been there, Sam had no more doubt of what they were witnessing.

"This is a residual haunting, isn't it?" he said softly, stroking Bo's braid.

Bo nodded. "I believe so. This area has a good bit of slate in the ground, if I remember right, and that's been associated with residuals."

"The way the thing behaves sure fits that theory." Pursing his lips, Dean rewound the video he'd just taken and started it playing again. His face glowed blue in the light of the small screen. "Yeah, this is just like before. And look here, when it passes the police tape it doesn't even obscure the yellow. See?"

Positioning themselves on either side of Dean, Sam and Bo watched the video over his shoulder. Sure enough, the police tape was clearly visible through the thing's shadowy form.

"Its shape changed some at Oleander House and South Bay, but it was never transparent," Sam mused as Dean switched the camera off. "And like you said, Dean, its behavior's more consistent with a residual haunting than with an actual live being. It never ignored us before."

"Right. But I'm glad it's ignoring us now." Bo tapped a finger to his chin. "Okay, here's my tentative recreation of the event. This area has a high EMF level, which gives it the potential to support a portal. Somehow, the portal was activated. We'll leave the how of it for now. However it happened, one of the inhabitants came through, it killed a person, and the killing was 'recorded' as a residual haunting."

"What about the portal?" Dean asked, fiddling with the zipper on his jacket. "I figure it must be closed now, since Sam didn't sense it, but why? And how? Who did it? Or do you think *they* did it?"

Bo stared into the gathering darkness. "I don't think the portal was under their control, because if it was I doubt they would've closed it, and I doubt very much that this would have been the first killing. I think the portal was most likely opened by a second person, someone other than the body we found. Whether Harry was the person who opened the portal or the person who was killed, or neither one, I have no idea. We'll have to wait for the police report."

Dean nodded in the direction of the trail. "Why don't we go back to your cabin and go through our video and pics? I don't know about y'all, but I'm freezing my ass off out here."

"Good idea." Moving back to Sam's side, Bo settled an arm around his shoulders as the three of them began the trek back through the trees. "I don't know if they're still serving dinner at the same time, but I assume Lex or Carl will tell us if they aren't."

Nodding, Sam tucked the notebook and pen into his jacket pocket and wound his arm around Bo's waist. "If the detectives are still questioning the staff, it's bound to delay dinner, especially since there aren't any guests to worry about. We should have time to go over at least some of our stuff first."

"Assuming we're right and what people are seeing is a residual haunting, what then?" Dean asked, training his flashlight beam on the tangled and snow-shrouded undergrowth in their path. "I guess we'll need to figure out how and when the portal was opened and why it closed again, but I'll be damned if I know where to start."

In the flashlight backwash and the glow of the fading sunset, Bo's face was solemn and thoughtful. His arm tightened across Sam's shoulders, and Sam wondered if he even realized it. "I suppose the logical place to start would be with the body in the woods. Once we know whether or not it's Harry Norton, we can move on from there."

"If he's the one who's dead, either that thing killed a person who was a psychic focus—something we haven't seen or heard of before, though admittedly our experience is limited—or there was another person there at the time of the killing who was able to open the portal." Sam firmed his grip on Bo in order to help him climb over a fallen tree. "If the body isn't Harry's, then it's possible he's the focus, wherever he is."

"Of course either way, there's no way to know for sure when the portal was opened, or closed." Sighing, Dean stopped beside the large white boulder and played the flashlight beam over it. "At least you're pretty sure it's closed, right, Sam?"

"It's about the only thing in this case I *am* sure of." Without letting go of Bo, Sam rested a hand on the rock. The stone felt frigid against his palm, the dusting of snow melting into prickles of icy cold in the heat of his skin. "Y'all know I've picked up that weird abnormal energy thread around here, but it's nothing like what I felt at Oleander House or the school. Those were..." He stopped, trying to find the right words. "They felt alive. This feels dead."

"And you don't know if those portals left behind that same energy after closing," Bo added, his eyes searching Sam's face. "You didn't go back to either place after it was all over, and you weren't in any shape to notice things like that at the time."

Sam let out a dry laugh. "You could say that."

Both times he'd faced one of the interdimensional portals and the beings inhabiting the other side, their presence in his mind had wrung the breath from his lungs and the strength from his body. When it had passed, his attention had been occupied with more important things. Amy's horrific death at Oleander House. Bo's injury and rapid decline into septic shock at South Bay High. He hadn't had the time to notice what—if any—energy was left behind by the closing of the portals, even if he'd had the presence of mind to check.

Soft lips, cold with the winter evening, brushed his cheek in a gentle caress. He turned to look into Bo's eyes. Bo smiled, tracing Sam's jaw with icy fingers. "It's not going to be that way this time. This portal isn't active. All we have to do is figure out when it became active, and how, and why."

"And then figure out why it closed, and make sure it's not

going to open again." Dean patted the boulder, then moved away through the forest toward the trail, which was just visible in the gloom. "Piece of cake."

Shaking his head at the dry sarcasm in Dean's voice, Bo followed Dean and the flashlight, his arm still snug around Sam's shoulders. "I know, it's going to be difficult. But at least no one's life is at stake here."

No one except that person who was torn apart in the woods, Sam thought, though he didn't say it. He knew what Bo meant, and he knew they were all thinking the same thing. Voicing it out loud wouldn't make it any less true.

Full dark had fallen by the time they turned onto the narrow walkway running from cabin to cabin. Two figures, one tall and one short, stood outside Sam and Bo's cabin. Darkness and distance hid their features, but the sweep of Dean's flashlight beam revealed a flash of familiar color on the smaller figure. Lex's jacket, a bright spring green.

Dean frowned. "Is that Lex and Carl?"

"Looks like them." Bo let go of Sam and drew away, grimacing as he put his weight on his bad leg. "I wonder what they want."

The loss of Bo's warmth left Sam feeling cold and bereft. He shoved both hands in his jacket pockets to keep himself from reclaiming his hold on Bo. "Bet I can guess."

"It won't matter," Bo said, his grim expression belying his words. "They're not homophobic."

Sam didn't point out how many people think they're okay with it until confronted with the reality, only to find they're not as open-minded as they'd always hoped. There was no harm in giving their hosts the benefit of a doubt.

The Lodge owners stopped whispering together and turned to face Sam, Bo and Dean as they approached. Sam plastered on a smile to hide the anxiety boiling inside him.

"Hi," Bo greeted them. "Were you looking for us?"

Bo's voice was bland, his expression neutral. His "investigation face", Dean called it, accurately enough. Bo didn't like jumping to conclusions without evidence to back it up, regardless of the situation. Whatever his personal thoughts or theories were, he always kept them to himself until he was sure, and he rarely let those thoughts show on his face. Not in front of clients and strangers.

"We were, yes." Clearing his throat, Carl glanced at his wife, then back at Bo. "I know you've been working and are probably tired, but would you mind coming up to the office? We have something we need to talk to you both about."

Silence. The muscle in Bo's jaw twitched. Seeing the tiny movement by the light of Dean's flashlight, Sam moved as close to Bo as he dared.

"What did you need to talk to us about?" Bo asked, his tone dangerously soft and blank. "Anything you want to say to Sam and me, you can say in front of Dean."

Lex and Carl looked at one another. Carl shrugged.

Stepping closer, Lex gazed up at Bo and Sam. "Anne came to us this evening. About you. The two of you, I mean. Do you understand?"

Inside his pockets, Sam's fists clenched of their own accord. Behind him, Dean muttered something which sounded suspiciously like *that fucking bitch*. Whatever Bo's reaction was, he kept it in check.

For a long moment they all stood staring at one another across a gulf many times wider than the foot or two it appeared to be, Lex and Carl on one side, Sam and Bo on the other with Dean at their back. No one said anything. When Bo broke the uncomfortable standoff by slumping against Sam's side with a defeated sort of sigh, Sam put both arms around him and kissed his brow. He watched Lex's face as he did it, daring her with his eyes to say one single word. She didn't, and he felt better.

"All right. We'll talk in your office."

Bo sounded more tired than he had in a long time, and Sam hated it. He left an arm around Bo, keeping him close. Bo didn't protest, for which Sam was grateful. With Bo held against one side and Dean's solid, supportive presence on the other, he followed Lex and Carl up the path to the office.

Chapter Ten

Sam could tell Bo was trying not to show how much his leg bothered him, but it wasn't working. He clung to Sam much harder than he normally would have as they made their way up the steps, and the crease between his brows announced his discomfort clearly in spite of his carefully neutral expression. Sam couldn't help giving him a worried look as they entered the office together and Bo sank into a chair with a tiny grunt.

"I believe we know what Anne said to you," Bo began before anyone else could speak. "She saw Sam and me in somewhat of a compromising position, right?"

Lex blushed and looked away. "Well, yes, actually."

Bo nodded, his face grim. "Thought so. And what do you intend to do about it?"

Carl blinked. "Nothing. Or, well, it doesn't change anything about our decision to hire your company to investigate the Lodge. She claimed you were acting unprofessionally, but since we have no guests here at the moment and you believed yourselves to be alone, Lex and I feel we have no business making that judgment. I hope you'll stay and finish the investigation."

Bo's expression softened a little. "Thank you, we fully intend to finish. But what I meant was, what do you intend to do about Anne?"

Surprised, Sam stared at Bo's profile. Bo looked calm, but determined.

Clearly flustered, Lex darted her gaze from Bo to her husband and back again. "Oh. Well, we told her in no uncertain terms that not only do we not consider a person's sexuality to be an issue, whether it's a guest or employee we're talking about, we also couldn't see that your behavior was in any way unprofessional. She was pretty upset, but she can't very well do anything about it. If our decision bothers her that much, she's welcome to quit."

"She's a good worker, but this homophobia of hers is getting to be downright disruptive." Leaning against the desk, Carl rolled his eyes. "After last time, I'm not sure we want to keep her around in any case."

Sam frowned. "Last time?"

Lex and Carl exchanged meaningful glances, and seemed to come to a silent agreement. "Okay," Lex said. "I'm telling you this because I believe you need to know, considering the circumstances, but it goes no further than this room. Agreed?"

Sam, Bo and Dean all looked at each other. Sam shrugged. "Fine with me. Whatever it is, I won't tell a soul."

"Same here," Dean chimed in.

"It stays between us," Bo promised. "What happened?"

Sighing, Lex went to stand beside her husband. "The last time Harry was in town to pick up his medicine—before *this* time, I mean—Anne happened to be in town as well, on her week's break. She saw him coming out of the pharmacy with a strange man, and thought they looked, as she put it, 'a little too friendly'. So she followed them. They went to a motel together and stayed there all night."

"So she saw them together, assumed they were lovers and followed them, then staked out the hotel to make sure." Sam's stomach rolled. "Jesus."

"Okay, that's just scary," Dean declared, rubbing his arms.

Bo sat perfectly still, his eyes glinting with something indefinable. "So this woman basically stalked one of her fellow employees, then came to you and told you all she'd seen, hoping what? You'd fire him?"

Carl cleared his throat and shifted his feet. "I guess so, yes."

"And yet she's still working here."

Bo's voice was flat and inflectionless, but Sam read his fury in his eyes and in the tension in the shoulder under Sam's hand. Sam moved his palm up to stroke Bo's braid. He took comfort in the small touch, and it usually helped soothe Bo's anger.

"She accepted it without argument when we reprimanded her." Lex twisted her fingers together. "And she hasn't done any such thing since."

"You told us before that she said derogatory things to Sandra when she was first hired." Dean perched on the arm of Bo's chair, opposite where Sam stood. "How derogatory, exactly?"

Lex hunched her shoulders. Something about the shrinking look in her eyes gave Sam a very bad feeling.

"It didn't seem that bad at the time," Lex said. "It only seemed problematic in hindsight. Sandra had already been working here for over a year when we hired Anne. When Anne found out Sandra's a lesbian, she called Sandra a dyke and expressed the fear that Sandra would hit on her if they had to room together. We reminded her that we had very limited space to house our staff, and told her if those arrangements weren't satisfactory to her we'd have to let her go. We also informed her that we didn't tolerate our workers being disrespectful to anyone, not guests and not fellow employees, and she never did it again as far as I know."

Bo leaned forward in the chair, elbows on knees and hands clasped together. "Lex, I think you and Carl should tell Detective Parsons what you just told me."

Carl's eyebrows went up. "Why?"

Sam thought he knew. Catching Dean's eye, he saw the same fear, and the same ugly suspicion.

"Because Anne has a history of not simply being homophobic, but acting on that phobia," Bo explained, his voice calm and quiet. "She came to the conclusion that Harry was gay—based on purely circumstantial evidence, I might add— then stalked him and attempted to have him fired for it. Most likely her behavior has nothing to do with Harry's disappearance, since no one's found any sign of foul play so far. But it *is* kind of an interesting juxtaposition, and I think the detectives would like to know."

Lex and Carl looked at each other, identical expressions of guilty realization on their faces. "You're right," Carl said. "I didn't think of that before, but it makes sense."

"We'll tell them as soon as they finish talking with the staff." Moving around behind the desk, Lex dropped into the chair with a deep sigh. "I swear, if the Lodge survives this whole thing still financially solvent, it'll be a miracle."

Carl perched on top of the desk, reached across and took his wife's hand. "We'll make it, honey. We always do."

She gave him a wan smile, but didn't answer. Sam read her worry in the crease between her eyes and the tension in her shoulders. He wished he could reassure her, but he couldn't think of anything comforting to say that wouldn't be a lie.

"Is that all you had to tell us?" Sam asked, his hand still toying with Bo's braid.

Lex nodded. "Yes. We've already reprimanded her and warned her that if any such thing happens again we'll be forced to let her go."

Rising to his feet, Dean crossed his arms and frowned. "Do you think that's enough? I mean I know y'all know her better than I do, but she said some pretty hair-raising things to me earlier."

Lex shot him a sharp look. "What do you mean? What things?"

"Well for one thing she said it was inexcusable that y'all hire gay people. She also said gays are, and I quote, 'an abomination' and the government should get rid of all of them." A visible shudder ran through Dean's body. "She came and ranted to me right after she saw Sam and Bo kissing, before she told y'all. It gave me the creeps. I didn't tell her this, but I'm bisexual. I'm sure she'd have a field day with that."

Carl hunched his shoulders. "Damn. Lex?"

A weary groan escaped Lex's lips. "We need to fire her, before she causes us real trouble with a guest or another employee. And we need to let the detectives know about the incident with Harry."

"And you need to tell them those inflammatory things she said to you," Bo added, pointing at Dean. "You didn't tell us before exactly what she'd said to you. I don't like it at all."

"Neither do I." Scrunching his face up, Dean sat on the arm of Bo's chair again. "So what do we do now?"

Lex rose from her chair and skirted the desk. "Carl and I will go wait for the detectives to finish questioning the staff, then we'll tell them all about Anne and her behavior. I can either send them to your cabin after we're finished, or send someone to get you so you can talk to them in the dining hall or our office. What would you prefer?"

Sam and Bo glanced at each other. One corner of Bo's mouth hitched up in an unexpected half-smile. His eyes glittered with a dark fire. Sam knew that look. Twice a day wasn't the norm for them, but it wasn't unheard of either. He bit his lip.

"I'm sure the police will have other questions for us," Bo said, his voice remarkably calm considering what Sam was sure he was thinking. "Would it be all right if we head down to the dining hall in a couple of hours? I'd like to review some of our tapes and videos before we speak with Parsons and Ramirez."

Lex's blush said she understood precisely why Bo wanted to do it that way, but she simply nodded. "Of course. Sandra and Jerome are cooking, but there's no set time for dinner. They'll keep the food warm, just go into the kitchen and get what you want whenever you're ready."

"You think it's ready now? I'm starved." Dean smiled, his face the picture of innocence.

Sam knew better. Dean's ability to read Sam and Bo both was uncanny. He generally knew when they needed—or just wanted—time alone.

Carl let out a halfhearted laugh. "I'm not sure. But you're welcome to go on to the kitchen if you like. Sandra or Jerome will feed you."

"Cool." Hopping up, Dean stuck his hands in his pockets and turned to Sam and Bo. "Are y'all gonna be in the cabin working?"

Bo nodded. "Yes, we will. Join us when you get finished eating."

Dean grinned, eyes twinkling. "What about you and Sam? You gonna eat in your cabin?"

Bo turned nearly as red as Lex and Carl, and Sam swallowed the laugh which wanted to come out. He shot a quick smile at Dean. The man always knew when his friends were upset, and did his best to cheer them up.

One day, Bo's gonna kill him.

"We'll *have dinner* when we go to the dining hall to talk to the detectives," Bo said, leveling a deadly glare at Dean before turning back to Lex and Carl. He stood, ignoring the hand Sam offered him. "Lex, Carl, thank you for telling us about Anne."

"Certainly." Lex walked to the door and stood beside it, hand on the doorknob. "Let us know what you find on your tapes, okay?"

"We will. And I'd appreciate it if you let us know what you find out about that body in the woods." Bo gave Lex a warm smile as she swung the door open for them. "We'll talk to you later."

"All right. Thanks." Returning Bo's smile, Lex stood aside to let them out, then shut the door behind her.

Outside, Bo's smile withered. He stomped down the stairs without so much as a word to Sam or Dean, or a glance in their direction. Sam and Dean looked at each other. Dean shrugged, obviously as confused by Bo's behavior as Sam was.

Sam hurried after Bo, with Dean hot on his heels. He caught up to Bo halfway down the steps, Bo's limp slowing him down in spite of his haste.

"Bo, what's wrong?" Sam asked, touching Bo's shoulder.

Bo didn't answer. Worried, Sam brushed past him just in time to stop him at the bottom of the steps. He laid both hands on Bo's shoulders. "Tell me what's wrong. Please."

For a second, Bo just stared at him, brown eyes wide and unreadable. Then, to Sam's surprise, Bo wrapped his arms around Sam's waist and buried his face in his neck. Sam held him, stroking his back and pressing kisses to his hair. Tension hummed through the taut muscles under Sam's palms.

"I'm sorry," Bo murmured against Sam's neck. "It's not you. Or us. It's just... This is ugly. Ugly. It scares me."

Sam's chest constricted. He tightened his arms around Bo, as if he could somehow protect him from all the hate in the world.

A hand touched Sam's shoulder. He swiveled his head around to meet Dean's gaze. Dean's eyes reflected the same hard-won knowledge Sam possessed.

"I'm off to the dining hall," Dean told him. "I'll be back in probably forty-five minutes or so. That enough time?"

Sam nodded. "Yeah. Thanks, Dean."

A smile lit Dean's face. "What are friends for?" He squeezed Sam's shoulder, then Bo's. "Bye, Bo. See y'all in a little while."

Bo turned to look at Dean without lifting his head. "Okay. See you."

Dean wandered off, hands in his pockets, and Sam pulled Bo closer. "Things like this are always ugly. But we have a lot of support from the other staff here, and there are no guests around. Try not to worry too much about Anne and her hang-ups."

"I know. Logically speaking, I know it's just words from a person who's proven herself to be intolerant and there's no real reason to worry. But I've never had to deal with anything like this before. It's harder than I thought it would be." Pulling out of Sam's embrace, Bo gave him a humorless smile. "And I know it won't be the last time."

"Probably not." Sam fell into step beside Bo as they started down the path to the cabin. He resisted the urge to slip his arm around Bo's waist again. Bo's limp seemed less pronounced, and Sam trusted him to say something if he needed or wanted help. "Nobody outside of this group has to know about us, though. We've kept our relationship a secret this long, we can keep on doing that."

Bo darted an inscrutable look at Sam. "Actually, I think I'm tired of trying to hide. It's too much work, for too little payoff. People find out anyway, so why bother?"

Surprised, Sam stared at Bo's profile. "What about Janine? What about the boys? You don't think our coming out as a couple would affect your chance at getting shared custody?"

Bo tilted his head back to gaze up into the night sky. A few flakes of lingering snow dusted his face, catching on his lashes and melting against his skin. Sam managed to suppress the urge to lick off the little trickles of water.

"I love my children," Bo said, very softly. "But I love you too, Sam. Why should I have to choose?" He stopped walking and pinned Sam with a determined gaze. "I'm a good father. There is absolutely nothing in my past or present which would be grounds for keeping me from my boys. My lawyer tells me I'm on solid legal ground here, and I know I'm on solid moral ground. I won't allow anyone to force me to choose between my children and you."

Sam licked his lips. His heart raced, the blood whooshing in his ears. "So, that's it? We're officially out now?"

"Yes. I'm sick of hiding. All this with Anne just made me realize how harmful these sorts of secrets can be." Stepping closer, Bo took both of Sam's hands in his. "When we get home, let's move in together."

Sam's mouth fell open. "Really?"

"Yes."

"You're sure?"

"Yes, I'm sure." Lacing his fingers through Sam's, Bo pulled him closer and pressed a light kiss to his lips. "I'm starting to get used to waking up with you. I don't want to give it up."

Laughter bubbled up from somewhere deep inside Sam. "Okay. But you're moving into my place. There's no way I'm living in that shithole apartment of yours."

"My thoughts exactly," Bo agreed with a grin. He leaned closer, his voice dropping to a seductive growl. "Now let's get to our cabin. I need to fuck you before I can concentrate on work."

Sam's knees went weak. "Good idea."

Drawing away but keeping one hand linked with Sam's, Bo led the way to the cabin. Sam followed, feeling as if he were floating. Maybe everything would work out for him and Bo after all.

In a dark corner of his brain, a tiny voice reminded him the Sunset Lodge case wasn't entirely over. They still had to deal with Anne, and she wasn't going to be happy.

Sam tuned the voice out. He didn't want to hear it.

CR

By the time Dean's knock sounded on the door, Bo was fully dressed again and Sam had only to put on his boots. Bo jumped up to answer the door while Sam sat rather gingerly on the chair by the window to get his shoes on.

"Hey," Dean said, stepping inside. He grinned as Sam rose carefully to his feet. "You look a little sore, Sam."

Sam managed to meet Dean's teasing gaze without blushing. "A little, yeah."

Bo laughed. "Hey, you shouldn't say things like 'harder' if you don't mean it."

Fighting back a smile, Sam snatched a fallen pillow from the floor and launched it at Bo's head. "Shut up."

An exaggerated sigh drew Sam's gaze to Dean, who stood gazing at them with a faraway look in his eyes. "I love how y'all are after you get done fucking. It's so sweet."

Bo blinked, the pillow still clutched to his chest. "What do you mean? You don't always know when we've been...um, intimate."

"Oh, please." Dean snorted and rolled his eyes. "Y'all are so obvious you might as well have a neon sign over your heads saying 'we just had hot monkey sex'. I *always* know."

Heat rushed into Sam's cheeks. It was one thing to be out as a gay man, or even as a gay couple. It was another thing entirely for everyone to be able to tell when he and Bo had been having sex.

"Don't worry," Dean added, walking over to pat Sam's shoulder. "Nobody but me can tell, I'm sure." A thoughtful look crossed his face. "At least, I don't think so."

Bo groaned. "Okay, I don't want to know. Let's check our videos and stills, then we'll head down to the dining hall and try to catch the detectives."

"Lex and Carl talked to them after they got done questioning Darren." Crossing the room, Dean plopped onto the bottom bunk. "They told them about Anne stalking Harry, then Parsons came and got me and I told them what all Anne had said to me."

"And what'd they say?" Sam asked.

"They thanked me and said they'd have questions for you and Bo later." Dean shrugged. "They put Anne in the hot seat as soon as they got done grilling me, so they must've been paying attention."

"Hmm." Bo paced the tiny floor, tugging on the end of his braid. "Well, hopefully Parsons and Ramirez will be able to tell us something when we talk to them later. In the meantime, let's get some work done. I'd like to be able to present our residual haunting theory to Lex and Carl, but I want to review the evidence first. Make sure we didn't miss anything."

Stretching out one leg, Sam hooked his foot under the handle of the nearby equipment bag and dragged it toward him. He reached in, removed the laptop from its protective case and thumbed it on. "Dean, hand me the camera, I'll upload the pictures."

"'Kay." Dean pulled the camera from around his neck and placed it in Sam's outstretched hand. "What about the videos? You think we have enough battery power to watch them on the view screen?"

"We have extra batteries, so I think it'll be okay to do that." Bo stretched, joints cracking, and sat beside Dean. "Sam, we'll wait for you to load the pictures before we watch the videos."

Sliding the memory card out of the camera and into the port on the side of the computer, Sam cradled the laptop carefully in his arms and stood. "Hang on, I can move over there and let the pics load while we're watching."

Dean's grin was pure evil. "Yeah, the bed's more comfortable on a sore ass anyway."

"Shut up, Dean," Sam advised, lowering himself to the mattress beside Bo. He set the laptop on the bed, well away from the edge. "Okay, let's see what we have."

CR

An hour later, they'd gone through all their videos and

photos with a fine-toothed comb. What they saw served to cement what they'd already suspected—a residual haunting. None of the stills had captured anything but the vaguest suggestions of shapes, and the videos weren't much better. The last one, the one taken that evening at twilight, showed only a vaporous and indistinct black mass shooting through the forest. The one taken when they'd first witnessed the killing showed only shadows. Bo speculated this was because it was filmed in daylight.

Armed with the video camera, the three headed down to the dining hall to present their conclusions to the Bledsoes. The snow had stopped falling altogether, and the clouds were breaking to let through scattered glimmers of starlight.

Sam drew a deep breath of icy, winter-scented air as they trudged through the snow. "You know what, I could get used to living up here."

Dean shot him a horrified look. "You're kidding."

"No, I'm not. It's beautiful here, and the air's so clean." Tilting his head back, Sam smiled up at the sky. "Of course, I guess I'd eventually miss showering."

"And TV, and bars, and civilization in general," Dean added. "Like they say, it's a nice place to visit, but I wouldn't want to live here."

Glancing at Bo, Sam caught his eye and smiled. "It has its benefits."

To his delight, Bo sidled up to him, hooked a hand behind his neck and planted a kiss on his mouth. "From now on we're getting the same benefits at home."

"Benefits?" Dean's eyes widened. "Oh my God, are y'all moving in together?"

"Wow, you're good," Sam declared, impressed. "Yes, we are. How'd you figure that out?"

"I don't know. From the way you say it, it just sounded like 'benefits' equals sex on demand." Dean shrugged. "Seemed pretty obvious to me."

Laughing, Bo ran his fingers through Sam's hair. "You *would* think that. Personally, I'm looking forward to getting back to running water and electricity."

"And showers," Dean said, rather wistfully.

Bo nodded, letting his hand fall from Sam's hair. "And especially showers, yes. I could use one right now. I'm getting pretty ripe."

Sam bumped Bo's shoulder with his. "I like how you smell."

"Probably because I smell like come," Bo murmured, low enough that only Sam could hear. He flicked Sam's earlobe with his tongue before pulling away.

Sam snickered. Bo did indeed smell of their mingled semen and sweat, though not strongly enough for anyone to notice unless they were mere inches away.

Dean grabbed Sam's shoulder with the hand not holding the video camera. "Look, there's Anne," he whispered, nodding toward the dining hall. "Let's hang back and wait till she leaves to go in."

Sam looked. Anne was striding up the pathway between the dining hall and the staff quarters. Even in the dark, Sam could see the angry set to her shoulders. At that moment, she glanced up. Her gaze locked with Sam's.

"Too late," Bo muttered. "Here she comes."

Indeed, Anne had switched directions and was walking toward them. They stopped, drawing closer together. Sam slid an arm around Bo's waist.

As she drew closer, Sam saw the hot fury sparking in her eyes. She raised a shaking hand and pointed a finger at Dean.

"You fucking bastard," she hissed. "I thought I could trust you to keep your mouth shut."

"You're a homophobic bitch, I swing both ways, and two of my best friends in the world are gay. So no, I'm not keeping quiet." Leaning against Sam's shoulder, Dean gave her a look full of cold disdain. "Just stay out of our way and try not to get yourself in any more trouble than you're already in."

Anne's face went dark. For a second, Sam thought she was going to hit Dean. Her eyes cut sideways, aiming a deadly glare at Sam and Bo. Then she turned on her heel and stomped off.

"By the way," Dean called after her, "you're a lousy kisser. I had better than that in eighth grade."

She stiffened, but didn't break her stride or acknowledge Dean in any way. After a moment, she disappeared into the staff quarters. The sound of the door slamming echoed in the still night air.

Sam whooshed out the breath he hadn't realized he'd been holding. "She's really pissed at you, Dean. You better be careful of her."

"Yeah, well, she can bite my incredibly hot ass. She doesn't scare me." Giving Sam's arm a squeeze, he pulled away and started back down the path to the dining hall. "C'mon, let's book. If Anne's out, that means Parsons and Ramirez might be free to talk."

Sam shook his head. He wished he had Dean's confidence that Anne would leave them alone. He had a nagging suspicion she wouldn't.

Just stop it. What can she do, after all? The cops are probably watching her now. Quit worrying and concentrate on wrapping up the case.

Bo's arm snaked around Sam's waist. "Stop staring at Dean's ass."

Sam turned a sharp look to Bo. To his relief, there was no accusation in those dark eyes, no suspicion, only a mischievous twinkle. Sam smiled. "It's a hot ass. He said so himself."

"Can't argue with that. But a guy could get jealous here."

"No reason to. There's not a butt in the world I like better than yours." Sam dropped his hand down to grab the posterior in question.

The lusty growl he got in return was almost enough to make him turn around and march Bo back to the cabin for a quickie.

"I can hear y'all." Dean turned to give them a coy look over his shoulder. "Of course, I should be used to it by now. Everybody wants some of this." He gave his backside a tempting little wiggle.

Sam burst out laughing. "It's really too bad you're so unsure of yourself."

"Hey, life's short. Why waste any of it on false modesty?" Aiming a hard smack at his own butt, Dean faced forward and kept walking.

Sam could've sworn he put an extra bit of shake in it.

Inside the dining hall, Lex and Carl sat huddled around a table in the corner with the two detectives. All four glanced up when Sam, Bo and Dean entered.

"Come on over," Carl called. "The detectives here were just saying they'd like to talk to the three of you as well as Lex and me."

The three headed to the table. Sam kept his arm around Bo, taking comfort in the feel of Bo's arm resting against his hips. He felt the tension building in Bo's body, and knew Bo was wondering how Parsons and Ramirez would react to seeing the two of them in a pose which announced the intimate nature of their relationship loud and clear. To his relief, Parsons' cool expression didn't change. Ramirez's eyes widened infinitesimally before his face resumed its mask-like expression.

"Gentlemen. Please sit down." Parsons gestured toward the empty chairs at the table. "Ramirez and I have some information which affects the three of you as well as the Bledsoes."

Sam let go of Bo so they could sit down. Once settled in their chairs, Bo's hand found Sam's under the table, weaving their fingers together. Sam gave Bo's hand a little squeeze and was rewarded by a quick, loving glance from Bo.

Setting the video camera on the table, Dean leaned forward. "So what is it you have to tell us? Does it have anything to do with Anne?"

Parsons nodded. "Yes, it does. As you know, we've questioned her about her activities in regards to Harry Norton, both previously and just before his disappearance."

"What did you find out?" Lex's fingers twisted nervously together. Carl laid his hand over both of hers, and she gave him a grateful smile.

"Nothing concrete. But her stories are inconsistent, and she became quite angry when we questioned her recall of events." Parsons turned a penetrating stare to Lex and Carl. "Are you aware of Anne Tallant's whereabouts on the afternoon Harry Norton disappeared?"

Lex and Carl looked at each other. Their faces reflected the same apprehension Sam felt. "She was here at the Lodge somewhere," Carl answered. "Though of course she could've been anywhere on the property. Our employees all do multiple jobs here, and they all have reason to be all over the property during a typical day."

Ramirez scribbled something on the big yellow legal pad in

front of him. "Any idea where on the property she might've been between two and three o'clock on that day?"

"If I remember right she and Corinne were cleaning the cabins that day. Corinne's our other employee," Carl added. "This is her week off."

Parsons pursed her lips. "Hmm. Would we be able to get in touch with her if we need to speak with her?"

"Well, we'd have to radio the main office and they would have to call her, but yes, we could probably find her if we needed to." Lex glanced anxiously between Parsons and Ramirez. "Why? Has Anne done something we should know about?"

"She's made veiled threats against the two of you," Ramirez said, nodding at Sam and Bo. "Nothing we can act on, but threats all the same. Watch yourselves, and report to us if she tries anything."

Dean shot a questioning look at Bo. Bo nodded, his expression grim.

"We ran into her outside," Dean told them. "She was seriously pissed off at me for ratting her out. She didn't say anything to Sam and Bo, but she didn't look any too happy with them."

Concern showed in Parsons' eyes. "Ramirez, keep an eye on her. Don't make a move unless she does, but watch her."

With a nod, Ramirez stood, his chair scraping across the wooden floor. Shrugging his jacket on, he strode out the door into the night. He left the yellow legal pad and pen on the table.

Carl gazed after Ramirez, a frown creasing his brow. "Surely Anne isn't actually dangerous."

"We don't know anything for sure at this point," Parsons said. "But while she is not currently a suspect, she *is* a person of interest in this case."

"What does that mean, exactly?" Bo asked, his hand gripping Sam's harder.

"It basically just means we want to question her further. She let slip a couple of details regarding the afternoon in question that don't add up." Picking up Ramirez's abandoned pen, Parsons tapped the end of it against the table. "That isn't enough to detain her, but it *is* enough for us to question her further, with a court order if necessary."

Lex was shaking her head, face set in stubborn lines. "I know she's homophobic. But she's never given us any reason to think she'd actually hurt anyone. We never would've hired her if we thought she'd do that."

"I'm sure that's true, Mrs. Bledsoe. But you can't tell a criminal just by looking. If that were possible, my job would be much easier." Parsons' expression was solemn and sympathetic. "People are capable of truly horrendous things. I hope Ms. Tallant is as innocent of wrongdoing as you think she is, but I can't afford to assume that. The things she said lead me to believe she may have seen Mr. Norton on the day he disappeared, yet she claims she didn't. His prescription medication, just filled that day, was present at the scene of a murder. If she saw Mr. Norton that afternoon, we need to know. Even if she didn't harm anyone, she may be a witness."

Shocked, Sam stared at Parsons' blank face. He'd come up here expecting to face a monster from another dimension. He hadn't expected to face the more familiar—and far uglier—human horror.

Lex stirred and seemed about to speak. Then the dining hall door flew open and Ramirez burst in.

Parsons looked up with a stern frown. "What the hell, Ramirez?"

The big man strode closer, and Sam noticed with a thrill of fear that his hand rested on the butt of his pistol. "We have a situation."

Chapter Eleven

In an instant, Parsons was on her feet. Her eyes were cold. "Explain."

"I went up to the staff quarters to keep an eye on Anne, but she wasn't there."

Carl rose to his feet, throat working. "What do you mean, she wasn't there?"

"I mean, she wasn't there," Ramirez growled. "She's missing. The other employees are in the common room. None of them have seen her."

Parsons reached into her jacket and pulled a pistol out of the shoulder holster Sam hadn't noticed until now. She checked the safety, muzzle pointed at the ceiling and finger off the trigger. "Mr. and Mrs. Bledsoe, do you have any reason to believe Ms. Tallant might be armed?"

Lex's eyes saucered. "No."

"Good." A muscle ticked in Parsons' temple. "The five of you, stay here. Don't anyone go off alone for any reason. We'll be back."

She and Ramirez rushed outside, shutting the door behind them. In the stunned silence that followed, Sam let go of Bo's hand and instead wound an arm around his shoulders.

With a deep sigh, Lex planted her elbows on the table and

covered her face with both hands. "I can't believe this. I knew Anne could be an unpleasant person sometimes, but I never thought for a moment that she was dangerous."

Carl rested an arm around his wife's shoulders. "Maybe the detectives are just being cautious."

Remembering the rage in Anne's eyes not so long ago, Sam wondered, but he didn't say anything. They were safe enough as long as they stayed together. There was no point in worrying Lex and Carl further with sheer speculation.

Lex gave Carl a fond smile. "You're probably right." Patting his hand, she turned her gaze to Bo. "What did you find when you reviewed your tapes?"

Bo shot a worried glance at the door through which Parsons and Ramirez had disappeared. "To make a long story short, we believe what you have here is a residual haunting."

"What does that mean?" Carl dropped into his chair and leaned forward, looking curious.

"A residual haunting is like a recording," Bo explained. "It replays an event over and over, and there is no interaction with the environment or anyone in it."

"So there's not a portal here?" Lex's voice sounded hopeful.

Sliding a hand onto Sam's knee, Bo gave it a light squeeze. "Sam?"

"Not an active one, no." Rubbing his thumb over the fabric of the jacket Bo still wore, Sam tried to think of the best way to summarize. "There's no way to know for certain, of course, but we think a portal opened very briefly in the area of that big boulder. If we're right, it was only open long enough for something from the other side to get through and kill someone before it closed again."

"We're not sure exactly how the portal was opened, or how

it was shut again," Dean chimed in, unzipping his jacket and wriggling out of it. "Hopefully we'll know more whenever the cops identify that body."

"God, I hope that's not Harry." Sighing, Lex rubbed the back of her neck. "Well, it's certainly a relief to know our guests aren't in danger from an interdimensional portal." She let out a bitter laugh. "If we manage to book other guests in time to keep the place from going bankrupt, that is."

Bo hunched his shoulders. "I'm sorry," he said, guilt written all over his face. "I hope your business can recover from this."

Carl shook his head. "No need to be sorry, Bo. I'd rather lose business this way than let people stay here if their lives might be at risk. You can't see into the future any more than we can. None of us could possibly have known there was no real danger."

"No danger from a portal," Lex corrected, her expression grim. "Who knows what sort of potential danger we've exposed people to by keeping Anne on here? I'm sure we've had many gay and lesbian guests before. It scares me to think what might have happened if Anne had found out and decided to make her feelings known."

Reaching across the table, Dean brushed his fingers over the back of Lex's hand. "She talks a good game, but I really don't think she's dangerous. Not to your guests anyway. Me? She'd probably like to gut right about now. But I don't think she was ever a danger to the customers."

Carl's brows drew together in a frown. "I think you're right. But you're also right that she's extremely angry with *you*, Dean. She's not happy with Sam and Bo either. And she's out there, someplace. I'm worried about the three of you more than anyone else."

Dean waved a dismissive hand. "I can take her."

Torn between amusement and irritation at Dean's casual attitude, Sam slugged his friend lightly on the shoulder. "How do you know she isn't a black belt or something?"

"How do you know *I'm* not?" Dean shot back, crossing his arms and arching a challenging brow.

"Are you?"

"Well, no."

"Okay then."

"Okay." Biting his lip, Dean leaned over to look at Bo. "Hey, y'all mind if I stay in your cabin tonight?"

Everyone but Bo laughed. He stared at Dean, dead serious. "I think you should, yes. I won't worry about you if you're with us."

Lex sobered fast. "I'm going to have the rest of the staff move from their quarters into empty cabins, at least until Anne is found. Just to be on the safe side, since she has a key to the staff quarters. All the cabin keys are in our office, which is locked right now, so I'm certain she can't get into the cabins."

Sam smiled. "Don't worry, Lex. I'm sure they'll find Anne soon, and everything will work out."

She nodded and returned his smile, but Sam could tell she wasn't entirely convinced. Not that he blamed her. He wasn't really convinced himself.

"Well. As long as we're stuck here for a while, we might as well have some dinner." Planting both palms on the table, Carl pushed to his feet. "Who's hungry?"

CR

The night was long and restless. Voices and bobbing flashlight beams announced the arrival around one a.m. of the uniformed back-up Parsons had requested following a fruitless search for Anne. After that, Sam, Bo and Dean stopped pretending to sleep. Dean crawled into the bottom bunk with Sam and Bo and the three of them lay quietly discussing the case until the sky outside began to pale.

They were just trying to decide whether to go on down to the dining hall to see if breakfast was ready when footsteps clumped up to their door and a sharp knock sounded. Dean, who was closest, rolled out of bed and hurried to answer it.

Darren and Jerome stood on the top step. They both looked as tired and worried as Sam felt. "Hey," Jerome greeted them, straightening his glasses. "Y'all want to come eat? Sandra and Lex have breakfast ready."

"We were just talking about that." Dean glanced over his shoulder, a questioning look in his eyes. "Y'all ready?"

"I am." Yawning, Bo sat up and swung his legs over the edge of the mattress. "You and Darren don't have to wait for us, Jerome, we'll be down in a minute. Thanks for coming to get us, though."

"Naw, we'll wait. We got something to tell you anyhow." Jerome nudged Darren's arm. "Can I tell 'em?"

Darren rolled his eyes. "Why're you asking me?"

A thoughtful look crossed Jerome's face. "Huh. I don't know." He strolled inside and sat on the chair by the window, eyes shining with the light of discovery. "We think the cops found something out in the woods."

Bo raised his eyebrows. "What makes you think so?"

"Me and Darren were out on the trail a little while ago, seeing if we could find Anne. That Ramirez guy was standing guard by the path near the big boulder, and there's a whole
186

area of the woods roped off with police tape. More than before, I mean. And the place is *crawling* with cops. There must've been twenty of 'em."

"More like five or six," Darren corrected, looking amused. "But yeah, they've cordoned off more of the forest, and there are definitely more officers out there."

"We heard them coming up the trail last night." Sam scooted up to sit beside Bo, found his boots and began pulling them on. "I remember Parsons telling Lex and Carl she was calling for back-up, after they came back from looking for Anne."

"Speaking of which, why were the two of you out looking for her this morning?" Leaning over Sam's legs, Bo grabbed his boots. "Lex would worry, and I *know* Parsons wouldn't like it."

Darren shot a pointed look at Jerome, who grinned sheepishly. "Darren caught me going off by myself. After he yelled at me for wandering off alone, he came with me."

"Because you needed to talk to the cops, and I didn't want you out on the trail by yourself." Darren turned to Bo and Sam with a serious look. "Jerome told me he thought of a place where Anne might be hiding."

Dean's eyes went wide. "What?"

Jerome nodded, bouncing slightly in his chair. "There's a cave a little ways from here, about ten minutes' walk past Sunset Rock. You have to go down a side trail to get there. Me and Anne found it a few months ago, when we were out exploring. It's not much, but it's deep enough to make a pretty decent shelter."

Sam stared, shocked. "Did you tell Parsons?"

"She was out in the woods someplace, behind the police tape. I told Ramirez." Jerome shrugged. "He sent a couple of uniforms to check it out."

Tying the lace on his boot, Bo glanced up with surprise on his face. "He didn't want to go himself? Or send Parsons?"

"They were both busy with whatever was going on out in the woods, remember? I told y'all that." Jumping up, Jerome stuck his hands in his jacket pockets. "Whatever they found, it's right there where you guys found that body yesterday. And it must be something major, because I bet you're right, I bet either Parsons or Ramirez would've gone to the cave themselves if they weren't in the middle of something more important."

Glancing sideways, Sam shared a curious look with Bo before turning back to Jerome. "You don't have any idea what was going on?"

"Nope." Jerome rose to his feet and stretched, joints cracking. "But we figured y'all would want to know, since that's the same spot you've been investigating."

"Definitely. Thanks." Bo pushed up to stand beside the bed. He tucked a stray lock of glossy black hair behind his ear. "Dean, will you hand me my jacket, please?"

"Sure thing, boss." Twisting around, Dean snagged Bo's jacket from the wooden hook on the door and handed it to him, then tugged his own jacket on. "Okay, let's get going. I need some caffeine."

Sam grabbed his jacket and pulled it on as the five of them filed out into the winter morning. The clouds from the previous day had scattered, leaving behind a sky of pure watercolor blue. Sunshine glittered on the unmelted snow, and the icy air stung Sam's lungs with each breath.

As they approached the dining hall, Sam spotted Carl and Parsons walking from the office building to the small utility shed situated about twenty yards away. Parsons was talking. Carl listened with his shoulders hunched, looking grim.

"Wonder what's up," Dean muttered, nudging Sam with his

elbow.

Sam shook his head. "I don't know."

"Bet it's about whatever was going on in the woods," Jerome said, staring at the pair with unabashed curiosity. "Wonder if Carl'll tell us?"

"Probably, if we don't piss him off in the meantime." Clamping a hand onto Jerome's arm, Darren dragged him through the door of the dining hall. "Leave them alone. I'm sure Carl will fill us in on whatever he's allowed to."

Jerome looked disappointed, but didn't argue. "Y'all sit down, me and Darren'll get the food and bring it out."

Sam, Bo and Dean gathered at the nearest table. Someone had left a steaming pot of coffee and a tray of clean mugs on the nearby sideboard. Dean filled three mugs while Sam and Bo took off their jackets and claimed chairs.

Sam was still stirring cream into his coffee when Jerome and Darren returned, carrying trays laden with grits, scrambled eggs, biscuits and sausage gravy. It smelled heavenly. Sam's stomach rumbled.

The front door opened as Sam was pouring gravy over his second helping of biscuits and eggs. He glanced up. Carl was walking toward them, his face gray.

Sandra, coming through the kitchen door at that moment, gasped and hurried to Carl's side. "Carl, what's wrong?" she asked, slipping a hand through his elbow. "Are you all right?"

Nodding, he let her lead him to the table. He sank into a chair and drew a shuddering breath. His eyes were glassy and shocked.

Frowning, Darren leaned over the table toward his employer. "Carl? What's happened?"

"They found another body," Carl answered, his voice

shaking. "At the bottom of the drop-off near where the first body was."

He trailed off. The others exchanged apprehensive glances.

"Carl, what is it?" Bo prodded gently. "Tell us."

Carl looked up, his throat working. "The new body. It's Harry."

Chapter Twelve

"Oh, my God." Sandra dropped into the chair beside Carl's. "Are they sure? There couldn't be any mistake?"

"No. No mistake." Sighing, Carl rubbed his fingertips against his temples. "They brought me to the utility shed to identify him. It was Harry."

A stunned silence followed Carl's quiet declaration. Sam frowned, his mind racing. *Does this mean Harry was the focus for the portal? If he was, what made him a focus? And how did he die?*

"I'm sorry," Bo said quietly. He traced the rim of his coffee mug with one fingertip. "Do they have any idea what happened to him?"

"The edge of the drop-off is very sheer right above where they found the b..." Carl swallowed, his face going even paler. "Where they found him. Parsons wouldn't tell me what she thought, but I figure he took a wrong step and fell. The spot where he fell was about twenty feet away from where you found Harry's prescription bottle, and the trees and undergrowth are really thick there. He probably just didn't see the drop-off."

Sam and Bo glanced at each other, and Sam saw his own questions echoed in Bo's eyes. After all the years Harry had worked here, wouldn't he know the drop-off was there? Wouldn't he know to be careful in that area? And if the undergrowth was so thick, how could a simple misstep cause Harry to fall off the edge of the cliff in any case?

Unless he saw something which scared him so badly that he wasn't paying attention, Sam mused, staring at the table to hide his excitement as the scene recreated itself in his mind. *Unless he was running for his life from something which had already killed one person.*

He cut his gaze sideways to catch first Bo's eye, then Dean's. Bo looked grim, Dean thoughtful. Sam could tell they were both thinking the same things he was. Dean raised his eyebrows at Bo, a question in his eyes. Bo gave a minute shake of his head, which Sam instantly understood to mean no, they would not voice their questions here and now, when Carl and his employees were grappling with the fact of their friend's death. Dean nodded, accepting Bo's decision.

The whole silent exchange took only a couple of seconds. If it weren't for the grief-stricken faces surrounding him, Sam would've smiled. It amazed him sometimes how he and his friends could communicate so much with nothing more than a tilt of the head, or a change in expression. He'd never had that level of trust and understanding with anyone before, and he cherished it.

The dining hall door opened. Every head swiveled to look. Lex entered and went straight to Carl, who stood and folded her into his arms.

"Detective Ramirez told me about Harry," she said in a voice thick with tears. "God, Carl. What happened? Why did he fall?"

Carl pressed a kiss to her hair. "I don't know, honey."

"I hope it was quick. I hate to think of him lying there, probably calling for help, with no one to hear him."

Jerome made a small distressed sound. "Christ."

Glancing at Jerome, Carl shook his head. "His skull was..." Carl's face took on a greenish tinge, his hands trembling. "His head hit a rock when he fell. It was about forty feet. Parsons says he probably died on impact."

Darren groaned, slumping in his chair. "God. Poor Harry."

"Yeah." Looking thoughtful, Sandra planted an elbow on the table and rested her chin in her hand. "He must've had a seizure. He knew better than to get too close to the edge at that spot."

Sighing, Lex pulled away from Carl's embrace. "I don't know if the police can ever tell us why he fell. We'll probably never know." She rubbed at the corner of one eye. "They checked out that cave you told them about, Jerome. They found Anne's sleeping bag in it, but she wasn't there and they have no idea where she might have gone."

"Crud," Jerome said, disappointment clouding his features. "So what now?"

"They're still searching for her. They don't think she's left the area." Lex turned wide, solemn eyes to Sam, Bo and Dean. "The detectives think it would be best if the three of you went back to Asheville, considering Anne's threats against you. They'll send two officers to escort you down and drive you back to the Kimberley Inn."

Looking resigned, Bo wrapped his braid around one hand, gave it a tug and let it unwind again. "I hate to have to leave, but to be honest we'll have better luck wrapping up the loose ends of this case elsewhere. We'll need internet and phone access to do some research."

"All right. You can email us or leave a message on one of our cell phones and let us know what you find about the portal. We'll be going back down the mountain for a few days whenever this thing with Anne is resolved." Lex glanced at her watch. "It's nearly nine now. Why don't the three of you go ahead and get packed? I'll let the detectives know you'll be ready to leave soon. Carl, Ramirez suggested canceling our reservations for tonight too, since we still don't know where Anne is or what she might do. They seem to think she might be dangerous, though they're not saying it in so many words."

"I've noticed that too." Carl nodded, his expression grim. "We'll go ahead and cancel the reservations now. I had the office warn all of our guests for the next two weeks that we may have to cancel at the last minute, so there's actually only three still booked for tonight."

Darren grimaced. "Not good."

"You can say that again." Jumping to her feet, Sandra laid a hand on Lex's arm. "Listen, I'll be happy to give up my paychecks until y'all recover from all these cancellations. I've got some money saved up."

"Me too," Jerome chimed in. He pushed his glasses up his nose and swiped a hank of hair out of his eyes. "I love this place. I don't want to see it go under."

Tears welled in Lex's eyes. Smiling, she took Sandra's hands in both of hers. "Y'all are wonderful to offer. Thank you, from the bottom of my heart. But we can't accept that."

"Certainly not," Carl agreed, his fond smile echoing his wife's. "We'll make it through, don't worry." He put an arm around Lex's shoulders. "Let's go radio the office, honey. No point in putting it off."

She nodded. "Yes." Her features pinched with grief and worry, she let her husband lead her from the building.

Sam watched them go. He wished he could do something other than feel bad for them.

"Well. I guess we better go get our stuff together." Picking up his coffee mug, Dean drained it and set it on the table with a thump. He turned and threw his arms around Darren, who was sitting beside him. "I'm really sorry about Harry."

Darren, clearly startled, patted Dean on the back. "Um. Thanks."

Dean let go of Darren, stood and went to hug Jerome. Not nearly as reserved as Darren, Jerome clung to Dean and sniffled on his shoulder for a bit.

"I wish y'all could hang out for a while," Jerome said, giving Dean a watery smile as they drew apart. "I hardly got to talk to you guys at all. I had lots of questions, too."

"Sam, do you have any of our business cards on you?" Bo asked, standing and pulling his jacket on. "I didn't think to bring any."

"I think I have a couple. Hang on." Digging in his jacket pocket, Sam found three business cards. He handed the least battered one to Jerome. "Our website, email and phone number are on there. Feel free to contact us any time. We'll do our best to answer your questions."

"That goes for all of you," Dean clarified, moving around the table to hug Sandra. "We've loved meeting y'all, and getting to stay at Sunset Lodge. It's gorgeous up here."

"It sure is." Taking Bo's hand, Sam nodded toward the three sad-faced people huddled around the table. Not knowing what else to say, Sam lifted his hand in an awkward wave. "Bye."

The three of them exited the building amidst a chorus of "goodbyes" and wishes for a safe trip down the mountain. Outside, Dean darted a nervous look around. "I tell you what, I'll be glad to get back to Asheville. It's making me nervous being up here with that crazy woman running loose out there someplace."

"Thought you said you could take her," Sam teased. He

glanced at the building housing the staff quarters, common room and office as they passed by. Two uniformed officers stood on the deck outside, eyes scanning the grounds while they talked. "Seriously, though, I'm with you. Lex was right, the cops are acting like she's some sort of dangerous fugitive, and *that's* making *me* nervous."

"Me too." His expression thoughtful, Bo studied the two policemen on the deck. "Why did Parsons ask if Anne was armed last night? And why do those two on the deck both have their hands on their weapons?"

"Parsons said something about Anne's story not adding up," Dean reminded them. He darted another worried glance around the Lodge grounds. "God, it creeps me out that I made out with a psycho-killer."

Normally, Sam would've laughed at the exaggeration. This time, however, it felt uncomfortably close to the truth, and he didn't laugh. "We don't know that about her, but yeah. It's pretty creepy."

As they neared their cabin, Bo pulled the key out of his jacket pocket. "Well, we'll be back at the Kimberley Inn in a few hours. I'm sure Parsons will let us know if she thinks we'll be in any danger once we leave here."

Sam nodded. "They'll most likely find her pretty soon anyhow. There's only so long she can survive out in the open up here, when it's so cold."

At the cabin, Bo unlocked the door and the three of them piled inside. Sam was relieved to see that Bo's limp had become less pronounced than it had been the previous evening. "How's your leg, Bo?"

"Better." Throwing the key on the table, Bo dragged his backpack from under the bed and set it on the mattress. "Of course, it's always better when I'm away from the area where the portal was."

"True." Sam cast a worried look in Bo's direction. "Are you going to be okay hiking down the mountain?"

"I think so, yeah." Bo flashed a lascivious grin. "You might have to hang onto me, though."

As usual, Bo's sudden shift from serious to playful startled Sam into laughter. "I think I can handle that."

Dean snickered. "I just bet you can."

"Shut up," Sam suggested, thumping Dean on the shoulder.

Screwing his face up in mock pain, Dean rubbed his shoulder. "Oh fine. Since you've broken my arm, you can just go empty the water bucket. I was gonna do it, but now..." Dean shook his arm with an exaggerated wince. "Oh, the pain!"

"Smart ass." Picking up the half-empty water bucket, Sam headed for the door. "Be right back. Try not to die of your injuries while I'm gone."

Laughter followed him outside, and he smiled. After the events of the morning and the previous night, it felt good to joke and laugh.

Sam took a quick look around as he stepped between their cabin and the one next to it. The place seemed strangely quiet. No animals scurried away from his approach, no birds chirped, not even a breeze stirred the branches of the nearby woods. Unease prickled the back of his neck.

Scolding himself for letting the tension of the past couple of days get to him, Sam turned to face downhill and upended the bucket. The water splashed into the snow, forming a crater and cutting a little river toward the pathway between the two rows of cabins.

Something rustled behind him. He turned just in time to

meet Anne's blazing eyes. Her teeth were bared, a large kitchen knife clutched in her hand.

Adrenaline jolted Sam into action. He let out a shout and dropped the bucket just in time to deflect a blow from Anne's knife. The blade sliced open the side of his left hand. Hissing at the sharp sting, he stumbled backward. Blood splattered the snow, creating red puncture wounds in the sparkling white crust.

"Fucking fag," Anne growled, and lunged at him.

Sam dodged the dripping knife, tripped over the bucket and went sprawling flat on his back.

Anne was on him in a heartbeat. She straddled his middle and sat on his stomach, her knee pressing his good hand to the ground. The point of the knife dug into his throat. He grabbed her wrist and managed to put a few inches distance between his flesh and the blade. The effort sent a river of blood gushing from the wound in his hand. It hurt with a deep, nauseating ache, and the muscles in his hand refused to work properly.

His grip slipped in the torrent of blood, and the knife once again pricked his throat. Anne grinned down at him, her eyes bright with triumph. "Gotcha," she whispered, and Sam wondered if he was really about to die.

He heard the cabin door bang open, heard the shouts and the sound of running feet, but didn't really register what was happening until Anne's weight suddenly lifted from his body. Blinking, he watched Bo haul her away by the back of her jacket.

Not missing a beat, she swung the knife at Bo. He dodged it, clamped a hand around her wrist and dealt a vicious punch to her jaw. She crumpled silently to the ground. The bloody knife dropped into the snow beside her.

Bo kicked the knife further away, then hurried to Sam's

side. "Sam, how badly are you hurt?"

Pushing himself to a sitting position with his uninjured hand, Sam examined the gash in his other hand. "Not too bad. I don't think it's all that deep."

Bo frowned at the cut. "It's bleeding a lot." His worried gaze met Sam's. "Christ, Sam, she could've killed you."

"I know." Sam glanced at Anne, who had begun to stir. "Good thing you came along when you did."

Bo said nothing, but put an arm around Sam's shoulders and kissed his brow. Sam leaned gratefully against his lover. Now that it was over, reaction had set in and tremors rocked him from head to toe. The way Bo's hands shook said he felt the same.

The susurration of boots through snow announced Dean's presence just before he dropped to his knees at Sam's other side. "I went out to the path and hollered for the cops," he said, tearing his jacket off. He whipped his sweatshirt over his head, folded one sleeve and pressed it hard to the wound in Sam's hand.

Sam yelped, surprised by how much the firm pressure hurt. "So, the cops are on their way?" A soft moan from Anne's direction made him look over. She rolled onto her side and stared at him with unfocused eyes.

As if in answer to his question, both uniformed officers came running up the path. Their weapons were drawn and ready. Sam froze, realizing the two had no way of knowing who was the bad guy here.

"All right," said the tall officer with the neatly trimmed beard and mustache. "What the hell happened here?" He holstered his pistol and glared between Anne and the three men huddled on the ground.

Groaning, Anne sat up and gingerly fingered the bruise

already forming on her jaw. "He hit me!" she shouted, pointing at Bo. "Damn queer asshole punched me in the face."

"She attacked me with a knife." Sam nodded at his hand, where Dean still held the bloodstained sweatshirt tight against the wound. "I tripped and fell, and she jumped me. Bo punched her when he pulled her off me and she tried to cut him too."

"It's true," Bo added. "Sam was out here emptying our water bucket. Dean and I heard him shout, so we came outside and found Anne attacking him. I ran to help him, while Dean went to call you two."

The second officer kept his gun out, pointed toward the sky, searching gaze darting from Anne to Bo and back again. "Is this Anne Tallant? The girl we spent all night looking for?"

Dean nodded. "Yes. She threatened all three of us yesterday, before she went missing."

Anne glared at him. She opened her mouth to say something, but shut it again when the cop aimed his gun at her head. "Lie down on your stomach," the officer ordered, his tone cold. "Put your hands behind your head."

She hesitated, her face crimson with fury. The bearded officer made a move to draw his weapon. "Do it," he growled.

For a second, Sam thought Anne was going to ignore the cops and go for him again. He was relieved when she turned and flopped face-down in the snow, fingers laced across the back of her head. In spite of what she'd just done to him, he didn't want to watch her get shot.

"Looks like she's done this before," Dean murmured as the officers clamped handcuffs around her wrists and dragged her to her feet, the bearded one rattling off her Miranda rights in a practiced monotone. "Getting arrested, I mean."

"You're right." Hooking a hand under Sam's good arm, Bo stood and helped Sam up. Dean rose with them, Sam's wounded hand clamped between both of his to hold the makeshift pressure dressing in place. "If she has a record, it's not going to go well for her."

The policemen dragged Anne past where Sam and his friends stood. "This is your fault," she spat. "All you filthy queers, getting decent people in trouble."

The bearded cop sighed. "Ma'am, I suggest you keep your mouth shut until you see your lawyer."

She ignored him. "Harry wouldn't be dead if he hadn't called up that demon!" she shouted over her shoulder, struggling now as her captors forced her toward the office. "Fags are in league with Satan, that's why it came to him! You'll all burn in hell!"

The other officer chortled. "Girl, you're gonna dig yourself a hole you'll never get out of if you keep talking like that."

This time, Anne fell silent. She shot a deadly glare at Sam, Bo and Dean as the two officers rounded the corner of the cabin next door.

Sam stared after her, shocked. "Oh shit. Did she really see it? Did she see that thing kill...whoever it was we found in the rhododendron thicket?"

"It seems so." Bo tugged at his braid with his free hand. "If she did, then she's the only one who really knows what happened. I wish we could talk to her. I'd love to know precisely what she witnessed. Maybe if we knew that, we could figure out whether Harry was truly the focus for the portal to open."

"Yeah, too bad she'd rather fillet you than talk to you." Easing the sweatshirt away from Sam's wound, Dean inspected it with a keen eye. "I think the bleeding's about stopped. It's a clean cut, no ragged edges and not too horribly deep, so hopefully you won't need stitches. We *will* have to take you to the ER and get it washed out good so it won't get infected,

201

though."

Sam grimaced. "That sounds painful."

"Can be. But they'll give you some pain meds first." Dean replaced the sweatshirt over the cut and squashed Sam's hand between his once more. "Let's get inside. I have a small first-aid kit with me, I can at least fix you up with a clean pressure dressing before we head down the mountain."

Gritting his teeth against the pain in his hand, Sam nodded. "Okay. I want to change clothes, too. These are all wet now."

Flanked by Bo on one side and Dean on the other, Sam let them lead him back into the cabin. He couldn't help glancing behind him as he walked through the door. Awful as the experience with Anne had been, he wished he could have just ten minutes alone with her. Ten minutes to learn the things she knew about the day Harry Norton had died.

If wishes were horses, beggars would ride. With a humorless smile at having his mother's favorite bit of wisdom pop into his head, Sam walked into the cabin.

ᐧᐧᐧ CR ᐧᐧᐧ

When the three of them arrived at Lex and Carl's office twenty minutes later, they were greeted by both detectives and a uniformed officer. Lex and Carl sat side by side at the desk, looking shell-shocked.

Parsons rose from her chair as Sam, Bo and Dean entered. "Are you ready to go?"

Bo nodded. "We are, yes. The sooner the better. We need to get Sam to the hospital and get his hand taken care of."

"Of course." Parsons gestured to her partner. "Ramirez and

Officer Chambers will accompany you down the trail. Chambers and the others who arrived last night came up on horseback, you're welcome to take what horses you need for the trip."

"We'll need at least two," Dean said. "One for Sam, and one for Bo. Neither one of them should really be hiking that far right now."

Ramirez frowned. "Did Anne cut both of you?"

"No, just me," Sam answered. "But Bo's leg's still recovering from an injury he got a couple of months ago, and it's been bothering him a lot since we got up here."

Bo wrinkled his nose, but didn't argue. Moving to the other side of the desk, he held out a hand to Lex. "Thank you both for having us up here to investigate your place. I have your email and cell numbers, I'll let you know if we find out anything else about..." He darted a swift, cautious glance at the detectives. "About the haunting."

Lex gave a wan smile as she shook Bo's hand. "Thank you, Bo. All of you. I'm so sorry about what happened with Anne."

"It could have been much worse. At least she's caught now." Letting go of Lex's hand, Bo turned to shake Carl's. "We'll be in touch."

Carl's expression was solemn as he shook Bo's hand. "Thanks. We'll look forward to hearing from you."

After Sam and Dean said their farewells, the BCPI team followed Ramirez and Officer Chambers outside and down the steps to the path. They trudged down a side path to the small barn used for the horses, which bore supplies and occasional visitors to Sunset Lodge. Inside, it was dark and relatively warm. The odors of horses, leather and manure permeated the air. An officer was already there, checking tack and inspecting the horses' hooves. She looked up as they entered the building.

"Saddle two, please. We have two injured to get down the

mountain." Ramirez walked over to stroke one big animal's nose. "Hey, girl. Yeah. Who's a pretty girl? *You're* a pretty girl, yes you are."

Dean's eyebrows shot up, but he wisely kept quiet. Covering his mouth with one hand, Bo coughed in a way Sam recognized as a not-so-subtle method of covering impending laughter. Sam bit the insides of his cheeks. Seeing the hulking, menacing Ramirez singsong endearments to a horse was beyond amusing.

Within a few minutes, the woman had two horses saddled, bridled and ready to go. Clutching the saddle horn with his good hand, Sam managed to swing himself onto the horse's back. Dean handed Sam's pack up to him, and he settled it onto the saddle in front of him.

He felt unsafe and distinctly out of place as the animal shifted restlessly underneath him. He'd ridden a little as a child, but it had been a good twenty years since he'd last been on a horse. Attempting to guide one down a steep, treacherous mountain trail with his one working hand did not seem like a good idea.

It didn't help his mood any to notice that Bo had mounted his horse with ease—carrying his backpack, yet—and was holding the reins as if he actually knew what to do with them.

Dean surveyed them both with pursed lips and hands on his hips. "Hmm. Bo, can you handle your horse?"

"I think so, yes. It's been a while, but I used to ride all the time. I'll get by."

"Okay, great. Because Sam's gonna need all the help he can get." Dean walked over and stood grinning up at Sam. "I'll lead her for you, Sam. Give me the reins."

"Gladly." Sam tossed the loop of leather over his mount's head, and Dean caught it. "You better not use this against me,

Dean."

"Huh? What do you mean?" Dean blinked at him, the picture of innocence.

Sam knew better. "I mean, you better not go around telling everybody you meet that I can't ride."

Beside him, Bo groaned and hung his head, and Sam instantly wished he hadn't used those particular words.

Sure enough, Dean grinned, eyes sparkling with mischief. "Oh, I wouldn't say you can't ride, Sam."

Shaking his head, Sam leaned down and dropped his voice low. "You are an evil, evil man, Dean."

"Guilty." Patting Sam's knee, Dean looped the reins around one wrist and picked up the equipment bag in his free hand. "Detective Ramirez, we're ready."

Shooting the three of them a look suggesting he thought they were all out of their minds, Ramirez gestured to Chambers. "All right, Chambers, you're in front. I'll bring up the rear. Let's head out."

Dean gave the horse's reins a tug. The broad back swayed underneath Sam as the animal began to walk. As they exited the barn and started down the trail, Sam turned to look behind him. He could just make out the roof of the Lodge office building over the tops of the trees.

Bo slowed his mount until he was riding beside Sam. "What are you thinking about, Sam?"

"Just wondering if we'll ever know whose body that was we found." Sam faced forward again with a sigh. "It really bugs me that Anne might know what happened, but we can't talk to her."

"Not that she'd tell us anyway," Dean chimed in. He glanced back at Sam and Bo. "Maybe Lex and Carl can tell us something when we talk to them."

Bo looked over at Sam, brown eyes solemn. "I hope so."

"Me too," Sam agreed. The horse shook her head, and Sam had to grab at his pack to keep it from falling off. He winced as the instinctive movement sent a piercing pain through his injured hand. "You know what? Sunset Lodge is a beautiful place, but I'll be really glad to get back to civilization."

Dean nodded. "Amen, brother."

Sam and Bo both laughed at the heartfelt tone in Dean's voice. The three of them settled into a comfortable silence, and Sam let the sounds of creaking saddles and chattering birds lull him into a half-trance.

By the time they reached the small gravel parking lot at the trailhead, Sam thought he knew why the portal had opened, and what part Harry Norton had played in the events of that day. He kept his thoughts to himself as Dean helped him down from his mount and the three of them were whisked off to a waiting police SUV. He had a lot of research to do before he could give credence to his own conclusions, and he didn't want to say anything until he was sure.

In the SUV, Sam shut his eyes and rested his head against the back of the seat while Bo pulled out his cell to call Andre. If he was right in his theory, there might be a way to suppress his own ability to open the interdimensional portals. The question was, did he really *want* to suppress it, or would it be better for all concerned if he continued to hone his talents to the point where they were under his complete conscious control?

He didn't know, and right then he was too exhausted to think about it. Resolving to give the matter his undivided attention later, Sam drifted to sleep to the feel of Bo's hand stroking his thigh.

Chapter Thirteen

Thus, we may conclude that the diagnosis of epilepsy could be missed in cases where the seizure activity is confined to the limbic system—particularly the amygdala, in which induced seizures are known to produce vivid hallucinations and intense, almost paralyzing fear—and the client may be wrongly diagnosed with schizophrenia or acute psychosis. Use of the proper anti-convulsant drug can greatly reduce or entirely eradicate the hallucinations and debilitating fear suffered by these clients. Therefore, evaluation for deep brain epilepsy should be considered in all clients who fail traditional anti-psychotic drug therapy.

Curled on the sofa of the Kimberley Inn conference room BCPI was using as their base of operations, Sam read through the "Conclusions" section of the research paper for a third time. He'd found the article that morning at a local medical library, in a year-old issue of a small but well-respected journal of psychology. The librarian had recommended the journal, claiming it published the most cutting-edge epilepsy research, which was what Sam was looking for. He'd spent half the morning finding and copying articles, which promised to be enlightening, and the rest of the day on into the evening reading them. This one, near the bottom of the pile, was proving to be by far the most informative.

He glanced up as the door opened and his coworkers filed in. "Hey," he greeted them with a smile. "How'd everything go today?"

"Toby saw the butcher's ghost, screamed like a girl and fainted." David shook his head as he plopped onto the sofa beside Sam. "Tell you what, I'm glad this is the last day. That boy's driving me up the damn wall. What're you reading, Sam?"

"Research article." Sam tapped the paper in his hand. "As a matter of fact, I'm glad y'all are back because I think we all need to discuss what I found."

"So you've finally found something that might explain how that portal was opened?" Setting his EMF detector on the table, Bo walked over to sit on the arm of the sofa. He settled an arm around Sam's shoulders and squinted at the sheaf of papers in his hand. "*Journal of Modern Neuropsychology*. I didn't know the library carried professional journals."

"They don't. The librarian sent me to the MAHEC library, and the librarian there recommended this journal after I told her what I wanted."

"What's MAHEC?" Andre asked, settling into one of the large leather chairs gathered around the table.

"Mountain Area Health Education Center." Unfolding his legs, Sam leaned his head against Bo's chest. "They have a pretty good-sized medical library."

Nodding, Dean claimed the chair beside Andre's. "So what article are you reading?"

Sam flipped back to the front page. "Epilepsy of the Primitive Brain: Diagnosis and Treatment."

A puzzled expression crossed Cecile's face. "I'm lost. What does that have to do with portals?"

"Maybe nothing," Sam admitted. "Everything I've come up

with is sheer speculation, but I think the evidence fits well enough."

"Hmm." Nudging Sam over, Bo slid onto the sofa beside him. "I think I know where you're going with this, Sam. It has to do with Harry Norton's epilepsy, right?"

Sam nodded. "Partly, yeah. I got to thinking about it on the way down the mountain. My grandfather had epilepsy, so I learned a lot about it growing up. Basically, when we found out Harry was epileptic, I started wondering if the abnormal electrical activity could play a part in opening a portal. My grandfather took Phenobarbital, not Dilantin, so I didn't recognize Harry's Dilantin bottle when I saw it. If I had I might've made the connection earlier."

"Seizures are more or less uncontrolled firing of neurons in the brain," Dean explained in response to the blank looks around him. "Nerve cells generate electrical impulses to make your body work, and normally that's done in a controlled and regulated way. When you have a seizure, the nerve cells are firing out of control, which means big wild bursts of electrical activity in the brain."

"Clear as mud," David muttered, crossing his arms. "What?"

Cecile laughed. "I think I get it. I'll explain later."

"Go on, Sam," Andre urged, shooting an amused look at David. "How would the electrical activity from a seizure open a portal?"

Sam pursed his lips, casting for the vocabulary to explain. "When we were in the area where we think the portal was, I could feel a lingering trace of its energy. You remember how the active portals felt, right?"

Cecile and Andre nodded, both clearly thinking of the overwhelming intensity of the portals in Oleander House and

South Bay High.

"This felt similar," Sam continued. "But very faint, not nearly as intense. It was like a faded Polaroid compared to a high definition movie on a big screen. The thing is, since it was so low-key, I could actually notice more details about it. One thing I noticed, and didn't really realize I'd noticed until we left, was that the energy I felt had a flavor of electricity to it. Not an actual taste, but the *feel* of that taste in my mind, the same sort of feel as if you touch your tongue to a battery." Sighing, Sam shook his head. "I don't think I'm explaining very well. It's hard to put into words."

"No, I think I get what you mean. The residual energy from the closed portal felt electrical to you, which means the portal might actually run on electricity. Which means the uncontrolled electrical activity generated by a seizure would be a perfect power source." Frowning, Andre tapped his pen against the table. "It makes sense in the context of you being a focus too. If I'm understanding Dean right, electrical impulses are what make things happen in the brain. Psychic abilities, obviously, are centered in the brain, which means they would be powered by electricity too. That would include psychokinetic abilities like yours, Sam."

"So in the case of a human focus for the portal, it could be the electrical activity generated by psychokinesis which physically causes the portal to open." Cecile's brows drew together. "You believe Harry Norton was the focus in the case of this particular portal, right?"

"Yes." Bo tugged on his braid, his other arm sliding off Sam's shoulders. He rested his hand on Sam's thigh. "You're right, Sam, the facts do fit. Harry hadn't had his Dilantin for a few days, which means the level of drug in his blood could've dropped low enough that he had a seizure, which could conceivably have caused the portal to open."

"But then why did it close?" Dean asked, scratching his chin. "I mean yeah, it makes perfect sense that the portal could've opened that way. But how'd he close it again?"

"I doubt we'll be able to figure that out for sure." Sam picked at the fraying edge of medical tape holding the gauze bandage on his injured hand. "He must've been terrified when he fell. Maybe that rush of fear closed it. If the portals can be opened by those strong emotions from a focus, it stands to reason they could be closed that way as well."

Bo glanced at Sam, brown eyes solemn. "I just got off the phone with Lex a few minutes ago. She told me what all the police told her about what they learned interrogating Anne."

"Well, don't keep us in suspense," David burst out when Bo paused. "Tell."

Bo gave him a smile, which swiftly faded into a serious expression. "I'm pretty sure the police wouldn't like her telling us this, so y'all keep it to yourselves, but apparently Anne did see Harry the day he died."

Dean shot a wide-eyed look at Sam. "I knew it."

Bo nodded. "Harry had no family, and Lex held his power of attorney, so the police could legally talk to her about how Harry died."

"Do they think Anne murdered him?" Cecile's voice was hushed and her face pale. "Not that that would be a big surprise, considering how she attacked you, Sam."

Bo shook his head. "They aren't saying right now. Apparently she's being evaluated by a psychiatrist."

Sighing, Andre ran a hand over his close-cropped hair. "Okay, what exactly did Lex tell you?"

"The story the police got from Anne was that she saw Harry coming up one of the trails on the day he died. She followed him, with the idea of confronting him with what she believed was his homosexual affair. She planned to intimidate him, to try to make him leave the Lodge for good." Bo's thumb rubbed Sam's thigh in slow circles. "Before she could confront him, she said he stumbled off the trail and stopped, just staring into space and smacking his lips."

"Sounds like a temporal lobe seizure." Dean curled one leg underneath him and tilted his head, giving Bo a curious look. "What'd she do?"

"She went over to see what was happening," Bo answered. "She said that at first she wondered if he was having a seizure, but, as she put it, he wasn't convulsing. So she decided it wasn't a seizure after all."

"Idiot," Dean huffed, looking irritated.

Bo let out a short, sharp laugh. "It gets better. She said just as she was about to speak to him, a 'demon' appeared from behind that big boulder, which was just behind them, and vanished into the woods."

Cecile's eyebrows shot up. "Excuse me? She thought that thing was a *demon*?"

"Yeah, she said something about that after she attacked me." Sam wrinkled his nose. "She said Harry called it up, and that proved he was in league with Satan."

"By way of his presumed evil gayness." Dean ran a hand through his hair. "That girl is totally whacked."

"So what then?" David prodded.

Shifting in his seat, Bo pressed closer to Sam. "She said Harry mumbled something and ran after it, so she followed him. She saw the thing go into the bushes, but claims she had no idea the creature killed anyone."

Glancing around, Sam saw his own skepticism echoed in

the faces around him. "What happened after that? Did she kill Harry?"

"She says she didn't. She says he seemed to wake from a trance. He acted very confused, like he didn't know where he was. She accused him of calling up a demon from hell, and she said he became very frightened and ran away from her." Bo frowned. "This is where it gets confusing. She pursued him, and she says he just fell off the edge. Lex said the police didn't outright say Anne was lying, but Lex got the feeling they didn't believe her."

"It's possible he could've fallen off, not realizing he was so close to the edge," Dean mused. "If he had a temporal lobe seizure, he would've had a period of confusion after it ended. It could've been enough to make him not remember where he was, or that there was a dangerous drop-off nearby."

Bo shrugged. "Maybe so. I doubt the police will tell Lex anything more, unless Anne's actually charged and declared competent to stand trial."

Sam nudged Bo's shoulder with his own. "Why didn't she tell Lex and Carl what happened to Harry?"

"I don't know. Lex said Anne flatly refused to answer that question when Parsons asked her." Bo leaned forward, his hand sliding down to Sam's knee. "Oh yes, they've identified the body we found. It was a man from Indiana, visiting the mountains alone. He wasn't registered as a guest at the Lodge, so Lex figures he must've been on a day hike. People do hike those trails occasionally without staying at the Lodge."

"Damn, talk about being in the wrong place at the wrong time." Stretching both arms above his head, David let out a huge yawn. "So, I guess that one's about as solved as we can make it, yeah?"

"Yes." Bo smiled. "Our amateur group will be back here any

minute, are y'all ready to go over today's work here at the Kimberley? I want to wrap it up soon. We'll need to be up very early tomorrow, to drive back home."

The group gathered around the table, already discussing the day's events. Sam rose from his spot on the sofa and followed, lost in his thoughts. He hadn't told them what he'd begun to suspect about himself and his own abilities. The manifestations of seizures in some of the primitive areas of the brain sounded unnervingly similar to the strange things he'd experienced occasionally for most of his life, but he didn't want to share that with everyone else yet. Especially since a cure might be easily available. Bo would almost certainly pressure him to take it, and he wasn't sure he wanted to be cured. Not when it would mean the destruction of his ability to connect with the portals, and the things on the other side.

Bo's arm sliding around his waist startled him out of his thoughts. "Sam, are you okay? Is your hand bothering you?"

Sam smiled in what he hoped was a reassuring way. "No, it's fine. I was just thinking."

"About what?"

"Nothing."

The expression in Bo's eyes said he didn't believe that for a second, but the arrival of their amateur ghost hunters stopped him from saying so. He gave Sam a look that said quite clearly he was in for a grilling later, then turned to greet the group.

Sam watched Bo walk over to stand at the head of the table. Maybe the upcoming conversation wouldn't be as difficult as Sam feared. Maybe Bo would understand Sam's reasons for wanting to leave things as they were, and not push him.

Yeah. And maybe the sun'll turn into a giant snowball, too.

He'd need every logical, dispassionate argument he could think of if he was to get Bo to see reason. Sighing, Sam settled into a chair and began marshaling his thoughts.

CR

Predictably, Bo accosted him the minute they reached their room that night.

"Okay," Bo said, crossing his arms and giving Sam a stern look. "What's going on?"

Sam considered pretending he didn't know what Bo meant, but only for a moment. Bo knew him too well, and was far too stubborn to be put off for long.

"I thought of something else while we were riding down the mountain," Sam admitted, settling cross-legged on the bed. "About myself, and what I can do."

Bo sat beside him and laid a hand on his thigh. "Your psychokinesis?"

Sam laid his hand over Bo's. "My psychokinesis opens the portals. Harry's seizure probably opened the one at Sunset Lodge. I think the comparison is pretty obvious."

"So you believe your psychokinesis is basically a burst of abnormal electrical activity in the brain, similar to a seizure." Bo stared at him, keen gaze searching his face. "I wondered about that earlier. You think psychic abilities could be a form of epilepsy, don't you?"

"I think it's possible, yes."

"And if it's a type of epilepsy, it could be controlled with medication."

Sam wished he didn't have to crush the blaze of hope in Bo's dark eyes. "Possibly. But I don't want to do that."

The muscle in Bo's jaw twitched. "Don't try to be noble,

Sam. You're under no obligation to seek out the damn portals and close them."

"I know that. But how could I look at myself in the mirror if I deliberately suppressed what I can do, knowing what I know about the portals?"

"Nobody could blame you for not wanting to put yourself in danger. I know you. You'll put yourself in harm's way in a heartbeat to close one of these things."

"Yes, I will. Because I can. Because there isn't anyone else." Sam rubbed his thumb over Bo's. "Remember what we learned at Oleander House? Most people who can open the portals end up catatonic. I don't know why I'm one of the few whose mind can process it, but I am. I can't just ignore that."

Bo stared at Sam's hand where it lay over his. "Please, Sam. I can't stand the thought of losing you to one of those things."

Sam's chest tightened. Brushing a stray lock of hair from Bo's face, he leaned over to kiss his temple. "You won't lose me that way, Bo. They've never harmed a focus before."

"That we know of." Bo lifted his head and pinned Sam with a pleading gaze. "We're still fumbling in the dark when it comes to these portals. We don't know all the rules yet. Anything could happen, Sam. Anything."

Turning sideways, Sam stroked Bo's cheek. "Say I start taking seizure medicine, and it actually works, it suppressed my psychic abilities. What happens the next time we encounter a portal? What happens to us all, including me, if I've lost the ability to close it?"

The helpless anger in Bo's eyes said he understood exactly what Sam was saying, and hated it. He opened his mouth, then closed it again and shook his head. "If you get yourself killed trying to close one of those fucking things, I'll never forgive you."

Sam laughed, though there was no humor in the sound. Cupping Bo's face in his hands, Sam leaned forward and kissed him.

Bo's mouth opened under his, tongue pushing in. One hand slid into Sam's hair, the other diving between his legs to squeeze his hardening prick. Sam moaned at the touch.

Shoving Sam onto his back, Bo straddled his hips and ground his erection into Sam's. "Fuck me."

Sam blinked, shock and disbelief warring with a surge of desire. "What?"

"I said, fuck me." Bo's voice was hoarse, his eyes on fire. He bent and bit Sam's bottom lip. "Don't you want to?"

"I... I just..." Sam whimpered when Bo's hips rocked against his, harder this time. "Yeah, God, yes. You're sure?"

"I am." Dipping his head, Bo sucked at the spot on Sam's throat which always made him squirm and beg. "I've wanted to for a while now. Sorry it took me so long to work up the courage to ask."

Sam gave Bo's braid a gentle tug, forcing his head up so Sam could look him in the eye. "Never be afraid to ask me for what you need, Bo. I'll do anything you want. Just don't ever make me hurt you. That's the one thing I won't do."

Eyes shining, Bo smiled and kissed the end of Sam's nose. "Don't worry. I'm not into pain."

"Neither am I." Sam slid his hand down to the end of Bo's braid, pulled off the rubber band and started unwinding the long black hair. "Why don't you get us undressed?"

"You're usually the one doing that." Bo sat up on his knees and skinned out of his long-sleeved T-shirt. "Not that I'm complaining, but why the change?"

In answer, Sam held up his bandaged hand. "You can finish undressing yourself before you do me, if you want. I don't mind."

Bo laughed. "I bet you don't."

Climbing off of Sam, Bo stood beside the bed and shed his sneakers and jeans. He slinked out of his underwear in a slow striptease which made Sam's crotch ache. Lifting his foot, Bo kicked the red briefs across the room before pouncing on Sam again.

"So," Sam panted, lifting his chin so Bo could nibble his throat. "Your leg's feeling okay today, looks like."

"Yes, fine." Bo's tongue explored the hollow in Sam's neck, tearing a heartfelt groan from him. "Can we discuss that later, maybe?"

"Uh-huh." Sam moaned when Bo's hand crept underneath his sweater to pinch his nipple. "God, Bo..."

"Mmm." With one last sharp nip to the angle of Sam's jaw, Bo rolled off him. "Sit up so I can get your sweater off."

Sam pushed up with his good hand and raised both arms over his head. Bo lifted the sweater with deliberate slowness, fingertips brushing Sam's skin in a light, ticklish caress. Sam thought he'd go crazy before Bo finally tossed the garment aside.

"Tease," Sam accused as Bo nudged him onto his back. "You want me to go off before I get inside you?"

"God, no." Bo twisted around to take off Sam's shoes. "Come on, I know you have more control than that." Turning to face Sam with a wicked grin, he flipped open the button on Sam's jeans and dragged the zipper down.

"Sure, usually." Sam lifted his hips so Bo could slide his jeans off. "But just the idea of getting my cock inside your ass has me so excited I feel like a virgin again."

Bo's expression turned serious. "I *am* a virgin, when it comes to this."

The mingled nervousness and excitement in Bo's eyes tugged at Sam's heart. He ran his fingers through Bo's hair, fanning it into a shining ebony curtain. "I love that I'm your first."

"My first, and my only." Leaning down, Bo brushed a soft kiss across Sam's mouth. "How do we do this, Sam? You can't put your weight on your hand, that wound might open up again."

Sam pushed himself to a sitting position, wrapping an arm around Bo to keep him close. Bo ended up straddling Sam's lap, arms wound around his neck.

"You should probably be on your hands and knees," Sam said, running his bandaged hand down Bo's back. "That's usually the most comfortable position for your first time."

Bo's cheeks pinked, his lips parting as Sam's finger dipped into the cleft of his ass. "Lube's in the bedside table."

"I'll get it." Sam rubbed his fingertip in light circles over Bo's hole, causing the muscles there to jump and twitch. "You lie down and spread your legs for me, so I can get you ready."

A hungry whimper escaped Bo's throat. Clamping a hand onto the back of Sam's head, Bo brought their mouths together in a quick, fiery kiss. His legs trembled as he climbed off Sam's lap and sprawled on his back.

It wasn't easy to open the drawer and take out the lube without looking, but Sam managed. He couldn't tear his gaze from Bo lying there with his thighs opened wide and his cock hard and flushed against his belly. Knowing Bo was ready to take this step, that he truly wanted it, made him more beautiful than ever in Sam's eyes.

Setting the lube on the mattress, Sam knelt between Bo's legs, leaned forward and planted a kiss in the middle of his chest. "Are you ready?"

"Yes." Bo touched Sam's cheek. "Kiss me."

Sam gladly obeyed. He stretched out on top of Bo, holding himself up on his elbows. As he leaned down and captured Bo's mouth with his, one of Bo's legs hooked around his waist. The movement sent their cocks sliding together. Sam groaned and thrust against Bo's groin.

"God, I want you inside me," Bo breathed, his heel digging into the small of Sam's back. "Hurry."

"No." Sam kissed Bo's chin, his Adam's apple, his collarbone. "We have plenty of time, Bo. Let's take it slow."

If Bo was inclined to argue, he didn't let on. He arched his neck, fingers threading through Sam's hair as Sam trailed kisses up and down his throat.

Sam slithered down Bo's body to suck one brown nipple. The little nub peaked between his lips. His bandaged hand sought out the other nipple and pinched it, causing Bo to moan and squirm under him.

Smiling, Sam moved lower. He licked up the middle of Bo's belly, the fine dark hairs there tickling his tongue.

"God, Sam," Bo groaned, his abdominal muscles rippling under Sam's mouth. "Please."

"Please?" Sam scooted down to bite the tender skin just above the thick black thatch of Bo's pubic hair. "Please what?"

"I... I need... Oooooh, oh yes..."

Bo's words degenerated into low, broken moans as Sam's mouth descended on his groin. The sound was nearly enough to make Sam come without even being touched. Suppressing his arousal with an effort, Sam dragged his tongue the full length of

Bo's shaft and swirled it around the head. Precome oozed from the tip, and Sam lapped it up before pulling away.

Bo whimpered in protest. His hips lifted, thighs spreading wider in clear invitation. "Sam."

"Right here." Sam dipped his head and nuzzled the warm, soft skin behind Bo's testicles, breathing in the rich scent of his desire. "Lift your legs."

Bo obeyed, hoisting his legs up and apart to expose his hole. Fine tremors shook his body, telling Sam all he needed to know about how turned on Bo was. Sam spread Bo's cheeks and teased the rosy pucker with the tip of his tongue. Bo's taste, heady and familiar, excited him almost as much as Bo's sharp, sweet cries.

Sam licked and sucked until Bo was incoherent and unable to hold still, and his muscles had relaxed enough for Sam's tongue to wriggle inside him. His prick twitching in its eagerness to be buried in Bo's ass, Sam indulged in one last taste of Bo's anus before pulling away and sitting back on his heels.

"Turn over now," Sam said, gently stroking Bo's inner thigh. "Knees and elbows."

For a second, Bo just stared at him with glazed eyes. Then he nodded and rolled onto his stomach. Planting both elbows on the mattress, Bo raised onto his knees and spread his legs.

The sight of Bo on all fours, his gorgeous ass in the air and his cock and balls swaying beneath him, had Sam clamping a hand around the base of his cock to keep from coming. When he felt he could control himself, Sam reached for the lube and began slicking his fingers.

His uninjured hand coated with liquid lube, Sam positioned himself behind Bo, leaned over and kissed one caramel-colored buttock. "One finger first, okay?"

Bo nodded, sending the lock of hair caught on his shoulder cascading over his face. Resting his cheek against Bo's lower back, Sam slid one finger deep into Bo's ass in one smooth, steady motion.

Bo groaned when Sam hit his prostate. "Oh yes. Yes. More."

A shiver of need ran up Sam's spine. It was all he could do to ignore Bo's command and keep up the gentle in and out, in and out of the single digit in Bo's hole. "In a minute. You've never taken two fingers before. We need to take it slowly, make sure you're plenty relaxed."

Bo let out a desperate sound. "Can't last, Sam. Please. Please, more, please."

Sam almost protested again. But Bo's muscles clenched, pulsed and loosened their grip on his finger, and he decided it was safe to continue.

He lifted his face from Bo's back. The air felt cool after the heat of Bo's skin. Drawing his finger carefully out of Bo's ass, Sam poured more lube onto his hand. He spread some of it onto Bo's hole, which made Bo moan and press back into Sam's touch.

"I'm putting in two now, okay?" Sam's voice quavered, and he wished it wouldn't. He didn't want Bo to think he was too excited to be fully in control.

Bo turned to pin Sam with a pleading stare. "Yeah. Hurry."

Pressing his index and middle fingers close together, Sam lined them up with Bo's opening and slid them carefully inside.

It was a tight fit. Bo sucked in a hissing breath, his sphincter clamping down so hard Sam could feel his own pulse in the tips of his fingers.

"Bo? You okay?" Sam ran his free hand over Bo's back, up and down in a soothing motion. "Do you need to stop?"

Bo gave a vigorous shake of his head, which sent his unbound hair flowing like a dark waterfall over his shoulders to pool on the bed. His hands curled into claws, bunching the comforter. "No. Don't stop. I'm fine. Just...it's tight."

"I know." Sam twisted his fingers just enough for the motion to coax some of the spasm from Bo's anus. "It just takes a minute for your muscles to figure out it's okay to let me in, that's all."

Bo moaned when Sam's fingers torqued inside him again, this time sliding in a tiny bit further. "Oh. Yes. Harder."

Letting Bo's noises and the movement of his hips guide him, Sam pumped deeper, faster. When he felt some of the tension ease from the ring of muscle, he began spreading his fingers as he moved.

After a few minutes, Sam's fingers were sliding in and out with ease. He pulled them out and slipped both thumbs inside, massaging the loosening ring with gentle, steady pressure.

Bo groaned, hips arching into Sam's touch. "Sam... God, please. Now. Please."

"Yeah." Sam picked up the lube, opened it and rubbed a generous amount onto his shaft and Bo's opening. His hands only shook a little. "Ready?"

Bo darted a blazing look at Sam over his shoulder. "Yes."

Heart pounding with a nervousness like he'd never known before, Sam scooted closer. He rested the tip of his erection against Bo's stretched hole, took a deep breath and pushed.

"Fuck!" Bo gasped as the head of Sam's cock breached him. The muscles in his arms and back bulged, his entire body going tense. "Wait. Wait a minute."

Sam held still with an effort, one hand on Bo's hip and the other rubbing soothing circles on his lower back. "Just breathe," he murmured. "Breathe. Relax. I won't move until you say it's okay."

Bo nodded. His eyes were squeezed shut, his face contorted. Sam knew the discomfort was temporary, that it would pass soon enough and would lessen each time, but it was still hard to watch.

He was on the verge of pulling out and suggesting they try it another time when he felt the clutch of Bo's anus slacken. Bo pressed back against him, forcing his cock in another couple of inches. They both groaned.

Bo opened his eyes and peered back at Sam through a veil of hair. "Move. Fuck me."

The raw need in Bo's voice sent a violent shudder through Sam's body. Clamping his hands onto Bo's hips in a light but firm grip, he tilted his pelvis forward so that his prick glided deeper into Bo's body.

"God, you feel so good," Sam breathed, trembling with the effort of holding back the orgasm that wanted to wash over him. "So fucking good."

Bo answered with a growl and a sharp backward thrust of his hips which drove Sam's cock the rest of the way in. His groin flush against Bo's ass, Sam curled his body forward and tried to tamp down the pleasure swelling inside him. He'd fucked plenty of men before, including a virgin or two, but it had never been quite like this.

Love really does make everything better. The knowledge made him smile.

When he felt he could move without immediately coming, Sam drew his cock inch by inch out of Bo's ass, until only the head remained inside, then nudged it slowly back in. Bo moaned, his lips parted and his face flushed. Sweat dewed his cheeks and neck, plastering strands of black hair to his skin.

He pushed up on his hands, and let out a sharp cry when Sam's prick hit his gland.

"Oh *fuck* yes," Bo panted, hands kneading the bed. "Fuck me, God please, harder."

Thinking past the lust buzzing in his brain wasn't easy, but Sam managed. He assessed Bo with a critical eye. The tightness in Bo's ass had eased enough to let Sam slide freely in and out, and Bo's features were now slack with pleasure instead of scrunched up with pain.

Forcing himself to keep his thrusts controlled, Sam picked up the pace a little. Bo's sweet moans and the wanton roll of his hips made Sam's head spin. Encouraged by how much Bo seemed to be enjoying himself, Sam moved harder, faster. Soon enough, he was slamming into Bo with quick short jabs which had them both grunting. Rivulets of sweat ran down Sam's back to trickle into the crack of his ass. His injured left hand ached from gripping Bo's hipbone, but he didn't care. Watching Bo lose himself in ecstasy more than made up for the slight discomfort.

"God, close," Bo groaned, his voice ragged. "Touch me."

Sam was already reaching for Bo's cock before the request was out of his mouth. Curling the fingers of his good hand around Bo's rigid shaft, Sam stroked it in the rough, rapid rhythm he knew Bo preferred. Bo's insides fluttered in response, and Sam gasped as a rush of heat burst in his belly. He came with a low, heartfelt groan, every muscle in his body tense.

"Sam, oh, oh *fuck!*" Bo's back arched, his head flung back as his semen spilled over Sam's hand, and Sam decided he'd never seen anything sexier in his life.

He kept pumping his fist until the last of Bo's come dribbled out and Bo started to squirm away. Pulling carefully out of Bo's ass, Sam snatched the towel off the headboard where he'd left it that morning after his shower. He wiped off his hand, snaked his arm around Bo's middle with the last of his strength and collapsed sideways onto the bed. Bo fell into his embrace and lay there panting.

Sam rested his hand in the center of Bo's chest, thumb caressing the damp skin. Bo's heart thudded against his palm. "Wow," Sam mumbled, licking a drop of sweat from behind Bo's ear. "I may never move again. You okay?"

Chuckling, Bo turned his head to collect a breathless kiss. "Fucked to within an inch of my life, but I think I like it."

"Good, because I know I did and I'd hate to think the feeling wasn't mutual." Sam moved his hand up to cup Bo's cheek. "So, it was all right? I didn't hurt you?"

Bo smiled, dark eyes shining. "No, Sam, you didn't hurt me."

"It's always kind of uncomfortable at first."

"Yes, I expected that."

"It gets better."

"I'm sure it does." Bo twisted surprisingly fast in Sam's arms and pressed two fingers over his mouth. "Sam, it was good. Incredible, actually. It hurt a little bit at first, sure. But like you said, it's that way for everyone. I was expecting it. And it was only a few seconds before it started to feel so good I can't even describe it." His fingertips skated over Sam's bottom lip, tickling the skin. "You took such good care of me, Sam. You made it wonderful for me, like you always do."

The adoration in Bo's eyes warmed Sam right through. He buried one hand in Bo's tangled hair and kissed him. Bo opened to him with a soft sigh, arms winding around his neck. Sam shut his eyes and let himself sink into it.

Of all their different kinds of kisses, ranging from bruisingly passionate to innocently playful, these were his favorite. The sweet, languid kisses shared when they were naked and tangled together in bed, sated from good sex and communicating their love for one another in the age-old language of lips and tongues and leisurely caresses. This, he knew, was what life was all about. The dream every human being chased since the day of their birth. Loving, and being loved in return.

He'd begun to think he'd never have that. Until Bo came along and they turned each other's worlds inside out. Now, he couldn't imagine his life without Bo.

When the kiss finally broke, Sam clutched Bo close, buried his face in Bo's neck and breathed in Bo's musky scent, redolent with sex and sweat. Bo laughed, both hands buried in Sam's hair. "Sam? What are you thinking?"

"That I love you, and I never want to be without you." Sam kissed Bo's neck and nuzzled behind his ear. "I want to protect you."

"Which is why you refuse to even find out if your psychokinetic abilities might be controlled with medication." Bo drew back enough to look Sam in the eye. His face was deadly serious. "I love you too, Sam. That's why I don't want you to have any reason to face those portals again, now that we know there might be a way out of it."

"We don't know anything yet. And we'll keep getting portal cases. That's not going to stop, which means I have to be ready. We all do."

Bo bit his lip. "We don't have to take those cases. We can just say no. Nobody has to know why."

"Yes, we *do* have to take them." Sam brushed a lock of hair from Bo's eyes and kissed his forehead. "I may not be the only person in the world who can connect my mind to the portals without going insane, but I'm betting there's damn few of us. When people come to us with these things, we have to help them."

"Why?"

"Because it's right. You know it is."

For a long moment, they stared silently at each other. Sam stroked Bo's bare back, hoping his touch could somehow make Bo understand how he felt. How much he needed, on a fundamental level, to continue trying to close all the portals he could.

Finally, Bo sighed and snuggled against Sam's chest. "I can't talk you out of this, can I?"

Sam kissed his hair. "I'm sorry."

"So am I. But I think I understand why you feel the way you do." One of Bo's hands wandered downward to squeeze Sam's ass. "Just promise me you'll always be careful, okay?"

"Always. I swear." Smiling, Sam wound a strand of Bo's hair around his finger. "So. It's still pretty early. What would you like to do?"

"Shower. I'm sticky."

"Mmm, me too."

Bo grinned. "Will you wash my back?"

"And your legs, and your chest, and this sexy ass." Sam smacked Bo's rear, making him yelp. "I'll even wash your hair if you want me to."

"Good, my arms are tired from bracing myself." Wriggling out of Sam's embrace, Bo rose somewhat stiffly and hauled Sam to his feet. His arms, Sam couldn't help but notice, shook just a bit. "Why the sudden generosity? Last time you tried washing my hair, you got your hand tangled up and swore you'd never touch my hair again in any sort of cleanliness ritual."

"Hey, my hair's never been past my ears, what do I know about washing something like this?" Sam protested, tugging on a waist-length lock which hung over Bo's shoulder. "Anyway, I guess I just want to thank you for understanding me."

Bo's gaze softened from teasing to tender. Framing Sam's face in his hands, he pressed close and kissed him. "I'll always do my best to respect and understand your decisions, even when I don't agree with them. And I know you'll do the same for me."

Sam nodded. Bo's near death two months before had cured them both of the worst of their stubbornness. They'd tried hard since then to compromise. To talk instead of argue. It didn't always work, but at least they tried.

"We're getting better at this, aren't we?" Sam asked as they joined hands and started toward the bathroom. "This relationship thing, I mean."

"We are, yes." Bo glanced at him and squeezed his hand. "I'm looking forward to spending the rest of my life learning how to get along with you, Sam. You'd better not let one of those portals spoil my plans."

"I won't. I promise."

Bo stared at him for a moment, searching and serious. Then he smiled, kissed Sam's fingers and led him into the bathroom.

I'll always be there for him, Sam swore to himself, watching Bo turn on the shower. *I won't let those things take us away from each other.*

He only hoped he would be able to hold to his silent vow. He had no illusions regarding the danger he would face—the danger they would all face—the next time they encountered one of the portals. The way the old bite on Bo's leg had flared up

229

around the area where the portal had been still worried him. If the lingering energy of a closed gateway affected the injury that much, what would an active portal do to it? The possibilities made Sam's stomach knot.

Bo stepped into the shower and held out a hand to Sam. "Come on, Sam. You promised to wash me."

The not-so-subtle seduction in Bo's voice succeeded in pushing Sam's worries to the back of his mind. Smiling, he took Bo's hand and let himself be pulled into heat and steam, and his lover's welcoming arms.

About the Author

Ally Blue used to be a good girl. Really. Married for twenty years, two lovely children, house, dogs, picket fence, the whole deal. Then one day she discovered slash fan fiction. She wrote her first fan fiction story a couple of months later and has since slid merrily into the abyss. She has had several short stories published in the erotic e-zine Ruthie's Club, and is a regular contributor to the original slash e-zine Forbidden Fruit.

To learn more about Ally Blue, please visit www.allyblue.com. Send an email to Ally at ally@allyblue.com or join her Yahoo! group to join in the fun with other readers as well as Ally! http://groups.yahoo.com/group/loveisblue/.

There's more to summer than just hot weather.

Hot Weather
© *2007 Matthew Haldeman-Time*

Fresh out of college and new to the working world, John faces reality—spending the rest of his life stuck behind a desk instead of having fun in the sun with his friends. His boss is on his back, his car is breaking down, and the oppressive heat is broiling him alive. There's no end in sight to his misery.

Tall, slender, green-eyed Keith runs the lunch shift at the local diner, an air-conditioned oasis away from what John's life has become. Keith's cheerful personality, constant smile and unbearably sexy body help to remind John that summer is what he makes of it. And with Keith's cooperation, John plans on making this his best summer yet.

Available now in ebook from Samhain Publishing.

Two men bonded by love. A long forgotten secret
neither knew they shared in common.

Sins of the Past
© *2007 Amanda Young*

Andrew Vought is a wealthy single parent who's all but given up on love. Ryan Ward is an up-and-coming landscape architect, who's never believed true love exists.

In each other's arms, they find the love they've sought. But can a budding new love survive the secrets both men harbor?

Warning, this title contains the following: explicit sex, graphic language and some hot nekkid manlove.

Available now in ebook from Samhain Publishing.

Enjoy the following excerpt from Sins of the Past...

Andrew weaved around bodies left and right. He spotted Ryan and Nick slightly ahead of him and off to the right. Ryan had his head thrown back, laughing uproariously at something Nick was busy whispering in his ear. Breathing a sigh of relief at having finally found them, he shuffled forward. Then he noticed the way Nick shifted closer to Ryan, his hands falling to cradle Ryan's hips as they moved to the music, and molten anger shimmered through his veins.

How dare he? How dare Nick rub all up against Ryan, like some bitch in heat? And why was Ryan just standing there, letting him do it? *The bastard.*

Andrew took a wobbly step forward, his hands balling up into fists at his sides. A man the size of a small mountain stepped into his path, blocking his view of Ryan. He stopped, ready to tell the guy to move the hell out of his way, and looked up, and then up some more. *Damn*, the guy was tall.

"How about a dance, pretty?" The man's voice was gruff and scratchy, like maybe he'd smoked one too many cigarettes. His words didn't sound like a question, more like an order. Normally that would've ticked Andrew off. He didn't like being bossed around. Tonight, however, it sent a little tingle of excitement shivering down his spine.

Andrew leaned to the side—almost tipped over, before he could catch his balance—and glanced around the goliath. Ryan was still absorbed in Nick's sparkling wit, or whatever the hell it was he found so entertaining.

He turned to the goliath. "Sure." What the hell. It wasn't as if his date would mind. The bastard was too busy letting Nick hang all over him to pay any attention to what he was doing.

"Bud," the man said, holding out his hand.

Andrew accepted the shake and watched his hand disappear inside the larger man's paw. "Andrew."

He started to pull back his hand, but found it trapped in the vise-like grip of Bud's closed fist. Bud smiled, the upward tilt of his thin lips taking away some of the severity from the chiseled planes of his face, and gave Andrew's hand a sharp tug. Pulled off balance, Andrew stumbled forward, his face smacking into the middle of the behemoth's sternum.

Bud's gigantic forearms closed around his back and pulled him up tight against him. Andrew held himself stiffly, not aiding but not exactly resisting either, as Bud began to sway to the beat of the music. Against his cheek, he could feel the steady thumpedy-thump of the man's heart beating. Every granite muscle in Bud's torso flexed and rippled as he shimmied them back and forth.

The song seemed to last forever before it finally began to slow to its end. Andrew let out a breath of relief, glad the dance was over. The arms around him loosened and he sucked in a deep breath, inhaling the pungent scent of sweat and cheap cologne.

It wasn't a bad smell, just not the one he wanted. Not like Ryan. Ryan always smelled of woodsy cologne with a hint of the underlying musky testosterone that exuded from his pores.

He mumbled a hushed thanks to Bud for the dance and spun around, intent on finding Ryan. He didn't have to look far. Ryan stood a couple of feet behind him, his hip propped against the wall, a glower on his handsome face and fire in his eyes. With his arms across his broad chest and his jaw clenched tight enough to grind nails, Ryan did not look happy. He looked mad as a wet cat, and that put a spring in Andrew's step as he strutted over to him.

"Who was that?" Ryan barked out as soon as Andrew got

close enough to hear him over the music.

For spite, he glanced back at Bud and waved. "Oh, that's just Bud," he answered as nonchalantly as he could. A smile tugged at the corners of his lips, trying to pop out, but he restrained it.

Ryan humphed and came up off the wall. He moved in close, so close Andrew could count the individual black eyelashes framing his eyes. "If you can dance with Bud," he said, spitting out the other man's name as if it left a vile taste in his mouth, "then you can dance with me."

Andrew shrugged. "I guess so."

Ryan must not have liked the response because his eyes flashed a deeper shade of brown and the grinding of his teeth started up again. The smile Andrew had been fighting broke free and spread across his face. He couldn't help it, seeing Ryan jealous was so sweet. It more than made up for the brief bout of insecurity he'd felt upon viewing Ryan and Nick dancing together.

"You little shit," Ryan muttered, hauling Andrew into his arms and up against the lean contours of his body. "You're getting a kick out of this, aren't you?"

Andrew rested his arms on Ryan's shoulders and sank his fingers into the soft hair at the base of Ryan's neck, kneading the taut muscles. With a contented sigh, he shifted himself a bit deeper into Ryan's embrace, resting his cheek against Ryan's stubbled one. "So what if I am? It's what you deserve."

Ryan's arms tightened around the small of Andrew's back and he began to move, swaying his hips, taking Andrew's body along for the ride. Their groins brushed together with every pass, allowing Andrew to feel how hard Ryan was for him. He swallowed back a groan, feeling his own cock stir at the contact.

Fingertips grazed the rise of his bottom. Andrew shivered,

clenching his ass cheeks to stop the needy ache he felt inside.

Ryan must have felt the tremor pass through his body, must have felt their pricks rubbing together as Andrew did, because the riled expression in his eyes wavered and was replaced by something that looked a hell of a lot like more like hunger than aggravation.

Ryan's breath was warm and moist as it wafted over his ear. "I don't think I've done anything to deserve seeing you all cuddled up with that dumb-ass lumberjack. Not when you hadn't even agreed to dance with me yet."

Andrew rotated his hips, pressing in a little harder against Ryan, dragging their pricks together and teasing them both in the process. "I'm dancing with you, aren't I?"

A growl rumbled through Ryan's chest. Andrew felt the vibrations more than heard it, and damned if it wasn't the hottest thing he'd ever experienced.

"You know what I mean," Ryan grumbled.

"Yes, I know what you mean. Just like I know while you were *supposed* to be in the bathroom, you were actually dancing with Nick."

"I went to the bathroom, Andrew. Nick caught me as I was coming out. That's all."

Andrew felt an irrational surge of the same anger he'd experienced earlier at seeing Nick latched onto his man. "He was hanging all over you."

Wait. Had he just thought of Ryan as *his* man?

"He was only talking to me, baby." Ryan paused, his lips feathering over Andrew's cheek. "I do think it's cute that you're so jealous though."

"You're one to talk," Andrew replied.

Ryan sighed, blowing hot air over Andrew's ear. "I don't

know what you're talking about."

Andrew shivered, goose bumps of arousal popping up all over his skin. He let go of Ryan's neck, ran his hand between their bodies and gave Ryan's nipple a sharp twist.

Ryan jerked his head back. "Hey! That hurt."

Andrew smiled and snuggled back into place. "It wasn't supposed to feel good."

"Then why the hell did you do it?"

"You were asking for it."

"I didn't ask you to twist my damn nipple off."

"I was hoping it would refresh your memory. Do you still not know what I meant?"

"About what?"

Andrew pinched Ryan's nipple between his thumb and forefinger and cocked an eyebrow.

"All right, all right, I might have been a tiny bit jealous when I saw you dancing with the marshmallow man over there."

Andrew grinned. "Marshmallow man?" That's not how he would've described Bud.

"Yeah, marshmallow man." The petulant look on his face warned Andrew not to contradict Ryan's description, though Bud's body was anything but soft.

He snorted and leaned in to rub his cheek on Ryan's shoulder. Who would have thought he would actually like a touch of possessiveness in a lover? He never had before, but then again, none of the few men he'd been with were Ryan. The man could make anything, even jealousy, look good.

"What? You have a thing for big, brainless meatheads now? You know his balls are probably the size of small acorns because of all the steroids he's taken, right?"

"No, I have a thing for tall, cute landscape architects, who ride motorcycles and get jealous at the drop of a hat."

"Oh really?"

"Mmm–hmm." He leaned up and pressed his lips against Ryan's, oblivious to the party going on around them. For once in his life, he didn't care if he was putting on a show. All he knew was Ryan and the chemistry and warmth sparking between them like static electricity, the delicious press of their chests and the desire he saw mirrored back to him through Ryan's eyes. "Know where I can find someone like that?"

"Oh I might be able to think of someone," Ryan murmured against the corner of Andrew's mouth.

Ryan's lips covered his, not with pressure but with a gentle coaxing sensation that melted Andrew's knees and forced him to incline against Ryan's chest for support as their lips, teeth and tongues dueled, heedless of the spectators around them. The roof could have caught fire and he wouldn't have cared. All he wanted was more. More of Ryan, more of that one single moment when everything began to slide into place and he realized what he felt for Ryan was growing in leaps and bounds. Steadily spinning away from like and well on its way to another four letter word that should have scared the shit out of him, but surprisingly didn't.

Love.

GREAT
CHEAP
FUN

Discover eBooks!

THE FASTEST WAY TO GET THE HOTTEST NAMES

Get your favorite authors on your favorite reader, long before they're
out in print! Ebooks from Samhain go wherever you go, and work with
whatever you carry—Palm, PDF, Mobi, and more.

Samhain
Publishing, Ltd

WWW.SAMHAINPUBLISHING.COM